Dead Girls

Dead Girls

Nancy Lee

National Library of Canada Cataloguing in Publication Data

Lee, Nancy, 1970–
Dead girls

ISBN 0-7710-5250-2

I. Title.

PS8573.E34845D42 2002   C813'.6   C2001-903830-5
PR9199.4.L43D42 2002

We acknowledge the financial support of the Government of Canada through the Book Publishing Industry Development Program for our publishing activities. We further acknowledge the support of the Canada Council for the Arts and the Ontario Arts Council for our publishing program.

The following stories were previously published:
"Young Love" in *The Dalhousie Review* and "Associated Press" in *Toronto Life* and *Write Turns: New Directions in Canadian Fiction*. Both stories appear here in slightly different form.

Typeset in Garamond by M&S, Toronto
Printed and bound in Canada

McClelland & Stewart Ltd.
The Canadian Publishers
481 University Avenue
Toronto, Ontario
M5G 2E9
www.mcclelland.com

1 2 3 4 5   06 05 04 03 02

For Mom
(and Tinsel)

Contents

———•———

Associated Press

That boy works as a photographer for the Associated Press. He is at home in a suite at the Marriott Hotel, in a city whose name sounds like machine-gun fire. You keep in touch through e-mail. He sends you photos of human rights violations: the scarred backs of Chinese women, a severed hand at the side of the road, a secret mass grave. You send him photos of local atrocities: your father's retirement cake in the shape of breasts, the words "Jesus Sucks" graffitied in etching gel across the windows of a church.

That boy is more social conscience than you can bear. His love letters are diatribes, global history lessons. He woos you with the blood of political unrest, the testimonials of broken refugees. Devotion disguised as the pain of strangers, something coded and hidden in newspaper clippings, wire-service announcements. When he does think to mention the curve of your back, the smell of your skin, his words are few and precious, grains of rice, drops of clean water.

In your last message, you wrote: *A terrible thing has happened here. I've been selected for jury duty – a man accused of killing prostitutes and burying them in his backyard. There will be crime scene photos.*

You sent this message three days ago. You have not heard from that boy in over a month, since he responded to the retirement cake photo with a curt, "ha, ha." You know he isn't dead; every day he checks in with a supervisor at the AP. You want to call it irresponsible, selfish, but he risks his life to expose terror and oppression in the world, and you live in a two-bedroom condominium with heated tile floors. Everything he does seems forgivable.

There are no new messages on the server.

This boy, with his high-rise-view suite, black leather furniture and state-of-the-art home theatre system, is seducing you the old-fashioned way. South African Chardonnay in hand-blown glasses, Nina Simone in quadraphonic sound. You let your head loll back against the sofa, indulge in the ease of its smooth surface. You watch him lounge in his custom-ordered chair, polished black hide pulled tight over a chrome skeleton.

Earlier that day, you had chosen the perfect outfit for court, a tailored black suit, a steel-grey blouse, serious, but impartial. Your make-up was decidedly neutral.

The air in the jury room was warm and overused. The room itself, dismal and dated – a concrete box, walls panelled in worn gold velveteen, red modular furniture from the seventies.

The other jurors chatted, drank coffee from Styrofoam cups. You fanned yourself with your notepad, tried to picture the accused. You had seen his photo months ago, in newspapers, a balding, dough-faced man with small eyes that receded like pressed raisins. You wondered if he would appear in regular clothes, if he would be handcuffed and shackled.

The door opened and a sheriff walked in; he was older and short, stocky in his tan uniform and black vest, his gun belt pulled tight around his gut. He called for everyone's attention and the room hushed. He announced that the accused had changed his plea to guilty, thanked you for your time.

You were confused. Some of the jurors cheered and clapped, others hurried into their coats, dialled cell phones. You looked to the man beside you, a well-dressed electronics salesman with perfect posture. He was softened by your alarm, tried to reassure you. "It's a little-known fact that most criminal cases are settled before lunch."

Outside the jury room, you stalled, studied the geometric patterns in the carpet, considered sneaking into another trial. You imagined opening statements, objections, false testimony, bloodstained evidence. Things you could e-mail about later.

He felt responsible for you, you could tell. As he stretched into his raincoat, he hovered, as if waiting to see how long you would stay. When only the two of you were left, he offered to walk you to your car; then, at your car, to buy you lunch. Lunch stretched out past dark and now you are in his apartment.

He has the bright, smooth face of someone well scrubbed. You suspect he showers too often, gets his hair cut before it needs cutting, tries clothes on in a change room before buying them. You already know everything about him. You tell yourself he isn't your type; you don't like dark-haired men, men with skin so clean looking, you can be sure they are without scent or heat.

He reaches under the coffee table and pulls out a box. "Do you like trivia?"

You smile despite yourself. "Yes."

"We'll have a contest. First to get ten in a row wins." He hands you a stack of cards.

The idea of competing engages you; you could use a victory, even a small one. You shuffle the cards in your hands. "Wins what?"

He smiles. "We'll decide that after."

You reach for your wineglass, bring it to your lips as he flips the top card in his deck. "What is the capital of Indonesia?"

You try to swallow before you laugh and end up coughing. The wine rises up into your nasal cavity. The alcohol burns. You snort, then, embarrassed, start to giggle uncontrollably. He laughs with you, his eyes curious. "Boy," he says, "you must really know this one." This makes you laugh harder. You curl over yourself, your hand at your stomach. He waits. The moment you feel tears in your eyes, you know you will let yourself lose this game, sleep with this boy.

There are no new messages on the server.

Months of absence made that boy a perfect lover. Distance times longing times uncertainty. You had both learned that love at its best was slow and drawn out, stretched thin for sadness to show through. Each moment you spent together carried within itself a nagging seed, a small, hard reminder of what you would inevitably lose. The sensation of your fingertips touching, life vibrating from one skin to another seemed at once an immeasurable gift, an unbearable injustice. Sometimes you took days to undress one another.

Your bodies moved with calculated stealth, a careful invasion. You lingered wherever the territory seemed foreign, the damp skin behind his knees, the pale insides of his wrists. He unfolded you like a map. Searched for changes in the landscape, new tan lines, a scratch from your neighbour's cat. The couplings remained wordless. Although he hadn't told you directly, you knew there were things he did not want to hear, things that would burden him, that he would never say in return. You kept them to yourself. If you felt those words rising inside you, you held them back like stale breath. Sometimes they found a way out, as mewing when you cried, as gasps when you were ecstatic.

You were someone else when that boy was in town. You took vacation time from your job at the library and forgot you worked there. You attended political lectures and rallies, watched slide shows of hidden, anonymous suffering. Your legs and underarms were waxed. Your hair was trimmed and highlighted in a way that made you look, you thought, more optimistic, proactive. You read at least two newspapers a day. You went to basketball games, and drank beer, watched him sit forward in his seat and nod silently while everyone around you stood and cheered. You listened as he rattled off player stats and conference rankings, as he talked about free throws and penalties; you heard him say that basketball was the one thing he missed about the Western world.

You lay stretched and naked in front of his camera, stared into the eye of his lens, tried to project who you were with him. Hoped that later, in the darkroom, it would bloom on the paper as something disturbing and spectacular, something from which he would try, but fail, to turn away.

You had a habit of going through that boy's things when he was in town. While he went out for coffees or newspapers, you would flip through his plane tickets and itinerary, read his date book, empty his toiletry bag onto your bed. You would piece together his life without you, names of co-workers and guides, addresses of consulates and labs, appointments, deadlines. Once you found his toiletry bag stuffed with condoms.

You clutched them in a fist when he came back in the door. "What are these for?" you asked him.

He laughed. "You don't know what those are for?"

"What do you need them for?"

He walked over to you and peeled a silver square off the strip. "The AP gives them out by the bushel. Look," he said, holding the square close to his face to read the fine print on the wrapper. "They've probably expired."

He looked at you and shook his head, slid his hand under your chin and kissed you firmly on the mouth. "God," he said. "You're tougher than customs."

There are no new messages on the server.

This boy wants to tell you he loves you even though it's only been a couple of weeks. You see it in the sad edges of his smile when he says goodnight. But you know by the thoughtful way he makes dinner reservations, by his gracious habit of being on time, he will wait until you are ready to hear the words, five weeks, maybe seven.

The first night he is in your apartment, he cooks dinner. He is confident in your kitchen, doesn't panic when he cannot find turmeric in the cupboard. He interrogates you as he dices and juliennes, his slender hand working your knife into the hearts of vegetables. You dodge his questions. Duck and cover. You are accustomed to listening and thinking carefully, painfully about what has been said; answering makes you nervous. "Who was your first best friend?" he asks, handing you a vellumous slice of jicama. "I don't know," you shrug. He looks at you as if you are strange.

You chew, your mind sifting for something erudite, articulate. "What do you think of East Timor?" you ask.

He shakes his head. "It's awful. I guess."

You nod. He smiles without looking at you, which, you've learned, is the physical cue that he's about to make a joke. "I'll start researching it tomorrow if it's important to you."

You pick up a garlic clove and hurl it at his head; it bounces off his forehead.

He slams down the knife. "Okay, that's it." He chases you around the counter until he has you pinned against a wall with your wrists behind you. He presses into you, you press back. He brushes the hair out of your face, moves his open lips to your neck and whispers slowly, "Tell me. The name. Of your first. Best. Friend."

While you are brushing your teeth and he is shaving, this boy asks whose clothing takes up a third of your bedroom closet, whose boxes and equipment fill your hallway storage space. You say they belong to a man, a friend.

"What kind of friend?" he asks.

"The kind that works overseas," you reply.

You stare at his reflection in the mirror and watch hard lines cut down to his jaw, a pained tension in his mouth as he rinses his razor under the tap. You are surprised to see that expression on someone else. You've worn it yourself so often, you sometimes slip into it for no reason, catch it reflected in the windows of cars, in glass doors.

Your own face is slack, as if your muscles have gone to sleep. This too is unfamiliar.

He sees your face in the mirror and stops shaving. "What?" His voice is sharp.

You continue brushing, very slowly as you weigh the pros and cons of saying simply, "Nothing." You slide the tooth-brush out of your mouth and spit into the sink. "I know what you're thinking."

He snickers. "What am I thinking?"

You turn and look straight at him, wanting him to know that you are connecting with him, relating to him, not mocking him. "You're telling yourself, leave it alone, leave it alone."

He stares at you. Shakes his head, throws his razor into the sink and walks out of the bathroom.

There are no new messages on the server.

To be honest, you weren't really interested in that boy until he told you he was leaving town. He was the too casual and tousled blond beside you in the rodeo-bar-turned-trendy-hangout. A going-away party for a fashion reporter, a button-down Ralph Lauren gay friend named Marcel who was, at that moment, riding a sluggish mechanical bull and twirling his camel-coloured suit jacket above his head.

You were drunk and unamused. The conversation with "Runs Hands Through Hair," the indigenous nickname you had thought up for that boy in an epic moment of boredom, was stilted and depressing. He wanted to talk about Pinochet. You wanted to talk about why you hated country music, all those lost wives and dogs. After several attempts at attack, you both capitulated, nodded when the other spoke, sipped your drinks in armistice.

After an hour, you cut in on Marcel's account of his latest nineteen-year-old, a Scottish model with "alarmingly strong hands and a delicious Italy-shaped birthmark on his hip." You Euro-kissed Marcel goodbye and pulled on your coat as you walked to the exit. That boy was standing on the sidewalk, finishing a cigarette. He offered to share a cab.

When he mentioned returning to Mexico, you imagined white sand beaches, blended drinks, ceviche; cheap hotels and burning tequila. You rested your head against the taxi window, let his voice dissolve into the drone of the road, and thought about slipping into a bath, washing away the smell of rodeos and politics. You were surprised when the cab pulled up to his building, a new brick townhouse near the centre of the city. You had cast him in a less cosmopolitan setting, a low-rent ethnic neighbourhood popular with the college crowd, an old house, a single room. He invited you in for coffee, to look at his photographs. He was being polite. You were curious. You assumed something *National Geographic*: majestic cliff-scapes, waterfalls, the craggy faces of friendly market vendors. Instead, you found a small, one-legged Mexican boy, shirtless with a bandana around his forehead, kissing the barrel of an automatic rifle. The decapitated bodies of three freedom fighters, their heads snatched as trophies, the hand of one victim making the shape of a gun. An old woman crying, cradling the body of a young woman whose torso had been blown open by explosives, the brilliant midday sun catching the young woman's wound, the centre of her body glistening like an oozing tropical fruit.

He placed a mug of coffee on the table in front of you. "It isn't how most people think of the world," he said.

You nodded, half agreeing with him, half acknowledging the embarrassing truth about yourself: you never really thought about the world. You rarely watched the evening news, only read the entertainment section of the paper. It wasn't that you didn't want to know what was going on, but that you couldn't make sense of it. The world had become too tangled for you to unravel in the hour before dinner, coups, rebellions, interventions, peacekeeping. Complex systems to manage hunger and murder and exploitation, but nothing to end them. That is what bothered you most, that there was no conceivable end.

You caught him looking at his own photographs, hands on his hips, chin lowered, chest dented into his body; you saw that the cost of these images went far beyond airfare and film. The blond hair above his ears was peppered with grey, incongruous with his age – which you had noted as you admired the numerous stamps in his passport – thirty-three. He struck you as someone who would grow old overnight. Perhaps after a long journey, an extended time away, he would return and seem closer to expiration: sudden creases in his face, a remoteness in the way he paused before speaking. The thought made you sad.

He straightened and asked if you wanted more coffee. You shook your head. You hesitated for a moment, then reached out your arm and slipped your hand inside his. The skin of his palm was tender and damp. He glanced at you sidelong for just a second, his eyes inquisitive, his smile small and private. You felt yourself blushing. As he turned back to his photos, he squeezed your hand.

You sat together on the couch. He explained each photograph, his voice quiet, but animated. His arm rested on the cushions behind your neck, his body inches from yours. He watched you as you studied his pictures, which made it difficult for you to study him. You imagined that under his white shirt, his frame was taut, trained. When he smiled, the angles of his face relaxed, his eyes warmed and you noticed for the first time that his lips were smooth and fleshy, like a boy's.

By three a.m. you had heard all about the Zapatistas and their struggle for independence. You were drawn in by their covered faces, their cunning tactics in the night.

You called in sick five days in a row; you spent every hour with him. The weekend before he left, the two of you drove to a bed and breakfast in the mountains. On a late-nineteenth-century silk brocade divan, in front of a window overlooking a glacier lake, you asked if you could meet him in Mexico. You made it sound casual, like you were planning to go there anyway. And you were, some day. He stared at the lake as if out on the water there were something familiar, something he knew he would see at this place. You breathed as slowly and quietly as you could. His seemed at ease, his mouth turned up slightly at the corners, a half smile. You took that as a good sign. He had been thinking about it, too. His eyes stayed on the water as he spoke. "This is something I do alone." You made an effort at a smile, then shifted your gaze away from him, to the dark hills that loomed around lake's edge. You didn't want him to see the tension in your face, to read your insecure thoughts.

There are no new messages on the server.

You call this boy because you should, because you haven't been completely honest. He arrives with flowers, birds of paradise. You've set the coffee table with two bottles of red wine and two glasses. You each sit on opposite ends of the couch. You tell him the entire story from beginning to end. Sometimes he nods, other times he sits motionless. Twice you cry. You are surprised; he is not. He says nothing, does not console you or try to hold you, but gently pries the soggy tissues out of your palm, replaces them with fresh ones. He refills the wineglasses. You both fall asleep on the couch. In the middle of the night, he wakes you, guides you to bed, his arm around your waist. He folds you into the blankets, then lies on top of the covers in his clothes.

You pull him towards you, press your face into his neck. You are comforted by the feel of his cheek against your forehead, the collar of his shirt against your chin. You fall asleep, your head full of the scent of his laundry detergent. Something bright and lemony that makes everything smell new.

The next day, you send the following message: *I can't compete with all the trouble in the world.*

Seeing this boy as often as you do, you worry about the dense scrub of relationship, an overgrowth of tenderness that will choke you into apathy, bind you towards contempt. You know sex is the place it will germinate, root itself. You are vigilant. You read women's magazines for advice on frequency, intensity, variety: *the trick to keeping a relationship hot is to save your tricks; every third time incorporate something new.*

But it is by accident, not during one of your "every third" times that you strike the mainline to this boy's desire, expose what is raw and eager in him with the slip of your hand.

It begins when you undress him one night and jokingly wrap his leather belt around your wrists. He moves on you swiftly, one hand at his zipper. He pushes your arms above your head, draws the belt so tight it bites your skin. He opens your legs with his knees, shifts his weight to one side, works himself past the crotch of your panties. He covers your eyes with his hand.

Nights later, he turns you naked on your stomach. Traps you between his legs while he loops his belt around your neck, enters you slowly from behind. His body on you and over you again and again. You lose your heartbeat in his rhythm, then feel its return, an urgent throb in your neck and head as the belt tightens. He curls the leather tail around his fist, once, twice. You watch the bedroom wall advance, retreat, as your vision narrows, then brightens. You wonder in a moment of swoon if you will die here, a willing captive in your own bed. You wonder how many women in the world die this way, blind and tied. He finishes abruptly; the belt goes slack. You watch colours turn on the insides of your eyelids as he kisses your neck, strokes your breast, slides down your body to finish you off.

This is how sex evolves between you. Loving torture. You invest in equipment: blindfolds, restraints. He practises cracking a belt so that it stings without breaking the skin. You learn to admire the marks across your back, around your ankles and wrists. There is something divine and surprising in the mercy you show each other afterward. A sincere caretaking that is ciphered into everyday language as you soothe your limbs against the cool of the sheets, fluff pillows for one another, check for any true harm. Something as simple as this boy offering to get out of bed and make coffee warms you like an unexpected gift.

You are lying on your side in the predawn morning, lulling between the blue light of your bedroom and a dream about microfiche. The phone rings. And though you usually let the machine pick it up at this hour, you reach for it in your half sleep, bring it to your ear. There is a buzz and a click, then the sound of an open tunnel.

"Tell me you don't have cancer." It is that boy.

"What?" you ask, struggling to ground yourself in time, space, and context. "What?"

"Cancer."

You sit up. This boy lies still in the bed, far away in sleep, his back to you. You speak softly, your lips close to the receiver. "I don't have cancer."

That boy sighs. "Thank God." He laughs. "While I was in Aceh I had this awful dream that you were dying and not going to tell me." His voice is forced. This, you think, is his best effort at being light.

You are silent.

"I'm sorry," he says. "For not writing."

You hear the echo of your own uneven breath.

"Aceh's a mess. It's East Timor all over again. Worse. They're making an example of the Acehnese. They're –"

"Do you know what time it is here?" you ask.

You hear him tap something in a broken rhythm, his finger or a pencil against a hard surface. He coughs. When he speaks again, he sounds tired. "Is he there?"

You swallow to mask your voice. "Who?"

"I don't know." He laughs. "Anyone." The casual tone is awkward on him.

You cannot think of where to begin, how to explain, so you just say, "Yes."

The click when that boy hangs up is so quiet, you don't realize he's gone until you hear the hum of empty air, feel the useless weight of the receiver in your hand.

You place the phone into its cradle, turn and press against this boy's body, your face between his shoulders, your chest to his back. You pull the comforter to your neck. Your right foot brushes against the bed in small circles, a nightmare remedy left over from childhood. His hand reaches behind for your waist and pulls you closer. You hunker down behind his shoulder, hide from the sun, a sliver of light above the windowsill.

You try to separate that boy from your life. The surgery is messy, like something severed in the jungle without anaesthetic. You mistrust your preferences, your habits, your usuals, wonder which ones you adopted because of him. When did you start preferring americanos to cappuccinos? When did you decide fifty dollars was too much to pay for dinner?

In a grocery store line-up, you dig through your purse for your chequebook. You have already asked yourself if it was his suggestion to buy organic, to skip the cereal aisle and never buy peanut butter or oranges from Florida. Inside your purse, your palm catches the tip of an open lipstick. The checkout girl drums the counter with a pen. The man behind you mutters something rude. You stare at the deep maroon smear across your hand, a painless wound. Ask yourself, did I buy that for him?

This boy's apartment is a refuge, a high glass tank that shields you from the world. While you work your days in the stacks, pulling books for inter-library loan, you dream of the view from his balcony, the dark water of the inlet, the city lights laid out like a jewelled carpet. You imagine your reflection in the sliding glass door, a version of yourself that is cool and smooth to the touch.

Inside these glass walls, you are frivolous and happy to be so. The two of you make dinner, drink wine, watch *Jeopardy!*, have sex. You tell each other the same animal bar jokes over and over, and pretend each time you've never heard them before. *A bear walks into a bar. Three pigs walk into a bar . . . An octopus walks into a bar . . .*

The two of you sneak down to the indoor pool and you swim naked for him, lap after lap, your body turning a slippery somersault at each end. He kneels at the pool edge, leans to kiss you as you approach. You wrap your arms around his neck and his lips brush your eyebrow. "I love you," he whispers. You hold him against you, your wet hair soaking his cheek. He loosens your arms to look at your face. You raise your feet and push against the pool wall, glide away from him. He pulls off his t-shirt and dives in. His body is silent under water. In a few strokes, he is beside you. You face each other, tread water in the middle of the pool. The laps have made you tired; you try to ignore the aching in your legs and shoulders. His eyes are bright and wide and wet. You feel your bottom lip touching the surface, struggle to keep your chin up. He is smiling. "Do you love me?" he asks. You laugh out loud, your body contracting, your head dipping under. You come up with a mouthful of water and spit it in his face. He wipes his eyes, then reaches his hand out and grabs your arm, pulls you toward him. You expect him to force you under, to hold you thrashing and airless as punishment for your dirty play. Instead, he moves his hand to the top of your back, buoys you up, allows you to float without having to move.

That boy came to your work once. He had been taking photographs of heroin addicts in the downtown eastside, part of a photo essay for a community gallery. You ate sandwiches outside the library, perched together on the edge of a concrete planter, the June sun easy against your back. You watched some kids in baggy shorts lounge in an alcove, their skateboards leaned up against the wall. A girl with cherry-red hair used a thick permanent marker to sign her curvy name on a boy's naked calf.

While you ate, that boy took photographs: the girl with her cheek against the boy's bare leg, a homeless man in front of the library's towering postmodern facade, your thin shadow on the sidewalk below the cement planter.

A group of pre-school children passed by, a parade of hand-made paper hats and knapsacks, swinging arms, profuse smiles, luscious and heartbreaking. That boy nudged you, pointed at the children, "How 'bout a couple of them?" You turned to see if he was joking; a dry piece of sandwich scraped down your throat. His face was attentive, awaiting your response. You felt yourself flush, and smiled, nodded slowly, your body very still. He pulled away from you then, the strap of his camera slapping your bare arm.

The children posed for him as a group, three rows of coloured hats, hands in mouths, eyes at the clouds, their teacher grinning and proud in a flowery dress that threatened to rise with the wind. You sat, hot and nauseated, embarrassed by what you thought he had meant, unable to look at him. He walked back toward you and you watched the children instead, moving away, their plump, lively bodies flattening into two dimensions, daubs of colour below the vast city sky.

You grow tired of this boy's apartment sooner than you expect. You tell him things are busy at the library. You stay late and roam the stacks, search for books that would interest you if you were the type to have interests. The history of carousel horses, small engine repair, winter gardening, the complete works of Dorothy Parker, Japanese paper art, the concise dictionary of Eastern mysticism, the songs of Bruce Springsteen, a century of fashion, a hundred and one metalwork ideas, the encyclopaedia of Victorian upholstery. You bring them home, their weight somehow comforting in your arms. The books pile up on your floor like clumsy pagodas, an obstacle course of precarious possibilities. In many you find things left by previous readers: bus transfers, an unused teabag, shopping lists, two fettuccini noodles, and once, a fifty-dollar bill folded between two diagrams of origami frogs. Sometimes, shockingly, in the margins of books, you find doodles, random sketches of geometric shapes or cartoon faces in pencil or pen. Messages scratched into a dirt wall, the impenetrable hieroglyphs of those who came before you and searched for something in this same place.

In a book on kosher cooking you find a piece of paper folded as a bookmark. A list of names: six nuns and two priests. You recognize the list; you used to carry it around in your purse; abominable murders posted on the Internet. And now you wonder if these were real names, real deaths, or simply an Internet hoax to manipulate political sympathy. You tell yourself you never really cared about those people, that love and propaganda are not the same thing.

In your own apartment, you monitor your autonomy. You have boxed that boy's clothes and camera equipment and moved them to a storage locker. And now, even the smallest infringements set you off. You balk when this boy brings over breakfast cereal without consulting you. You return the CDs he buys for your meagre collection. You are cautious about decisions and choices; the integrity of the border can no longer be compromised. To establish definite boundaries, you refuse to have extra keys made, dig a trench in the comforter when you sleep in the same bed at night. You sometimes imagine a halo of white chalk around your body as you walk through your apartment, feel it between this boy's fingertips and your skin when he touches you, something dusty and smooth. He is understanding. Tells you he respects independent women. Wonders aloud if the two of you should move in together. You point to the piles of books on your floor and tell him, there is hardly room.

If you had imagined a life for you and that boy, it was not the one you had. If you could do it over, you would be the kind of girl he would want to take with him. You would be stronger or smarter or harder. You remember his photos of female Zapatistas, skinny, rigid women in fatigues and bandana masks, their eyes fiery with disobedience. Look in the mirror at your own eyes, vague, watery. Your body, still young but softening, curving gently in and out on itself, womanly. A home body.

You've been unusually tired in the mornings and evenings, prone to crying in the afternoon. You decide to join a gym. Start in the class that combines kickboxing and aerobics. A sinewy man several inches shorter than you shouts in your face as you force your limbs out into fierce upper cuts, jabs, hooks. You feel both keenly charged and on the verge of collapse as you dodge, fake and swing, dodge, fake and swing. Sweat gathers in a stream between your shoulder blades; you watch your arms lash out in front of you, tell yourself, this is useful. This will come in handy some day.

You join this boy for dinner at a trendy, upscale restaurant, this boy and his friends. You are out of sorts when you arrive, a combination of agitation and fatigue. You pace the foyer, smile at the wait staff as they pass, scratch at the fake gold leaf with your thumbnail until this boy comes out into the lobby. "I was just going to call you," he says, waving his cell phone, all surprise and relief.

"I just got here," you say.

He guides you through the restaurant. Everything is dark red: the carpet, the velvet upholstery, the heavy satin curtains that drip down the sides of walls, and the walls themselves, reddened with a paint so dark and matte, it sucks away the room's already dim light.

The friends, three men arranged around a table, are easy to look at, the type who use hair products, wear dry-clean-only clothes. Two of them look a little younger than this boy; the third, older. This boy moves to fill your glass with wine. The older friend stops him. "Give her the good stuff." This boy fills his own glass with the remains of a local Gamay, christens your glass with an imported Cabernet Sauvignon.

The banter is light and energetic. Each friend draws you into alliance – a nod in your direction, a sidelong glance, a more direct, "Am I right?" from the older friend. You trail on the fringe of conversation, swallow your wine in mouthfuls. All the friends are attractive, all the friends are funny and sharp. This generic quality makes you stare at this boy until he is nothing but a blur between two faux-finished pillars. You see that his hazy face is smiling broadly at you, but then again, so are the others. Men like this are not uncommon in the world.

You wonder if his friends share the same proclivities in bed. You think that you could probably sleep with any of them. Apart from minor differences, age, hair colour, height, they are interchangeable. You suspect that they would also like to sleep with you. Two of them bump wrists in an bungled attempt to fill your wineglass. They laugh at your quips, mistake your apathy for keen wit. At intervals, they each turn from the conversation to smile at you, hold your gaze for as long as they can, create the brief illusion of intimacy. The message is clear, "If it doesn't work out for you two, we're just as good."

You peruse the menu. One of the younger ones touches your arm. "The decor in this place is something else, hey?"

"Yes," you say, dryly. "I believe they call this period Early Haemorrhaging." The friend chuckles. This boy stares at you with more than a hint of annoyance; you feel, momentarily, like a child.

After you've ordered, the conversation turns to electronics, DVDs, amps. You rearrange the napkin on your lap, study the other restaurant patrons: couples and groups who look far too young and coutured to be real. You wonder if they all give to Amnesty International.

You wish that you had met that boy's friends, anonymous phone voices who called at night and beckoned him out for drinks and card games.

"You wouldn't enjoy it," he told you. "They're crusty old photographers and pressmen. It's all shop talk."

"There aren't any women?" you asked.

"Sure there's women," he told you. "But they're crusty, too."

On those nights, you thought about calling your own friends. Girls from the college library program, girls who worked with you. Friends you ran into on the street and exchanged phone numbers with, knowing full well neither of you had any intention of getting together. You couldn't be bothered to keep in touch; you ignored invitations, forgot birthdays. When you did call, you found yourself rambling to answering machines or friends who were already in pyjamas.

You spent those nights alone, imagined that boy in a smoky room, laughing, rested back, his ankle on his knee. Relaxed in a way he never was with you. The people in the room were sarcastic and funny and informed. The women were never crusty.

The food arrives and the smell of it, garlic, anchovies, olive oil, causes a turn in your stomach. You excuse yourself from the table, move calmly through the restaurant to the ladies' room, a den of mirrors and chrome washed in a lighter, pinker red. In the stall, you grip the cold tank of the toilet, lean your face down to the bowl and catch a whiff of bleach and air freshener. Your body unleashes two and a half glasses of sanguine wine.

At the sink, you rinse your mouth and wash your face with cold water. Pat your skin dry with a paper towel. As you reapply lipstick, you feel relieved that the alcohol is out of you. You tell yourself, it's better this way. This is no time to take up drinking.

By the week's end, this boy is frustrated with your cultivated despondency. He suggests a trip, somewhere warm. His coffee table is covered with travel brochures, glossy pages of vacant beaches, crystal tides. You are afraid to pick them up. You wander around his apartment, look under cushions, behind the television. You flip through fashion magazines to watch the pages fan. He offers to fix you a drink, but you decline, pacing instead a track around his coffee table. He fixes himself one, three fingers of gin, no ice; you haven't had sex for days now and he is antsy. He carries his drink to the table and stands in your way. "We could go for a swim?" You stop in front of him, shake your head. He runs his hand around the back of your neck, up into your hair; he massages the base of your skull. "I know what'll make you feel better."

He pulls gently on your hair. You feel your skin loosening its grip on your bones. You lay your head into his palm and let him hold you. Your shoulder blades relax back and down. His lips land on your neck, soft, brushing kisses. His fingertips unbutton your blouse, trace the edges of your bra. You feel yourself hanging in air, your head tipped back, and wonder when he will let go, when you will fall. He keeps your head cradled in one hand as the other moves to your skirt, crawls under the hem. You stop him there, your hand grabbing down for his wrist and wrenching his arm up between the two of you. He smiles at the speed and severity of your gesture.

You look at him as directly as you can. "I'm late."

There are no new messages on the server.

This boy holds your hand in the waiting room. Whispers he loves you. Gets up to check with the nurse about the time. Shakes his foot while he reads a magazine. You breathe deeply into your stomach, sure you can feel something there, something floating in a liquid pouch. You tell yourself there are already too many people in the world, too many hungry children. You sift through a stack of old newspapers on the waiting-room table, pull out the international news sections. Wars, atrocities, disasters calm you. It is exactly as you suspected, the world is no place to raise a child.

You stare at the colour photograph that fronts a world news section already a few days old: *Army helicopter hit by rebel ground fire crashes in jungle outside Aceh.* The image is the view from the jungle floor. Leafy trees and vines decorated with glinting pieces of fuselage. Here and there, dark red blooms hang from branches like great weeping flowers.

The doctor who performs your procedure is cheerful, tells a joke about three men with Alzheimer's who share a house; he makes the nurses laugh. He gives instructions in a tender voice. *Slide down to the end of the table, good, good, feet on here.* He stops for a moment with your heel in his hand, the paper bootie crinkling, turns your leg to examine the fading marks. Looks at you kindly, his eyebrows raised as if asking if he should be concerned. You push a weak smile, he smiles back, and sets your paper foot in the stirrup.

Let your knees relax outward, that's it, good, you'll feel a little pressure, just my hand, good, perfect. His voice is hypnotic in its rhythm, its soothing timbre. The gown is crisp against your skin, the table cool and hard beneath you. A nurse strokes your forearm as the doctor moves a needle between your legs. *Just a pinch,* he says before you feel it.

You close your eyes and feel the glow of the examination lamps on your body. You try to draw in that focused warmth, absorb it, as if it were the sun. The lip of the table underneath your backside drops with a metallic click. Your legs tense. *Just relax,* the doctor's hand on the inside of your calf, your lower body flushed and heavy. The table seems softer, you are sinking into it. The noises of the room slip away in gentle increments. The chatter of nurses fades out to a distant twitter, grows dim and cottony as if they have left the room, then comes back slowly, sparkles into the chatter of young girls on a beach, their busy hands spreading oils and lotions, adjusting straps and sunglasses. The whir of a machine vibrates into the engine of a seaplane as it parts with the water, leaving a bright white cleft in the cyan tide. You are lying on sand, the earth's warm pressure against your back, the heat of the sun penetrating points deep in your centre. Every now and then, a young brown boy selling cold drinks comes by to ask if you are alright, you tell him, yes, yes. As he moves away from you, your head is filled with the perfume of jasmine and tropical fruit. There are other sounds: the music of handmade instruments, the easy laughter of island wives, the clicks and clacks of an unknown language. And beneath all this, the deep and insistent surge of your own breath, the echo of a pulse in your belly. You are amazed to find that here you can sit up, stand, walk around. You push your feet into the sand, stare at painted birds, brilliant flowers. You watch as glassy waves crawl onto beach, play broken seashells like wind chimes. The taste in your mouth is salty sweet, sea air, cane sugar. There are no rebels here, you tell yourself, no guerrillas, no mercenaries. No one dies here, no priests, no women. No children die here.

The sky melts into a puddly horizon of pink and tangerine. This boy is silent as he drives, but holds your hand, rubs his thumb over your knuckles. You stop at a drugstore for painkillers. The nurse at the clinic assured you there would be almost no pain, but you are unconvinced.

Back at your apartment, this boy tucks you into bed, tells you he will stay on the couch so you can get some rest, leaves you with a glass of water and the bottle of pills.

You shake two white tablets into your hand, then place them on the nightstand, beside the phone. You want to feel the pain first without the drugs, to confront it dead-on before numbing it out. You wait for the muted ache in your abdomen to grow, think about the two teenage girls in the recovery room, their worried murmurs to the nurses, their uncertain smiles. All three of you had glanced over your blankets at each other, fleeting but polite looks of sympathy. You had all endured something, you had all survived.

Your body feels alarmingly normal, a fullness around your middle, but other than that, nothing. You had expected something traumatic, an unhealed wound, a permanent injury. You had expected to suffer.

The bedroom glows with the warm tones of dusk, the hard corners of walls and furniture rounded and smoothed by the light. A photograph of this scene would disturb no one. You reach your hand between your legs, touch the hospital pad, remind yourself there is still blood.

You reach into the drawer of the nightstand and pull out a folded piece of paper. You stare at the phone for a long time before picking up the receiver. You dial a series of numbers, listen for chimes, dial more numbers. A hotel switchboard operator connects your call.

You count the rings. You have decided to hang up after seven.

At six, he answers. "Hello?" That boy's voice is distant and curious.

"Hello."

A pause and crackle on the line. "How are you?"

You slide your hand under the sheets, rub the flat of your stomach. "I saw the photo. In the paper. The helicopter."

"Yeah, what a mess." He sighs. "I've really wanted to call you, I just thought."

"I know." A twinge, small and sharp, flickers in your abdomen. "It's okay."

"I miss you."

You turn onto your side, push your hand into the sting. A cramp begins, a closed fist, a warm, twisting grip. Tears fall over the bridge of your nose.

"Something's happened here," he says. The connection falters; his words are delayed, then repeated in a digital stutter. "Happened here happened here."

"Something's happened here, too," you say, but he is already talking over you.

"I've applied for a new assignment in the Middle East. If I schedule it right, I might get a week or two off before I start." The ends of his sentences retreat into echo; the phone line is more like a vast space than a thin tunnel.

You and that boy are worlds apart, your closeness, an incidental by-product of technology, an illusion of satellites and fibre optics.

"Are you still there?"

You swallow to clear your throat. "Yeah." You look over at the pills, but the pain has disappeared, a fleeting and shadowy exit.

"Did you say something while I was talking? I couldn't hear you, this connection is terrible."

"No," you say.

This boy sleeps with a clear mind, dreams in quadraphonic sound. In bed, with the lights off, you stare at his shoulder, the turns and curves of muscle and bone. You marvel that his body is so sharp against the fade of the room, so vividly distinguish-able from the rest of the world. Your own skin seems to blur into the air around you, wash into the sheets. You watch the flutter beneath this boy's eyelids, run your fingers through his hair, damp around the temples like a feverish youth. You kiss the ridge of his brow.

Tomorrow you will tell him it is over. He will not believe you. He will negotiate, then shout, then cry. You will not know when to touch him. You will follow him around as he gathers his things, and beg him to look at you, to talk to you. He will shake his head and push you away. He will call you something horrible and you will slap him so hard his mouth will bleed. You will cry; he will take off his coat.

By the end of it, sometime between ten and midnight, after a full day of emotional hostage-taking, without food or water, while you are filling a glass with ice and he is dabbing hydro-gen peroxide to his lip, you will look at each other and find someone so unfamiliar, you will wonder if you are in the right apartment, the right country.

It is then that the two of you will finally reach a settlement, decide to call a truce, lie down in each other's arms and, soon after, manoeuvre your way out, in the dark.

Sally, in Parts

SALLY'S EYES

Sally's eyes have recently required glasses. For the fine print on hospital waivers, for the long curls of *l*'s that look like *t*'s, short humps of *e*'s that look like *a*'s on her father's medical charts. For a more intelligent appearance when talking with doctors and respiratory technicians. She has practised putting the glasses on, taking them off. She touches the tip of the plastic arm to her lips when she is alone with the doctor whose left eye is partially hidden by his dark hair, whose on-call stubble looks tactical. She turns the glasses in her hands when she is uncertain, when technicians and nurses buzz and ring in and out of the room, turning dials, pressing buttons. She folds the glasses in a loose fist when she is too tired to ask questions, when nurses and doctors blur into a murmur of white gauze.

When her father first went into the hospital, Sally stayed away. Slept in her own bed, Scotch Tape pressed against her temples to stretch out deepening crow's feet. Her eyes, once a perfect almond shape, keen and brilliant, now shrinking, collapsing at the corners like old sheets. Sally's mother sent her copies of lab reports, doctor's notes, but Sally had trouble reading them, all the small type, scrawled instructions. She held them close to her face, sniffed them instead. She told herself she was too young to need glasses; that he was strong and would get better without her. She dreamt she was driving a car and suddenly unable to open her eyes. Her lids so heavy, it was like they were sewn shut. Her father, in the back seat, demanded to know what was going on, what she was doing, and she told him, "Nothing, nothing," all the time straining to see the road through the red skin of her lids.

Now, so that her mother can go home for a proper meal, a proper sleep, Sally spends half the night sitting up, eyes open, then closed, then open, a ceaseless meditation. She has short, angry dreams, which are more like memories. Keeps watch over her father's bed. Looks for something changed.

What Sally's eyes search for: signs of weakening, softening. Her next lover. Discoloured skin, lumps and bumps.

In the hospital, before her father goes to sleep, Sally's eyes spend a great deal of time watching television, reading the paper. She cannot see the picture in the Magic Eye Puzzle that comes with the comics. Cannot figure out what is different in the "What Is Different?" cartoons.

SALLY'S LUNGS

During Sally's infancy, her lungs and their ability to produce sound were the focus of much amazement. "She'll be an opera singer," her father boasted. "Or a shrew," her mother countered.

In school, she was on the swim team because she could stay underwater longer than anyone else. Sally's mother arranged all the swimming badges and medals on the mantel. Once, while a family friend was admiring the awards, Sally heard her father say, "Keeps her out of trouble." Sally imagined herself throwing bricks into shop windows, robbing elderly people on the street.

During swim practice, Sally's favourite game was to promise boys a peek under her bathing suit if they could catch her beneath the surface. They never could.

At night, she held her breath as these same boys climbed the veranda railing and curled around the corner of the house to her bedroom window. Sally sat on the windowsill in her nightgown, with her hair brushed. She amazed these boys. Mashed her mouth against theirs, rolled her tongue around and around, let them squeeze and knead her unformed flesh through the worn flannel. Their skin hot, they breathed like dogs. Smelled like the pool, damp and tangy with chlorine. They marvelled at Sally's ability to kiss for minutes without needing to take a breath. Some boys timed her. She didn't have the heart to tell them she cheated, drew quiet sips of air through her nose. Some boys told her they loved her; this made her laugh. Sometimes, glazed-lipped and giddy with the smell of her mother's rose bushes, cherry gloss and boy sweat, Sally thought of her father, one floor below, cigarette burning, reading the newspaper in front of the television, and wondered why he had stopped coming up to kiss her goodnight.

The doctor with the swishy hair is wearing a new cologne. Something like citrus candy with an undertone of lake water. Sally fills her lungs with it as they stand side by side at the X-ray screen. The light shining through her father's chest casts a bluish glow that sets off the doctor's eyes.

Sally has seen her father's lungs many times. Has stared at the clumps of barbed asbestos particles that cling like moss to the upper walls. The doctor brushes his hair out of his face, compliments Sally on her glasses. She says thank you while touching her fingers to her bare neck. The doctor's eyes follow her hand; his lips press together, then part. He is not her usual type, but she likes his tired eyes, his earnest clinical demeanour. She has overheard him lecturing patients on the evils of smoking, his voice irritated and chastising.

He takes a pen from the pocket of his white coat and points at the X-ray. He explains that her father's smoking has para-lyzed the cilia in his lungs, making it impossible for his body to expel the asbestos it has breathed in. He describes her father's lungs as vacuum cleaner bags that will never be emptied, then coughs, apologizes for being crude, removes his own glasses and rubs the bridge of his nose.

Before Sally's mother leaves for the evening, she thumps her husband's chest and back to loosen the mucus that drowns his breathing. Sally watches her mother lift his thin body care-fully, as if afraid he might snap in two. The tapping sound is horrible, a hard knocking on the outside of a brittle reed. Sally imagines that beneath her father's skin, he is nothing but hardened muscle, stubborn bone, pushing back against her mother's hand, making the job more difficult for her. He coughs, long, gravelly drags that force mucus into his mouth. He spits, and coughs again, his eyes squeezed shut, his cheeks puffed, an alarming flush from his neck to his hairline.

At night, while the nurses are collected down the hall in the quiet glow of their station, while her father sleeps, Sally removes his oxygen mask and cups it over her own face. She is hit by the reek of his breath, the insides of his body spoiling, curdling. Then the clear, almost-wetness of the oxygen. November air, damp leaves. She inhales until she is dizzy. Revels in the full, unfettered girth of her lungs' expanse.

SALLY'S HANDS

"Never done a chore in her life." Sally's father offered her ten-year-old hand by the wrist to relatives, friends, solicitous strangers at the door, and they all said the same thing, *soft*. His way of keeping her thankful, showing off how well he provided.

Sally's hands are still "soft," and narrow and unblemished. Her palms are thin and smooth, her skin fair but not translu-cent, no snaking veins peeking through. Her fingers straight without a bulge at the knuckles, her nail beds long, her nails hard and shaped into perfect ovals.

Sally's hands are nothing like her mother's. Cracked and crooked from years of scouring, kneading, peeling. Sally's mother has never needed help opening a jar, has always favoured a dishtowel over oven mitts, still washes dishes in scalding water.

Because of her work, Sally must avoid cooking and cleaning. She eats out and has a girl come in once a week. She wears gloves to do anything that might get her hands wet or dirty. She doesn't order anything in a restaurant that cannot be eaten with utensils. Sally is a hand model. Her hands have paid for a car, one that makes men stare, and a waterfront apartment in the city.

Sally knows her hands are her best feature. She plays them up whenever she's with a man. Cradles a wineglass, grips the gearshift, plays with the buttons on her shirt. Men seem to have expectations of how her hands will feel, what they will do. She does not disappoint. Her hands keep a man happy until he starts to look too vulnerable, too lost. Then her hands close doors, fold tight into themselves, rest in her lap, refuse to answer the phone. Eventually, her hands start flitting and casting for something new.

On a job, Sally's hands will lie still for the camera, lathered in dish soap, decorated with jewellery, resting on the naked back of another model. Away from work, Sally's hands fidget, manoeuvre, as if they are unsettled by too much leisure time. At the hospital, Sally flips through the paper or straightens her father's bedding, arranges the items on his tray. When he is asleep, she sometimes sneaks flowers out of the gift vases in his room, plucks the petals one by one, wonders about the doctor.

Sally keeps a nightly regime of exfoliation, self-massage, touch-up manicure, and re-hydration. The antibacterial soap at the hospital has forced her to double- and triple-moisturize during the day. She had tried keeping her hands slathered in Vaseline under thin plastic gloves, but the crinkling sound of the gloves, her father told her mother the next day, like someone fiddling with a candy bar in a movie theatre, kept him awake all night.

The first man to hold Sally's hand was a stranger. A man who found her lost in a hardware store when she was seven years old. On Saturday mornings, Sally went with her father to Jal's Hardware, a sprawling lumberyard and store where everything looked already used and dirty. She had trouble keeping up with her father, who moved erratically through the store, stopping at a rack of saws or drills to evaluate each model, moving it in his hands, only to eventually shake his head, and march on to something else. Sally amused herself with the lower shelves of sponges and cloths. She drew pictures in the nap of the chamois, pretended the sponges were rabbits, until she noticed her father's legs were no longer beside her, and abandoned the soft objects to search for him in the store. On the day the stranger found her, she had already paced the store twice, looked down every aisle, and was crying softly beside a bucket of bolts. The man folded her hand into his and led her out of the store to look for her father's car in the parking lot. She spotted her father right away, turning and catching them as he tied some lumber to the roof of the car, a blank look on his face, his features falling away. He came across the parking lot, the sun blazing behind him as if he were walking out of it. His hand reached out as he neared. Sally smiled, let go of the stranger's hand and reached her own hand toward the sun. And, in a broad sweep of air, Sally's father slapped her face. "Thank you," he said to the stranger. He pulled Sally by the wrist to the car where he slapped her again and said, "Don't ever go with strange men, you hear me?" Sally nodded.

SALLY'S BREASTS

Sally has only one breast. After finding a pea-sized lump between her right breast and underarm four years ago, she came apart in pieces, lumpectomy, lymphectomy, mastectomy, her entire right side caved in, surrendered. She became an expert at nursing scars, binding them carefully with surgical tape, rubbing the taut, red skin with lotions and oils. She bought special bras, practical, rigorous contraptions with secret pockets for expensive silicone or gel-filled forms. Bras that sought to assert her breasts as a pair.

Sally got her first bra at thirteen. The white mounds of her developing breasts shook under her cotton t-shirts as she walked, jiggled as she climbed the stairs. Her mother noticed this problem first, took her to a department store and bought her a white cotton training bra with thick straps, more like a harness than an undergarment. When Sally got home, she ran to her room to put it on. In the mirror her breasts looked controlled and less alert under her t-shirt. She heard her parents arguing in the hallway. Her mother's voice was calm and insistent, her father's gruff and irritated. When she came out of her room, her father stopped her at the stairs. "Don't you get any ideas," he said. Sally stood for a long time after he left her, afraid of ideas she might already have had.

Sally's father stopped looking at her. He sometimes stayed home because of coughing or back pain or slow months at the factory. He ignored her when she walked into a room, spoke without looking at her, kept his eyes on his paper, the television. His words, when they came, were usually commandments. "Wash that junk off your face," if she tried to leave the house wearing make-up, "Get back up there and comb your hair proper," if she used the hairspray she kept hidden under the sink. Sally chewed her lips to keep them red, carried a small jar of Vaseline in her bag to use as lip gloss. She enjoyed telling him that it was chapped lips, not make-up, she suffered from. When she was finally fed up with waiting for him to go to the bathroom so she could leave the house, with washing her face in the school sink, being teased about her flat hair, Sally ignored her father, walked out the back door with make-up on and her hair sprayed high, her bag hanging heavy on her shoulder. She walked stiffly, quickly, expecting at any moment to feel his hands grab at her, drag her back to the kitchen sink. She walked a block, then exhaled, turned and looked back at her house.

Her father was standing on the front steps, his arms crossed in front of his chest. That night, for the first time, Sally's father did not eat dinner with Sally and her mother at the kitchen table. He ate alone, in the living room, with the television on.

Sally's father refuses to talk about Sally's illness. He does not ask her how she's doing. If she happens to mention it, the cancer, the surgery, the treatment, he fiddles with the newspaper or the television. Today, he pretends to be engrossed in a news-magazine exposé about a mass murderer, a middle-class man gone amuck. "You can't trust the middle class," he mutters to himself. Sally has taken up the same habit, reads editorials on the death penalty instead of talking with her father, holding his hand. An eye for an eye. In the hallway, Sally's mother scolds her for being insensitive. "Can't you make an effort?"

"I just don't see the point of being here." Sally is tired of waking in the middle of the night, of trying to keep her eyes open as she drives home through deserted streets.

"It comforts him to have someone here when he falls asleep."

"He doesn't want me."

"For godsakes, he could be dying."

Sally looks hard at her mother. "So could I."

Sally is waiting for reconstructive surgery. She meets with a surgeon to choose a nipple for her new breast. The nurse offers a tray of samples, strange rubbery invertebrates from the bottom of the sea, asks her to choose the nipple that looks most like her remaining one. Sally has to excuse herself and find a bathroom. She watches herself in the mirror as she lifts her shirt, unhooks her bra. Stares first at the trailing scars, the thick, raised skin, then at the other side, at the breast that is left. Lonely, inert. She memorizes it.

This is the closest Sally has gotten to having the surgery, but she will postpone it again. She has made a deal with God: she will delay her procedure if God agrees to keep her father alive. She feels this is a fair trade, after all, there is her mother to consider. Who will comfort her while Sally is unconscious? Sally knows if she has the surgery, her father will die while she is on the operating table. It's the kind of thing he would do to them.

SALLY'S TEETH

Sally had perfect teeth before cancer, not one cavity until the chemo and radiation. Now there's a sudden pain on her left side when she bites down. Her oncologist says it is normal. "But don't worry," he jokes, "a little tooth decay never killed anyone." He gives her the name of a dentist who specializes in post-cancer treatment dental care. Sally tells her oncologist she hates dentists; this makes him laugh.

When Sally was eight, the top of her tongue found a small, hard ridge in the roof of her mouth. Her tongue lolled there, pushed and pressed until one day the ridge felt sharper, harder. When she opened her mouth to show her mother, her mother said, "Oh." Made an appointment with the dentist. The dentist, a friendly young man with glasses and a moustache, explained that Sally had a supernumerary tooth, an extra, in her case, incisor, which occurred in one out of every hundred thousand people. Usually the extra tooth cut through close to regular teeth, but Sally's had broken through the centre of her palate. The dentist conferred with Sally's mother in another room and afterward his receptionist booked them a follow-up appointment.

When Sally got home, she ran to the living room, found her father in his chair. He sat up immediately, eyes wide with summoned concern. "Well, what'd the dentist say?" Sally climbed into his lap, looked at him seriously. "It's a Super Tooth," she said. Her father laughed. "A Super Tooth? You mean like Superman?" Sally nodded. Her father laughed again.

That night they watched television together, Sally's mother on the couch with her knitting in her lap, Sally and her father in his recliner, her body curved into his. She pressed her tongue against the roof of her mouth, felt a rawness there. She leaned her face close to her father's ear. "It itches."

"What itches?"

Sally hesitated, then whispered, "The Super Tooth."

Her father chuckled. "Open your mouth."

Sally opened wide. Her father slid his index finger into her mouth and rubbed the Super Tooth, the pad of his finger making a "come to me" motion.

Sally's mother looked up from her knitting. "What on earth are you two doing?"

"What does it look like?" her father said. "The Super Tooth is itchy." He smiled at her mother.

Sally's mother shook her head and looked at Sally. "For godsakes, you're acting like a baby."

Sally scowled back and pressed into her father's chest, closed her lips around her father's finger. His skin was rough, tasted musty, like stale tobacco. Sally liked the taste, drew a breath in so she could hold the flavour in her mouth.

The calloused skin of her father's index finger moved roughly over the ridge of her tooth, and a series of tiny vibrations carried up through her palate, down her neck. The rhythmic motion of his stroking sent an easy tickle across her skin, made her want to squirm and wiggle, though she didn't because she knew if she moved too much, her father would send her to the couch. She closed her eyes and pretended to sleep, tried her best to stay still, while in her mind she traced the tingling that moved to the tips of her fingers, her cheeks, down her back to her knees. A thickness seemed to gather around the inside of her thighs, prickliness between her legs. She pressed her knees together and the thickness grew. She clenched and unclenched her legs slowly.

Her father clamped his hand down on her knees. "What are you doing?"

"Nothing," she said softly.

"Well, quit squirming."

After a few minutes, Sally tried the clenching again, only this time, just her insides, without moving her legs, like she was trying not to go to the bathroom. She did this until she got tired, and then she fell asleep.

The Super Tooth was itchy every evening after that. She climbed into her father's lap, whined and pleaded while her father feigned exhaustion, a broken finger, and her mother shook her head. Sally loved the cradle of her father's body, the smell of his tobacco, woody and sweet, like old perfume in a basement, the heat that poured off his chest and up from his lap, enveloping her in his own gruff swaddling, the secrecy of her own body's hidden movements, the intense warmth that rose inside her.

Sally and her mother returned to the dentist two weeks later. When she realized that the large needle and metal instruments meant the Super Tooth was coming out, Sally cried. The dental assistant held her in the chair while the dentist froze the roof of her mouth. Sally did not feel the tooth come loose, was shocked to see it between the dentist's latexed fingers. "There. Not worth crying over."

That night, Sally's father wouldn't let her onto his lap. "Nuh-uh," he said, "Super Tooth's gone, you're a big girl now." Sally lay on the living room floor, her face against the bristly nap of the carpet, pretended to watch television. She pushed and wiggled her tongue through the layers of wet gauze to the roof of her mouth, hoping for a tingle. But all she felt was the stiff wiriness of stitches and, beyond them, something open and sour.

SALLY'S VAGINA

Sally's vagina is proud and demanding. A warm, wet channel where her tension gathers, her instrument of release. While other women pay for massages, go to the gym, Sally has sex. As often as she can. Sometimes with herself, but preferably with a man. Sally's vagina is most satisfied at the instant of penetration. She discovered this first at ten, with her own fingers, then again at fourteen with one of the emergency candles her father kept in the hallway closet. During sex play, she requests that her partner fully penetrate her over and over, separating from her a certain distance, then entering her again. At penetration Sally feels her body divide and fall away, so that she is no longer limited by her own physical vessel, no longer trapped by skin and bones, blood and muscle. She feels herself as energy fulminating, scattering into the air, a moment of true and elusive peace.

The type of men Sally chooses as sexual partners are not preened businessmen or pretty boys. Sally craves something rougher: men with large hands and foul mouths. Men who smell like hard work, who grunt and cuss when they come. Whose penises, like their bodies, are thick and marbled, bruised and angry. Some are younger, some older, some smarter, some dumber. Each one with an expiration date, though some last longer than others. An electrician lasted two years, until he too started to look eager around the mouth, spoke too often of their future, mentioned buying a house.

In the beginning, Sally lays it out: nothing serious, no love talk, no staying over. They all smile then. Think it's the jackpot, the holy grail. Until it isn't. Until they start to talk about their jobs and their mothers, their lost friends, their dead pets. Until they happen to have a toothbrush with them, or leave behind a shirt, telling her they'll pick it up next time, telling her it's hard living alone. She can feel them, circling her life, hovering, hoping for more of her, ready to snatch it up. They start hanging out at her neighbourhood coffee shop, buzz her apartment in the middle of the night. They come to confess their fears, their helplessness, the sadness they've carried since childhood. They exhaust and bore her, then ask her how she feels, what she is thinking. She tells them she wants to have sex. They are speechless and she has to go over it again: nothing serious, no love talk, no staying over. They flinch and stare. They tell her she's scared, that she needs to open up. They offer to take care of her and this makes her laugh. They call her cold, an unfeeling bitch. She tells them it's over. That simple.

Sometimes it doesn't go that way. Sometimes a man who seems ideal drifts in for a while, then drifts out again. Sally sees him weeks or months later at the movie theatre, at a restaurant with another woman. Sally doesn't say hello or approach them. She watches them from across the room, studies the natural way the man holds the woman's hand, the serene expression on the woman's face as she nuzzles under his chin. Sally wonders which one will break the other's heart.

Lately, Sally has been fond of sex in awkward places. Places where complete undressing is too risky, too time consuming. Sally favours succinct couplings. A flash of the necessary parts, a fierce joining. Saves herself the trouble of explaining, of shrugging off a comforting hand, sympathetic eyes. Since her surgery, Sally's vagina has become more responsive, charged. She's wondered if the arousal that once warmed her breasts has now compounded between her legs.

Sally sits in the cool humidity of her father's room. She crosses and uncrosses her legs; inside her, a nagging ache. She wishes the doctor worked the night shift, tries to conjure his image in her mind, but comes up with only an eye and a shoulder. Instead, she watches her father, his face turned toward her, his fingers near his throat, his white knee jutting out of the blanket; somehow, he is more animated asleep than awake. She closes her eyes to the room's grey light, the grate of his uneven breath.

SALLY'S EARS

Sally has her mother's ears. Small, high-set, indiscriminate. Sally confuses a cat's call in the night with a baby's cry, mistakes the doorbell for the phone, can never tell whether it is John or Paul singing a Beatles song.

Sally stands close, listens to the doctor as he speaks to her outside her father's door. The end of his shift, the beginning of Sally's; the doctor's head is bowed with fatigue. His hair, in need of a cut, flaps like a small dark flag as he speaks. "There's been some improvement," he says, his voice hushed and tired. "But I don't want to be overly optimistic." He takes a breath. "How are you holding up?"

Sally lets her fingertips dance near her earlobe. She is looking at the doctor's shoes, plain black dress shoes. "I have a cavity," she says.

He shifts his weight from one foot to the other, clears his throat. "I'm sorry to hear that." His voice is uncertain. "Are you in any pain?"

Sally looks up; his eyes are knitted with doctorly concern; she feels the corners of her mouth rise. "Sometimes."

He lowers his chin and looks up at her. "If it gets serious, you let me know."

Sally tries hard not to smile. She brings her left hand to her mouth and bites gently into the pad of her thumb. Her bottom teeth click against her thumbnail.

The doctor removes his glasses, starts to clean them with the edge of his lab coat. "Did you know it was a dentist who first came up with the electric chair?" he asks her.

"No," she says, pulling her thumb from her mouth with small sucking sound. "I didn't know that."

Inside the room, her father sits in his bed, watches the tiny television with the volume on low. Sally has long envied her father's ears, wide and flat, in tune with sounds that elude both Sally and her mother. She watches him, a vague silhouette against the brightness of the window. He is probably listening to the news, and the traffic twelve floors below, and the pump and hiss of equipment in the room behind them.

Sally's father can still name birds by their song, trains by their whistle. He can name cars in the parking lot below his window by the sound of their engine.

He stares straight at the small black-and-white screen. "Stop carrying on with the doctor."

Sally halts, her coat half off. "Excuse me?"

"I heard you outside the door. He's here to take care of me, not to entertain you. Let him alone."

Sally opens her mouth to speak, but cannot think of anything to say. She pulls her coat back on, wraps her scarf around her neck. "Suit yourself," is all she can come up with. She swings the door wide as she leaves. She will go out for some dinner, then a movie, maybe two. She will come back in the night, when he is long into sleep.

When Sally was a girl, every Sunday night, after dinner, her father would stand from the kitchen table and announce, "Going to relax." He'd lock himself in the room he called "the study," although it contained no books, only a battered easy chair, his record player and records, and a broken train set he had promised to fix for Sally years before. He'd played Maria Callas recordings until bedtime. "I don't know why he listens to that bawling," Sally's mother would say, scrubbing the roasting pan a little harder with a disintegrating handful of steel wool, her skin sweaty with the steam and grease of the kitchen. Sally would sit outside the study, her back flat against the door. She wondered if the songs were full of lust and scandal, if there was something obscene and secret about her father that he hid until alone in that locked room. Sally pressed herself hard into the door, let the vibrato of this other woman's voice tremble through her body, down her legs. She hoped that with each vibration she would absorb something of what her father coveted so dearly, held so close. Under the music, Sally heard the slosh of her mother mopping the kitchen floor.

For her father's sixtieth birthday, Sally found a rare Callas recording commissioned by Aristotle Onassis. She withdrew the money she had been saving for her first apartment, bought the record from a dealer in London. At her parents' house she presented her gift after all the others. Her father opened it and thanked her, nodding, remaining in his seat. She suggested he play it while everyone was there, but he shook his head. She persisted, offering to join him in the study, just the two of them. He asked her mother if there was any cake left.

Later that night, awake with the intermittent murmurs of a man she had picked up at a bus stop, Sally imagined her mother, at home, sleeping alone in the bed, the voice of another, more cherished woman calling up through the floorboards.

SALLY'S LIPS

If Sally's lips spoke her mind, they would interrogate, demand answers of him. "How can you be so hateful?" "Are you proud of the way you treat people?" Her lips would be fierce and wet; they would spit her words. If Sally's lips spoke her heart, they would be bare and tender. They would kiss his cheek, absolve his judgements, his distance; they would whisper forgiveness.

But Sally's lips have a will of their own.

"What do you want for breakfast tomorrow?"

Her father keeps his eyes on the television. A public memorial service at a community church, an all-women's choir singing a hymn, an ocean of flowers for lost girls. Her father coughs.

"Dad? Are you listening? Breakfast, tomorrow."

"I'm watching the news."

Sally waits.

"Your mother's angry with me. She hasn't been to see me for three days."

"She was here half an hour ago. She needs to go home and rest."

Sally's father coughs again. "She's hoping I'll die." His voice wavers with mucus.

Sally fans herself with the daily menu. "No one's hoping you'll die. What do you want for breakfast?"

On television, people are standing outside a church. A reporter talks to an elderly couple shivering in heavy coats. They hold a homemade cardboard poster, a blown-up, yellowing photograph of a girl with feathered brown hair, her name, SUSAN, spelled out in black electrical tape, like the giant, clumsy printing of a child. "This is our daughter," the man says, his mouth, trembling. "She's been missing for twenty-three years. She wasn't one of the girls found, but we came here to remember her." The old woman covers her face with a handkerchief. Her husband puts his arm around her, kisses her woollen cap. The camera closes in on the photograph of their daughter.

Sally looks at her father, catches him dabbing his eyes quickly with the corner of his sheet. "Dad?"

"Bacon and eggs," he mumbles.

"You know you can't have that. How about oatmeal?"

He shakes his head. "That's got to be worse than dying, losing a child."

A photo montage: family pictures, baby photos, school portraits, grade-school girls whose bodies show no hint of adolescence. Then inside the church, the lighting of candles, a roll call of victims' names, the unveiling of small memorial plaque – all of it set to a weepy popular ballad, a sentimental manipulation that makes Sally want to groan. Her father sits transfixed, his breath shaky, his eyes rimmed in red.

In the hallway, Sally's lips pale, stretch in a closed smile to thank the nurse who collects the menu cards. She watches the doctor as he approaches her father's door, tries to see past the doctor's white coat to the cut of his hip. He runs his hands through his hair; he has had it trimmed, it falls perfectly. He stops in front of her. Sally breathes deeply, lake water, bright citrus. She smiles, removes her glasses, pinches her finger and thumb together and runs them along the thin plastic arms.

The doctor is cheery, teases her about spending too much time at the hospital. Offers her a position on the surgical rotation. She tells him she would like to specialize in transplants, that she looks good carrying a mini-cooler. He laughs and recounts a joke about a lawyer, a marathon runner and a heart transplant. He stumbles on the punchline. She laughs anyway, watches his face as her index finger traces the frame of her glasses.

She sucks on her bottom lip as he tells her about a possible change in her father's medication. A trial drug that might increase his possibility of improvement. He tells her he doesn't want to cultivate false hope, but with this new drug, there might even be a chance of her father going home.

Sally nods, tries to look thankful.

The doctor asks her about her tooth; she tells him she's starting to enjoy the pain, like an annoying but reliable friend. He looks at her strangely, then reaches out and squeezes her elbow, keeps his hand there, holding her. He asks her if she is getting enough rest, taking care of herself.

For a moment, Sally cannot speak; no one has ever held her elbow. She nods, then says, "You got a haircut."

"Yes." He sounds pleased that she has noticed. "What do you think?"

She smiles and lowers her eyes. "It's nice."

When she looks up again, he is smiling.

"So," she says, draws the word out, holds her lips in a tiny o.

He remains there, his hand resting at the bend of her arm, his expression amused, coaxing her.

"Is there somewhere we can go?"

The doctor's head pulls back slightly. He tries to hold his smile. "Go? You mean, for a coffee?"

Sally glances at the door to her father's room. "No, not coffee."

The doctor drops his hand from her arm and brings it to his face, covers his mouth, takes a deep breath, and blows into his closed palm. He speaks with his hand still in front of his mouth. "I'm really sorry. If I've given you the wrong idea."

"Don't worry about it," Sally says quickly, eager to deflect his assumptions of disappointment, his pity. She smiles, her lips pressed into a thin, hard line; she slides her glasses back onto her face; the world comes sharp again. He is ruffled, unhinged by her advance. His face, still painfully attractive. He opens his mouth to say something, then stops. Sally takes a step back, dismissing him, but he doesn't move.

He dips his chin, speaks quietly, "Sometimes when people grieve –"

Sally turns away, shaking her head. She cannot believe she's hearing this.

"No, wait, listen to me," the doctor says.

"You know what I could really use, doctor?" she asks suddenly, turning back to look at him.

"What?"

Sally reaches up and brushes the hair out of his eyes. "A cigarette."

The doctor winces as if she had slapped him.

She wants to tell him she needs the taste of something burnt and ashy in her mouth, to balloon her lungs with black smoke, but he is already halfway down the hall.

SALLY'S FEET

Sally's booking agent, Carol, once commented that she had never managed a parts model with more exquisite hands or more ugly feet. As an adult, Sally has never worn sandals or gone barefoot in public. Her feet are bony and square, thick and slug-toed. She wears an extra-wide shoe, buys her shoes at a special store.

As a child, Sally's feet grew faster than the rest of her. Her mother complained that it was costing them a fortune to keep her in shoes. Her father teased her, told her no man would want to marry a girl with enormous feet. She told him it didn't matter, she was never getting married. That made him smile.

Because of her large feet, Sally was always tripping, falling over, bruising and skinning knees. She made an ordeal of each accident, with tears and yowls, until her father marched outside and gave the sidewalk a stern talking-to. He'd return to the house with a serious look and tell her, "If that sidewalk gives you any more trouble, you let me know."

When Sally was six, she had the stomach flu. For two nights she vomited green bile and was weak with fever. Her mother begged her father to take her to the hospital, but he hated hospitals, didn't trust them after his own father died in one. On the second night, her mother cleaned out the vomit basin, and her father came into her room, sat down at the end of her bed. While Sally whimpered with the ache in her body, her father's large hands took up one of her feet and, through layers of blankets, rubbed and squeezed one foot, then the other. Massaged Sally into a deep and peaceful sleep. She awoke in the morning, her father dozing on the floor beside her bed, her bedding damp with sweat, her fever, broken.

Nowadays Sally walks as if in a fever. When she is not at the hospital or on a job, she meanders aimlessly through the city streets, her gloves on, her coat cinched tight. She has no real destination, just puts one ugly foot in front of the other and tries to move forward. More than once Sally has looked up and been shocked by her surroundings: the interchange of an overpass, a children's water park, the front door of a community centre. She's told her agent it's like sleepwalking; her agent has suggested anti-depressants.

After the doctor's rebuff, Sally finds herself in a laneway behind a grocery store. Two older Italian men in bloodied butcher garments are perched on milk crates, sharing a Thermos of something hot. They speak loudly to one another, pat each other on the arm and shoulder. As she passes, one of them calls out something in Italian; his breath rises in a cartoon cloud. He gestures with his hand for her to join them, holds up the Thermos, its mouth steaming; the other blows her a kiss. Sally smiles, but keeps walking. A veterinary clinic. A boarded-up Greek restaurant. A skateboard park where boys with ski jackets and painted fingernails ask her if she'll help them buy some beer. Double-back to the hospital. A microbrewery. A cooking school. A car dealership turned toy store.

A few blocks from the hospital, Sally steps off a curb and stumbles. She rights herself. A man who had been crossing the street in the opposite direction asks if she's okay. "Yes," she says. She feels the heat rise in her face, looks down at the ground. The heel of her left shoe is twisted out to the side, like a fractured limb. For a moment she is overwhelmed by the damage; her eyes fill with tears. She steadies herself against a lamppost, takes a deep breath, rotates her stinging ankle, tells herself it isn't worth crying over, the shoes were old. She reaches down, slips both shoes off her feet and lays them on the curb. She walks back to the hospital in stockinged feet.

SALLY'S BONES

Sally's bones are long and dense. They have survived two skiing accidents and a fall down a flight of marble stairs. As a child, Sally's bones were her most obvious feature. "Skin and bones," her mother's mother would say, squeezing Sally's forearm between her chubby immigrant fingers.

On a day that Sally's mother stays home with a cold, Sally lifts her father, and comes to understand skin and bones. His body like a collapsed tent in her arms, all sheathing and poles. Hard to believe this man hoisted the engine out of the family car with help from nothing but a simple pulley, that he almost broke her wrist the first and only night she came home after curfew. She unties his gown as he leans forward. She is shocked by the colour of his skin. Across his back, yellowing blooms of blue and green. For a second, she is furious, ready to call the nurse, demand an explanation. Until she realizes what the marks are. In some, she is sure she can see the outline of her mother's small hand, the skeleton of her fingers radiating from the dark centre of each bruise. She tells herself that it is all show, that he is not really hurt. Her father's bones are narrow and hard, set like bars around his heart. She bangs the butt of her palm up and down his back. The pounding of a petrified drum. His body sounds are deep and grotesque and he is no longer embarrassed by them. He bends forward to spit into the metal dish, his cheeks collapsing to rid his mouth of the thick yellow phlegm. She stands with her hand on his back, waiting for him to finish.

When he is done, she moves the metal dish to the bedside table. Lowers him back into the bed. He lies there, breathes in snorts and gasps as if he's just run a race. Sally turns on the television, finds the evening news. More funerals, small private ceremonies around the city. She turns the volume down to a low murmur.

Sally arranges her father's blankets, a lighter one up around his chest, a heavier one folded over his feet. When she looks again at his face, it is unnaturally pale, the flesh of his lips tinged with blue, his eyes pulled wide. Her right hand reaches for the call button, presses it in a frantic rhythm, grabs the oxygen mask, pushes it against his face. Her left hand pats the bedsheet, searches for his hand. Finds it in a tangle of tubes and blanket. She strokes the top of his hand with her fingertips, feels the pattern of his bones. She makes soothing noises in her throat, watches his frightened eyes over the lip of the mask. Once the nurses are in, pushing carts, checking tubes, she backs away. Sally stands in the corner of the room as they stabilize him. Runs fingers over the bones in her own hand.

Later that night, Sally falls asleep in the chair beside her father's bed. Stumbles through short, sad dreams. Is drawn out of sleep by the sound of her father whimpering. As she rises to the surface of consciousness, she recognizes the sound as her own soft crying. She sits straight in the chair, wipes her eyes with her hand, feels the hardness of her knuckles against her face. She looks to her father and is startled by his face staring at her in the dark, the whites of his eyes reflecting the dim light from the hallway, the clear tube growing from his mouth. His forehead, cheeks, chin, a collection of bones on the pillow, a short, wet trail leaking from the corner of his eye to the pillowcase. His hand shakes as it leaves the bedsheet, lifts towards her.

Sally climbs out of her chair and stands beside her father's bed. Folds her hand over his outstretched fingers, his skin papery in her clasp. She kneels down on the linoleum floor and rests her body against the side of his bed, feels the shudder of the ventilator as it paces his breath in and out. She brings his hand to her face, presses his palm against her cheek, the warmth of his flesh rising in her skin. She aligns her fingers on top of his, moves his hand slowly. His fingertips touch her eyebrows, her nose, her cheek, her lips. She watches his face, his wet eyes blinking slowly. Takes his index finger, guides it past her open lips and with the flat of her tongue, presses it up against the roof of her mouth. She swallows the musk of her father's dry skin, tobacco, engine grease, mentholated cough drops. She rests her face on the edge of the bed, watches him close his eyes and closes her own, as she suckles him slowly. His finger is stiff and unmoving but she imagines the warmth of her mouth easing him, softening his flesh. As soon as she feels him stir inside her, she stills herself, waits; he continues: the slow, trembling curl of his finger against her palate, a small but significant beckoning.

Valentines

J ess holds her lipstick like a crayon. Pushes the dark pink stain over the edge of her mouth, puckers, then smacks. She slides her index finger into the pursed circle of her lips, draws her finger out, cleans the colour from her skin with a piece of toilet paper.

She relaxes her lower lip into a pout. Steps back from the mirror as she tucks her right palm into the left cup of her bra, lifts. Does the same for the other side. Better. How old does she look? Seventeen? She scrunches and tweaks the ends of her hair, untangles the strands twisted around her gold feather earrings. Eighteen? She's already scammed her way into two clubs, been served chi chis at a restaurant. Soon she'll be fourteen. Maybe she looks twenty.

Her finger traces a tiny heart in the empty cleft between her collarbones. She had hoped Joey would get her that heart-shaped locket she'd been hinting about. The gold one in the velvet-lined display case at the mall. He could have at least bought her some flowers or chocolates. Taken her out somewhere.

"Come back here, Jess!" Joey calls from the living room.

"Just a sec!"

She daubs on another coat of pink. She will try to not be mad at him. He did buy the beer. Maybe he's saving her gift, for after. She teases her reflection with the offer of a kiss. Leans in close and practises her reaction. "Oh, Joey," she whispers, "you shouldn't have."

Jess holds her breath as she enters the living room, stands straight, tries to keep that thin roll of skin from slouching over the waistband of her skirt. Joey and Kyle are lazing in recliners, listening to the all-rock radio station. Kyle's parents have gone to their cabin in the mountains; Jess knows that Joey hangs out with Kyle because his parents go away a lot. Kyle's town-house is also nicer: wall-to-wall carpet, glass tables, overstuffed beige furniture. Bigger TV, better stereo. Jess likes how the house always looks so clean; she imagines an army of maids with spray bottles and rags.

She leans against the wall, plays with the nub of the light switch, watches Kyle sip his beer. Kyle is fourteen and still has the body of a boy, lanky and slight. To make up for it, he keeps his dark hair long, like that band, the Ramones. Tonight he is wearing a striped collared shirt over a white t-shirt and jeans; he looks sharp. Jess wishes Joey would wear something like that, something other than his usual black t-shirt and faded black jeans. Still, Joey is fifteen and way more mature than Kyle. He wears his light hair cropped down to an army cut, never gets ID'd. He tells Jess about all the clubs he gets into without her, places where the bouncers playfight him on the street then let him in without cover. She hates that. She tries not to think about Joey cruising bars: heavy music, vanilla smoke, older girls staring at his muscled frame.

Joey says something quiet to Kyle; they both chuckle. Each of them is holding two open cans of beer. Neither offers her any. She forces herself to stand casually. "Well?"

"We just wanted to check something." Joey grins.

Kyle stays silent.

"What?"

Joey clears his throat, looks at her with serious eyes. "Stand with your legs together."

Jess turns to Kyle, tries to work out what's going on. Kyle looks to Joey.

"Just do it, Jess. Come on." Joey takes a sip of beer.

Jess keeps her eyes on Kyle. "Why?" She can tell Kyle is trying hard not to smile.

"Because." Joey sighs, rubs his palm over his face. "Because, I want to show Kyle how great looking you are."

Kyle nods once in agreement.

She can tell they're bullshitting, but decides to play along. She plants her hands on her hips and looks down. Her shiny black heels meet, her lacy ankle socks touch, her bare calves join.

Kyle points. "Told ya."

Joey sits forward. "Come on, Jess, get 'em closer."

She squeezes her legs together as hard as she can. Her thighs quiver under her denim miniskirt. "What? What are you looking at?"

Joey slumps back in his recliner. "The gap between your knees."

Jess looks down and sees a diamond-shaped space between her legs, just above her calves.

"Means you've been screwed," Kyle says. He smiles sheepishly without looking at her.

"So what?" Jess says. She crosses her arms in front of her chest and looks hard at Kyle. "At least I have been."

Joey chuckles, slaps Kyle on the shoulder. Kyle keeps his eyes down, brushes something off the arm of his recliner. Jess sits on the edge of the couch. She picks at her nails, tries to keep her face from scowling.

"Hey Kyle," Joey says. "What does a Surrey girl do in the morning?"

Jess rolls her eyes; he's told this joke a million times.

Kyle laughs.

A few minutes later, Kyle offers her a beer.

Joey stares at his reflection in the dark face of the big-screen TV. Tells himself he looks good. Cool, hip, tripped back in the recliner with a beer in his hand. It's unfair that someone as backward as Kyle should have all this great stuff. The TV, the stereo, the computer upstairs. Joey thinks he'd really be someone if he had parents like Kyle's, parents who went away all the time, left him alone, didn't check his coat pockets or knapsack, didn't take the lock off his bedroom door. Kyle had all the opportunities, but he was too fucking lame. If this was Joey's place, he wouldn't be wasting Valentine's with friends. He'd be scoring with some hot girl. Maybe some older chick. He'd let her take a bubble bath in the master suite jacuzzi tub, use some of his mother's expensive perfume. He'd tell her about every piece of electronic equipment, making sure she knew it was top of the line, expensive stuff.

Joey looks around for Jess. "Christ, girl, what are you doing in that bathroom?"

She marches out with a mascara wand in her hand. "What's your fucking problem?"

Joey shrugs. Lets her stand there, looking ridiculous.

"For your information, it's a powder room, not a bathroom."

"Whatever." He waves her off. He hates it when she corrects him.

Kyle sets up to roll a joint. Joey watches him lay out the implements: a small baggie of weed, rolling papers, a paper towel, a tiny pair of scissors. He notices how precise and careful Kyle is, attention to detail. Joey wonders if Kyle would be into pulling a B&E on his own place. They could sell the stuff and split the money. Joey would get a little more, of course, since it was his idea. But sixty/forty, that was more than fair. Kyle's parents could get even better stuff with the insurance money. They could do it every few years. Newer, better stuff, who wouldn't want that?

Kyle uses his shirt sleeve to buff the glass tabletop. His forehead is creased, his mouth set in a tight, worried line. His hand polishes in urgent circles until every finger mark is gone. Joey shakes his head. B & E probably isn't Kyle's bag.

Joey's heard that pot stunts your growth, wonders if that's what's happened to Kyle. Kyle lays the paper towel on the coffee table, begins to cut up the weed with the scissors. Joey watches Kyle's hands. He has hands like a girl, narrow and small. His wrists are so thin, Joey figures he could snap them with two fingers. Everything about Kyle is narrow: his face under the cloak of his hair, his chest, even his sorry little ass is narrow. Joey knows it's hard for Kyle, still looking like a kid. Kyle goes to a different school than Joey, a co-ed private school that his parents saved for. Kyle's told Joey that he gets hassled by the jocks in the Phys Ed change room, they try to snap at his crotch with their towels, tell him he's a girl because he's got long hair, offer to pay him to suck them off. Joey wishes he went to that school; he'd beat the crap out of those preppy fucks. Shit, that must hurt like hell, getting your balls stung by a towel. Joey catches himself. Tells himself to stop thinking about another guy's balls.

Joey sits up. "So, that Sheila girl, still in your English class?"

The hair nods.

"When you gonna ask her out?"

Kyle snickers.

Joey shakes his head. "Just trying to help, man."

Jess comes out of the bathroom, looks at Kyle. "Do you have a needle?"

Kyle's eyes stay on his rolling. He points absently to a sewing box beside the couch. Jess carries the box into the bathroom.

Joey shouts at Jess. "What're you doing in there, sewing your knees together?"

Kyle's shoulders bob with laughter. He looks up and gives Joey a high five.

"Fuck! Off!" Jess yells from the bathroom; she is laughing too.

Kyle smoothes the joint with his fingers, is soothed by its delicate paper, familiar shape. He wants to light this thing up, put his lips on it, let his mind go. He's been thinking too much about marks on the furniture, drops of beer on the carpet, his father's warnings about having friends over. He knows that with the first toke, he will worry about smoke lingering in the drapes, hot ash on the carpet, but by the third toke, he won't care any more. He wonders if his parents will ever notice.

Jess comes out of the powder room. Kyle smiles at her. She smiles back.

"Let's smoke that thing," Jess says, "I've got work to do." Her top seems to be dipping lower than before, her breasts about to float away. Kyle makes sure to pass the joint to Jess, so she will taste him on it. As she inhales, her breasts rise up. Her lips leave a wet, pink stain on the rolling paper.

"That's fucking gross!" Joey says as he scrapes off the lipstick with his thumbnail.

Jess exhales. "You don't think it's gross when it's on your dick."

Kyle grins.

"Sister, that says more about you than it does me." Joey inhales.

Joey puts his hand up for a high five. Kyle glances at Jess; she seems unscathed. Kyle slaps Joey's hand.

Kyle offers the joint to Jess when it should be his turn. She sucks deeply, her lips pursing a kiss in his direction. Kyle feels the corners of his mouth twitching. Jess grins as she hands the joint back to him. He doesn't wipe the lipstick off, savours the sticky sweetness on the wet part of his lip.

Jess stands up. "Do you have any ice?" Her voice is thin and tight; she is trying to hold the smoke in.

Kyle points to the freezer in the kitchenette. His eyes follow her snug denim rear as she walks away. The freezer door swings open, leaving a Jess that is only legs, ass, and tits. Kyle is mildly disturbed by the amputation. He hears her loosening the ice tray and is relieved when she closes the freezer door, appearing whole again. She cradles the ice tray as if it's a baby, waves as she passes them on her way back to the powder room.

"What the fuck is she doing in there?" Joey asks.

Kyle shrugs.

Joey takes the joint from Kyle. "I think she likes you."

Kyle folds up the paper towel, tries not to look at Joey. "Who?"

"Jess! Didn't you see the way she was smiling at you?" Joey takes a long drag.

"Nah." Kyle reaches for the joint, worried that Joey will finish it.

Joey nods.

"She's friendly." Kyle takes a drag.

"Horny," Joey says.

"Yeah?" Kyle tries hard not to exhale, but feels something about to leak out.

"She'd do it with you if I asked her to."

Kyle coughs, his face caught in a sudden cloud of smoke. "Yeah?" He tries not to laugh. Joey gets off on saying he can make people do stuff. Stupid stuff.

"She does what I say." Joey leans forward in his chair and reaches out a hand to slap the back of Kyle's neck. "Just like you."

Kyle pulls away. "Fuck off."

Joey laughs, takes the last drag and hands the roach to Kyle.

Jess moans from the powder room. "Jesus."

"What the fuck are you doing in there?" Joey yells.

"Nothing, nothing." Jess moans again, more quietly this time.

Kyle wants to get up and look, but Joey doesn't move from his chair, so Kyle stays put.

Joey looks at Kyle, shakes his head.

Kyle shrugs, begins to pick the roach apart over the small square of folded paper towel.

"So what's it worth to ya?" Joey adds.

"What?"

"Your first time."

Kyle rubs the leftover pot between his fingers. Tries to pretend he doesn't know what Joey's getting at.

"I mean, tonight. With Jess."

Kyle wipes his fingers on the paper towel. He cannot tell if Joey is serious or trying to make him feel like a jerk. Joey is better at these games than he is. Kyle folds the paper towel into a small, dense pad, rubs it along the edge of the coffee table. "I don't know. Twenty?"

Joey laughs.

Kyle squeezes the paper towel, braces himself for whatever humiliation Joey has planned.

"Twenty? No. Twenty's what you paid for that weed. I'm talking about a once-in-a-lifetime experience here."

Kyle holds his breath, feels a nervous smile break across his face. He wonders how far Joey will take this. Looks up through his hair. "Fifty?"

Joey leans back in the recliner and lets out a long breath. "Fifty's still low. But, you are my friend."

"Ow!" Jess bangs into the door frame as she stumbles out of the powder room.

Joey brings his index finger to his face and taps it against his lips.

Kyle nods.

Jess poses in front of them, hands on hips, legs apart like Wonder Woman. "So? What do you think?"

Kyle stares through Jess's clothes to the heavy outline of her breasts, the push of her hips.

"What?" Joey asks.

"My ears!"

Kyle checks Jess's ears and sees that they are red and puffy. Atop each dangling gold feather is a fresh second piercing, a gold stud embedded in an angry red circle.

Joey stands up to get a closer look. "Jesus, woman, you did that in the bathroom?"

Jess smiles and nods. "What do you think?"

Joey sits back down and shakes his head. "You're fucked."

Kyle lifts his beer in a toast. "I think you look good. Look great."

"Thank you, Kyle." Jess glares sideways at Joey. "You're sweet to say so."

Joey gives Jess the finger.

Jess walks toward Kyle, swoops in and presses her lips against his.

Kyle's head fills with a jumble of perfume smells. He feels himself sinking into the blush and glitter of a drugstore cosmetics counter. By the time he's resurfaced, thinks to kiss her back, Jess is sitting on the couch. She sticks her tongue out at Joey and sips her beer.

Jess flips through the *TV Guide*. She touches the tip of her left ear, feels heat through the thin, tight skin, presses the lobe gently to feel pain push back, a small but intense burn.

Joey has the remote control. He flips from channel to channel, pauses at nothing. Kyle lies on the carpet, his hands smoothing the pile, picking at pieces of lint. "There's nothing on," Kyle murmurs.

"I'll find something," Jess says, going back to her *TV Guide*. She likes to watch TV here, likes the sharpness of the picture, as if everything is clearer on TV than in real life.

"Hey, check this out." Joey sits up in his chair.

Jess looks up. On the screen, people in dark rain gear are crouched in a huge dirt pit, their bodies barely moving. Along the sides of the pit are shovels and hoses and piles of black plastic.

"What movie is this?" Jess asks.

Joey laughs. "It's not a movie, it's the fucking news." Joey points the remote at the screen. "That crazy motherfucker's backyard."

Jess listens to the names of some of the girls whose bodies have been found – sweet names like Tricia and Carly and Lianne. None of them are named Jessica. The reporter, a clean-cut man with dark brown skin and a long name that Jess can't pronounce, explains the excavation process, how the remaining mud and dirt is being moved away carefully, by hand. He clears his throat before announcing that forensic examinations of recovered skeletons have revealed that some of the girls were buried alive in groupings with other, already decomposing, bodies.

"Cool," Joey says. He turns the volume up.

Jess remembers seeing a movie where a pretty college girl who wanted to be a veterinarian tried to investigate the unexplained deaths of several animals in her neighbourhood. In the end, she fell into a pit of dead animal bodies. She didn't make it out, which was really sad because she had just made love to the class president and he had given her a ring. The zombie animals bit her all over and tore off her clothes, scratched her face, clung to her legs, dragged her back into the pit when she tried to escape. Jess wonders if it was like that for those girls, being stuffed into the ground, clawed and eaten by the dead. She doesn't want to think about how long they might have stayed alive under there, screaming and crying for help. "It's gross, Joey, change the channel."

Joey gives her an annoyed look, then shakes his head and turns off the TV.

Kyle gets up and heads toward the powder room.

Joey twirls the remote control in his fingers, calls to Kyle. "Hey, didn't you hear somewhere that the psycho guy broke out of jail?"

Kyle chuckles. "Yeah, I did hear that." The bathroom door closes.

Joey turns to Jess. "I heard he's pissed 'cos the cops dug up his backyard and he's going after more women. Only this time, he doesn't care if they're hookers or not."

Jess can feel him staring at her, keeps her eyes on *TV Guide* listings. "Fuck off. It would have been on the news."

"Nuh-uh. They didn't want people to freak out, so they're keeping it quiet. A bunch of prison guards got fired over it."

Jess scans the late night movie titles, *Jaws, Christine, Friday the 13th, Part II.* Where are the funny movies, the love stories? The rims of her ears feel hot and itchy. She's pretty certain Joey is lying, but wants to make sure. "So if it's not on the news, how do you know about it?"

Joey takes a sip of beer. "My dad bowls with one of the guards who got fired."

Jess looks him straight in the eye. He stares back at her.

"You're so full of shit," Jess says. "Turn the TV back on." She reaches for the remote control and the lights go out. "Joey!" She stays in her seat, looks around the room, but everything is blackness. She hears a door open, then shuffling. "Kyle?" The room is silent. She hears sounds from outside the house, a fading siren, an engine idling, kids on skateboards, their whoops and shouts, their wheels growling. She breathes as slowly as she can. Her eyes adjust to the darkness;

the living room is empty except for her. "Very funny, guys."

She hears heavy, gasping breaths, but can't place them in the room. She scans the grey light and startles at the sight of someone standing in the kitchen archway. A shadowy figure lit from behind by the stove light in the kitchenette. She pats her chest with her palm. She cannot tell which one of them it is; the silhouette is tall like Joey, but skinny, like Kyle. She swallows. "I can see you standing there."

"Are you a good girl, Jess?" A low, raspy voice seems to come from all around her.

"Cut it out, okay?" Jess's hand searches for a light switch on the wall behind her; there isn't one.

"Are you a hooker?"

Jess grips her *TV Guide*. "Fuck off!"

"You've been a bad, bad girl." The figure draws a hand out from behind its back and holds up a large, metal blade, a kitchen knife.

Jess slides to the back corner of the couch. "This isn't fucking funny anymore." She thinks if she runs, she can make it to the front door first.

"Prepare to die, bitch!" The figure lunges out of the doorway and waves the knife in her direction.

Jess jumps to her feet. A hand grabs her neck. She screams and plunges forward, bangs her leg against the coffee table, slips down beside one of the recliners.

The lights flash on. Joey is doubled over the back of the couch; Kyle is standing on a milk crate in the kitchen archway; they are both laughing.

Jess feels a vibration in her lower lip, presses the back of her hand against it. She cannot look at either of them. She stares at the upholstery pattern on the recliner, keeps her eyes open, hoping the wetness pooled at her lower lids will dry up and not escape. Joey and Kyle laugh as if she isn't in the room. She is going to leave. As soon as she can stand up without crying, she is going home.

Kyle tries to do two things at once: clean up a half can of beer that has emptied onto the carpet, listen to Joey and Jess fight in the hallway. Though Kyle cannot see her, he knows that Jess is standing in her coat, trying to get out the front door. He can hear Joey laughing, saying "Come on, come on . . ." Kyle presses the towel into the carpet over and over. He feels bad about the joke now; the word "bitch" had stung in his mouth the moment he'd said it. He wishes he could take that back. Kyle lifts the towel but the patch of carpet is still damp and brown; he wonders if he has done something irreparable. He hears Jess's voice, low and hard. Joey has stopped laughing; Kyle imagines him nodding, guilty. Kyle turns the towel in his hands as he waits for Jess to finish, for Joey to respond. "Okay, okay . . . okay," Joey says, his voice softened. This is a good sign. "Hey, Kyle!" Joey calls to him.

"Yeah?" Kyle calls back.

"Tell her you're sorry."

Kyle takes a deep breath. "I'm sorry we scared you, Jess." He waits for her response, the towel tight in his hand.

"That's okay, Kyle." Jess's voice is girlish and small.

Kyle feels something surprising and warm when she says his name. Something tender and liquid, as if his whole being has passed through her mouth. He hears the sounds of Joey and Jess stepping outside, Joey clomping around in his untied sneakers, Jess saying something about her ears.

Kyle looks at the irregular pattern of the beer soaked into the carpet. Pats half-heartedly at the wet patch. Leaves the towel on the carpet and goes out to join them for a smoke.

"It didn't hurt this much when they did it at the store."

Joey is sick of listening to Jess complain about her ears. She's close to tears and, as usual, he's the only one smart enough to work out a solution.

"You need to sterilize the wound," he tells her.

"How?" Jess whines.

Kyle is unwilling to unlock the liquor cabinet at first, but when Joey slides his index finger in and out of a closed fist as a reminder of what they talked about earlier, Kyle fetches the key from his parents' bedroom.

Joey insists tequila is the way to go. "They use it for surgery in Mexico all the time."

He makes Jess bend over the sink and tells Kyle to hold her still.

"Don't get it in my hair," Jess says.

Kyle stands behind Jess, looks over to Joey for a nod before daring to touch her. This makes Joey smile. He watches Kyle rest his hands on Jess, one on the plump round of her hip, another, small and alarming on the naked skin of her neck. Joey feels the beer not sitting right in his stomach, a surge of something bitter and acidic.

"Well?" says Jess, trying to look up from her bent-over position.

Joey picks up the tequila bottle and takes a long drink. The liquid passes sharp in his throat, then spreads warm and thick through his chest. As the heat wraps around his eyeballs he sees his girlfriend contorted over a kitchen sink; his friend looking like a frightened park ranger with a raccoon in his hands. Out of the blue, he wishes he had had a better plan than this for Valentine's, wishes he could have done something nice for Jess. With the second swig, he notices how Jess doesn't seem to mind having Kyle so close.

Joey steps to the sink and pours tequila over Jess's left ear. Jess shrieks.

Joey laughs; the fire in his stomach sends a satisfying charge down his legs.

"Hurt?" Kyle asks.

"No," Jess's sarcasm echoes in the sink, "it fucking tickles!"

Joey holds the bottle still until everyone is quiet, then pours the liquor over Jess's right ear.

Jess whimpers. Kyle grabs for a dishtowel and hands it to her as she straightens up.

Joey waits for Jess to thank him. Instead, she reaches for the bottle.

⁓

Kyle is unsure about what's going to happen. While Joey and Jess finish the tequila, he nurses his shot, examines the wet patch on the carpet to see if it will become a stain. Jess is sitting on the floor, her skirt hiking further up her thighs with each changing position. She is wearing a dishtowel around her head and has announced several times that her ears feel much better, thank you. He wonders if she's drunk. Wonders if Joey has already talked to her.

Jess crawls to the entertainment centre and changes the radio station from all-rock to all-dance. The disco beat makes Kyle nervous.

Joey cringes. "What is this crap?"

Jess stands, hikes up her top to reveal her pale midriff. "I want to dance!"

Kyle is mesmerized by the soft, pouty flesh around her bellybutton, the unfathomable differences between girls and boys. He watches her as she closes her eyes, lifts her arms above her head, then brings them down, running her hands over her neck, her breasts, her stomach.

She swings her hips lazily back and forth, turns her ass to the groove of the music. She gyrates in Joey's direction and pushes her stomach into his face. He laughs and pulls her down onto his lap, his hand rising immediately to her breast.

Kyle watches them kiss, catches the pink of Jess's tongue moving into Joey's mouth, feels somehow comforted by this scene and rests his head against the back of the couch. Joey's hand kneads Jess's breast through the thin cotton of her top. Jess lifts herself higher in Joey's lap. Joey's fingers creep under the edge of the fabric; Kyle watches the rhythmic movement of Joey's hand; Jess's breast looks as if it has come alive.

In the middle of making out, Joey smiles at Kyle, winks. His fingers grip the bottom edge of Jess's top. His hand lifts the thin fabric over Jess's breast, so that Kyle can catch the heavy white sling of her bra. Jess's hand reaches absently for her top and pulls it down again. Kyle closes his eyes.

Kyle isn't sure if it's the pot or the tequila or the excitement of watching Joey and Jess, but something has made him feel light inside. With his eyes closed, he feels his body hover above the couch, float on a cushion of vibrating air.

When Kyle opens his eyes, Joey is stroking Jess's cheek, whispering to her. He holds her chin in his hand and turns her to face Kyle. She squeals out loud then buries her face in Joey's chest. Joey continues to talk, quietly, the words are indecipherable; his lips move, the room suspended in the long hum of his voice. Jess raises her eyes to meet Kyle's. Her eyebrows are furrowed, her mouth turned down. She looks dismayed, confused, like she is hearing something awful about him. Kyle's chest is suddenly full and tight; the couch pushes up against his thighs. He turns his head away, toward the kitchen. It's all a joke. Joey is making fun of him, of both of them.

When Kyle is sure Jess's eyes are no longer on him, he looks back. Jess is staring at Joey's chest, her fingers trace a pattern there; Kyle can see from across the room the shape is a heart. She shifts her weight in Joey's lap, her bottom lip tucked between her teeth. She shrugs. Joey touches her neck, cooing, negotiating. Jess turns her head away from him, stares at her leg, tucked under her on the recliner.

Joey finishes with a word that draws the corners of his mouth wide. Jess looks up. Joey holds her there with his gaze. Says nothing. Then pulls her toward him, presses his moving lips against her neck. She closes her eyes and smiles, rubs her forehead against his. She turns to look at Kyle again, still smiling. Joey whispers one last thing to her and she nods slowly, her eyes hard on Kyle.

Kyle watches Jess climb out of Joey's lap. She sways her hips to the music as she moves toward him. Kyle leans back, ready for her to take a seat on his lap. But she offers her hand and pulls him up. For a moment Kyle worries he will have to dance with her, is embarrassed that Joey will watch them. Instead, she leads him upstairs, to his bedroom.

While Jess is in Kyle's room, Joey checks out the master bedroom. He thinks there should be money somewhere, searches under the mattress, in the bedside tables, finds nothing. In Kyle's dad's closet he comes across an electric tie rack. Joey flicks the switch and watches it spin a while, then picks out a couple of ties that might look good on him. He stands at the vanity mirror and lifts each one to his neck. The ties look stupid against his black t-shirt. He finds a white collared shirt in the closet, pulls it off the hanger and slips it on.

He loops a single knot in each tie to hold them at the collar, poses in front of the mirror. This is the job he needs – wear a tie, boss people around. He'd get ahead because of his talent for managing people, getting them to do what he wants. He'd drive an expensive sports car and drink beer at lunch. He winks at his reflection. He'd make his secretary wear short skirts. He'd have a big house with a pool and he'd let the neighbourhood kids, the poorer ones, swim in it. People would listen to what he had to say. No one would call him stupid or lazy, not even his parents.

Below the vanity mirror, on the dressing table, Joey sees a carved wooden box, the lid open. Maybe this is where Kyle's mom keeps her spare cash. He sits down on the padded stool, lifts the lid of the box with the tip of his finger. Inside, a tangle of jewellery: gold, silver, pearls, rings. Not shiny or glinting, but faded, tarnished, less important than Joey imagined jewellery would look. With one hand he scoops up the lot of it, feels the heft of its weight in his palm. He looks down into the red velvet lining of the box, sees a gold ring with a flat blue stone, a silver bracelet, a single diamond left behind. He picks up the diamond, an earring, in the pinch of his fingers, and lays it on the dressing table. Pulls through the jewellery in his hand for its mate, finds it caught in the clasp of a gold chain.

Joey studies the earrings side by side on the table. Real diamonds. Worth some money. Kyle's mom won't miss them. Probably doesn't even remember she has them. He picks up the earrings and holds them in his palm, squeezes his hand closed until the gold posts dig into his skin.

Behind the bedroom door, in the dark, Jess lies naked on Kyle's bed. She has let him touch her all over, his hands so light on her body, she barely felt them. She watches as he fiddles with the cuffs of his collared shirt, as he struggles out of his t-shirt. Her ears start to burn again as he slips off his jeans. He sits on the side of the bed in his underwear for a long time, hair hiding his face. He looks small.

Jess lies still, feels cool air on her stomach, her nipples, feels a small shiver in her arms. When Joey had first talked to her about doing this with Kyle, she'd thought for sure she would need to be wasted, shit-faced. She'd spent the last couple of days worrying about being too nervous, too shy, of being half naked and wanting to stop, humiliating herself. Even tonight, she'd thought of backing out. But now, she feels spacey, not really drunk or stoned, but just not quite herself. She is surprised by how easy it is to keep going.

She reaches her hand toward Kyle's shoulder; he jumps at her touch. She stays silent, turns his body toward hers, guides him on top of her. He is almost weightless, a thin blanket. His hair falls down around her face, cutting the dim light to darkness. This is what it's like to be buried alive, she thinks. She kisses him, softly at first, like she would kiss a puppy, then deeply, her tongue pushing into his mouth. He shudders on top of her.

"Are you cold?" she asks him, strokes his back. He shakes his head vigorously. Slowly, carefully, Jess slides his underwear down his narrow hips. She moves out from under him and manoeuvres him onto his side, runs her tongue along the inside of his lips. She reaches behind him for the condom on the nightstand. Opens the packet with her teeth. Grins. Kyle's face is pale, his mouth open. Jess can hear his breath, rough and amplified.

She kisses him gently on the mouth, then chin, then Adam's apple, then in the cleft between his collarbones. She lingers there, settles her tongue in the empty space. She feels Kyle's body lift up to her, a gentle poking against her hip. She kisses down the centre of his chest, through the hollow between his ribs, down the flat of his stomach. She feels his pubic hair against her chin. His penis is small, a boy's penis, but hard. She touches her lips to the taut, red, skin and it jerks as if startled by her presence. Kyle's hand moves to cover himself. Jess coaxes his hand away, thinks it will be over quickly. She pulls the condom out of its package. It fits loosely over Kyle's erection.

❧

On the way to the bus stop, Joey feels twitchy and bound, like his clothes aren't on right. He wishes he had another beer, something to get a buzz on. Jess stops walking and asks for her money. He digs a twenty-dollar bill out of his pocket, watches her tuck it into her bra.

Joey decides a smoke will settle his nerves. It takes him four tries to get the thing lit; the flame trembles in the cup of his hand. He blows the match out quickly. "So. What was it like?" he asks her.

"Fine." Jess touches her earlobe. Her fingertips come away stained. She digs in her purse while they walk. Pulls out a Kleenex and presses it to her ear.

He takes a deep drag of his cigarette, stuffs his hand into his pocket, feels for the earrings, pinches them hard into the pads of his fingers. "No, really, what was it like?"

Jess doesn't look at him, stares straight ahead as she walks. "I would have done it for nothing."

Joey stops, tries to feign a laugh. "Would you do it again?"

"No." Jess walks faster, wobbles on her heels.

He trots to catch up to her, ducks his head to get a peek at her face. "For fifty?"

"Fuck you."

"A hundred?"

Jess swings around to face him. "No!"

Joey is relieved, blows a thick stream of smoke into the air, smiles. "Good."

Jess has started walking again. "You're a bastard, you know that?" she shouts.

Joey moves up beside her and slides his arm around her shoulder. "Yeah, but you still love me, right?"

Jess's head is turned away. She wipes her cheek with her palm, nods.

Joey spots a small wooded area on the other side of the road. He tugs Jess's arm. "Come on, let's go in there."

"No, Joey, not tonight."

He lets his arm fall to her waist, tries to warm her up by slipping his hand down the back of her skirt. "Come on," he says, "I got a surprise for you."

"My ears are bleeding. I wanna go home."

"Just come on, Jess, it won't take long. You'll love it." Joey knows he can change her mind. He pushes his body against hers so that she has to walk backwards, moves her across the road, towards the trees, with large deliberate steps.

Jess struggles against him. "Quit it, Joey!" She tries to walk forward, forcing herself into him; he holds his ground.

She wrenches her arms out from under his; he grabs for her wrists, but misses. She ploughs her arms into his chest and pushes him back. "Cut it out!"

Joey loses his balance, stumbles, then catches himself. He takes an exaggerated step away from her, holds his arms up in a gesture of mock surrender.

He shakes his head, stares at the road, then looks up, points his cigarette at Jess. "Sometimes, you're a fucking cunt, you know that?" He jerks his hand as if to throw the lit cigarette at her face. Watches her flinch.

❧

After Jess and Joey leave, Kyle takes a bath. He holds his breath and lies at the bottom of the tub for as long as he can, eyes closed, arms floating, hands away from his body. He counts the hours until his parents will be home, wishes the weekend were closer to over. He drains the tub and turns on the shower, soaps his hands and face and chest, points the shower head at his crotch.

After, he dries off, throws the towel in the laundry hamper; he brushes his teeth twice, flosses once, rinses his mouth with mouthwash.

Downstairs in the living room, he collects beer cans and empties them out in the sink. He wipes down the coffee table and counter with his mother's bleach solution. Washes the ashtray. Goes over the couch and recliners with the hand vac. He checks the carpet where the beer spilled; there's a large, dark stain. Tomorrow morning he will go out and buy club soda.

In the kitchen, he fixes himself a sandwich, peanut butter and jelly with raisins; he is careful to clear the crumbs from the counter, retie the twist tie around the plastic bread bag. He turns off the lights around the house and checks the windows and doors before taking his sandwich and a glass of milk up to his room.

In his bedroom, Kyle boots up his computer. Loads Planet Blaster. Checks the date of his high score: four months ago. He will break that score tonight; he hopes it will take till dawn. He bites into the sandwich, follows with a swig of milk, wipes the corners of his mouth with his hand. When he picks up the game pad, it is reassuring, familiar under his fingers.

As he's about to start the game, out of the corner of his eye, Kyle sees a figure move. Someone waving a raised hand. He swings around in his chair, but finds that it is only his reflection in the bedroom window. The thin white streak of his own arm, his face shaken and cut narrow by the dark hood of his hair, a uneasy tiredness around his eyes. He stares for a long time at this other, hovering, Kyle, a disembodied torso and head drifting off into the pitch of the night.

Dead Girls

You are addicted to television news. The speculation, the body bags, the hopeful high school photos; dead girls, everywhere. The police have arrested a man in a suburb of your city – a retired dentist, a small bungalow, a large backyard. A mass grave discovered by a dog named Queenie, who followed a tennis ball through the snow and retrieved for her owner a browning scapula. The first of an undetermined number of female skeletons. Just off the patio, behind the picnic table, a manicured lawn, a soft-spoken man. So far, the victims are all prostitutes, bodies for hire, disposable girls. Between four and midnight, you watch five hours of local coverage. You switch from channel to channel at peak times, five and six, ten and eleven. You keep the volume high. When your husband comes in to ask if you want dinner, you watch his lips move, demand that he speak up.

You have no tolerance for whispering, for delicate sounds. The soft swish of the broom as you drag it across the kitchen floor makes your teeth hurt. You look down at the small pile you've made: two popcorn kernels, a broken matchstick, an old twist tie; you and your husband leave so little behind. You dig the broom under the lip of the stove, force it between the refrigerator and counter, wish for something that isn't yours. A hair clip.

The agent has told your husband it is difficult to make a sale when you refuse to leave the house during showings. She is forced to whisper, which, she has explained to your husband, makes her seem less than honest. She has also said that you unnerve the browsers with your awkward stares and constant pacing. You try to sit still while the agent is there. You are an exhibit, you tell yourself, a rare and pitiable specimen perched at the counter, sipping your tea. You do not smile, but focus intently on your cup, best they see you in your natural environment. The agent is huddled close to a young couple with twin toddlers; you hear yourself described as a "motivated seller." You hear the mother say, "It's much nicer than the photo." The toddlers, a girl and boy, pull on their mother's cuffs and pant legs, stuff their free hands into their mouths, sway toward you as if you are some curious animal. You bare your teeth at them. The girl moves behind her mother's thigh, the boy smiles, a thick, saliva-lipped smile. The mother looks over her shoulder at you; you stare back. You want to tell her that your family is broke and your husband is eager to sell the house you raised your child in, but if it were up to you, you would fight her for it.

Your husband's whispering is the worst. The sound of his pencil as he hunches over ledger books at the kitchen table, pressing so hard the silhouettes of his numbers carry through several pages. You hear every *scratch scratch* in every column; it drowns out the late night news. During a commercial break, you tear a stack of papers out from under his hands, the hospital invoices, the loan applications, the amortization forms, throw them in the air, cruel and ecstatic, scream at him, "This is a family, not a bank. You can't keep withdrawing!" He rests his forehead in his palms, then stands, places his pencil neatly in the seam of his book, and walks away from you, goes upstairs to bed. You stare at the papers on the kitchen floor, consider for a moment finding a glue stick and arranging the documents into a fiscal wall mural, something to horrify prospective buyers. Instead, you leave the paper scattered like debris and take your husband's seat at the table. You read his account of each transaction: name, expense, credit, debit. Your small family's history in numbers,

balance falling from positive to negative in staggering increments. You study the back of each page, the relief of your
husband's entries raised up like Braille. Every thought, every
feeling he has had, focused into that tiny point of graphite. You
run your fingertips over the contours of lines and loops, forward
and backward, try to decode his closed, quiet language.

The lending officer at the bank had understood completely. A
small man with dyed black hair in a neat crew cut. A crisp
white short-sleeved shirt, a plain blue tie. As soon as he heard
the words recovery centre, detox program, he approved your
second mortgage. He showed you a pin and a small photo in
his wallet of him holding a gaily iced supermarket cake. He
told you in a hushed voice that he, too, was in recovery, then
nodded as if you were conspirators. These things take time, he
said. What he meant was, these things take money.

You have stopped measuring her distance in days and weeks, you
are on to months and years. You last saw her a year and a half
ago in the bright light of the glass-walled treatment centre. Her
last phone call was seven months ago, while you were waiting
for the ten o'clock news. When you lifted the receiver to your
ear, all you heard was a girl crying. It made you cry. Then you
heard, "Mommy, Mommy," and you couldn't speak, could only
press the cool receiver hard against your face. "Please Mommy,
I'm sick." You knew that "sick" could mean a lot of things. There

was a click. Your husband had run upstairs to the bedroom phone. His voice was gentle and focused. "Clare? Where are you?" And your daughter spoke again, sounding suddenly grown-up and pulled together, "Outside the art gallery." You wanted to tell her then about selling the house, but you didn't want to upset her, to tip her away from you. Your husband spoke, "Do you want us to pick you up, or meet you at the hospital?" And Clare started to cry again, her voice hiccupy and childlike, "Pick me up, Daddy." You and your husband drove to the art gallery with a blanket and winter coat even though it was July. You spent two hours waiting on the art gallery steps. Your husband walked to a Starbucks and brought back iced coffees. He didn't speak, except to comment on the how warm the summer evening was. You could barely hear him over the scraping of skateboards below you. A group of skate kids were doing tricks around the lit fountain. You listened to their boards grating over the carved stone rim, the slaps of their palms as they passed one another, their jeering voices. You wondered where their parents were. Your husband walked down the small concrete steps to where the kids gathered, lighting cigarettes. He had a quiet talk with their slouched bodies, lifted a photo out of his coat pocket. They all shrugged and shook their heads, their hair swaying in front of their eyes like fine beaded curtains.

When you got home that night the front door was broken open. Small things were missing: money from your dresser, the spare-change jar, your husband's electronic organizer, the portable television from the kitchen.

The body count is at twenty-three. A female broadcaster, whose hair has turned from dark auburn to medium blond in the days you've been watching, announces that skeletons have been found in sets of twos, threes, and fours, an elaborate corpse orgy, orchestrated by the accused. Hip against hip, skull upon skull, fingers entwined, a morbid collage. She warns that the following scenes may be difficult to watch, that parents should ask their children to leave the room. A live camera pans through a backyard with cedar fencing, past a white plastic patio set and a painted picnic table to a huge rectangular dirt pit, its muddy sides reinforced with wood planks; small orange flags dot its surface. To you it looks like the beginnings of an in-ground swimming pool. The camera moves in closer. Protruding here and there beside the orange flags, pale slivers and rounds, the bones of the unexhumed. Drowning hands. Then there are the victim photos – police record mug shots, thin, angry girls. The parents of a recently identified victim weep openly on the screen. The mother is dark-skinned, maybe Malaysian or Filipino; the father wears a baseball cap. They bow their heads, hold up a photo of their daughter at her high school graduation and repeat over and over that she wasn't a prostitute, that the police have confused the facts, that she was a good girl. Her face is homely beneath the tasselled cap, a smatter of acne across her brown forehead; she is a little on the plump side; her lipstick is pink, not scarlet. This is how they want their daughter remembered, they say, as they push the photograph towards the camera. You wonder if you would do it differently.

You and your husband have not had sex in over a year. You have thrown out your birth control pills, lubricants, anticipating you will never have sex again. It is as if the two of you have been accomplices in an unspeakable crime and can no longer return to the backroom of its conception. You move around your house like cautious guests, clothing wrapped tightly, eyes averted. Signs of affection have been reduced to domestic favours, someone has made breakfast for two, someone has put the bathmats in the wash. Each regards the other's suffering as something foreign and solitary; this awareness dilutes everything between you, reduces your connection to a thin wet strand, a tenuous liquid thread. If there were times you considered consolation in lovemaking, they were brief: a moment when he rested his hand on your hip, the second it took for you to brush an eyelash from his cheek. Until you remembered the act itself, the furious press of bodies, the hushed, plaintive cries. And its results: the frantic upstream swim, the penetration of nucleus and with it, the reckless joining of genetic material, the shrouded crapshoot of chromosomes. So much easier to believe that it all went wrong back then, in that hidden and automatic chemistry. Better there than under your roof, in your care. Nature versus nurture – where is it that life begins?

The day your house is sold, the news breaks that the accused kept a record of his victims: first name, eye colour, left-handed or right-handed, bra size. The newscaster, an older man with a slouchy face and gelled hair, tells you that police hope this inventory will speed up the identification of Jane Doe skeletons. The document was leaked to the media early that morning by an unknown source; the police retaliated immediately by acquiring a court order barring the press from releasing what the police have been referring to as "the ledger." You are sitting at the kitchen table with your husband and the real estate agent; she is opening a bottle of expensive champagne and telling your husband a joke about a man and an alligator. The television in the other room is turned up so you can hear the news. Several newspapers and television stations have lawyers in court seeking permission to broadcast the ledger's contents, citing that it is the public's right to know. The agent fills three glasses and raises a toast. "To new beginnings." You carry your glass to the counter and pour your champagne down the sink.

When you were a child, your parents got divorced and the nightmare you had was this one: on a regular, sunny day, you walked home from school, the same route, the same trees, the same tire swing in the neighbour's yard. But when you reached your house, strangers lived there. An immigrant family, dirty and unkempt, filled the front doorway, stuffed together like old coats in a dark closet. When you asked them about your parents, they all screamed gibberish and flapped their arms wildly. The children, dwarflike, hidden in the shadowed archways of their parents' legs, hissed and spat at you. The smell from inside the house was like burnt milk. The door slammed shut. You stood on the steps and cried.

Unlike your parents, you and your husband are not getting divorced. You have decided, and suspect he has too, that it is far better punishment to stay together.

You have sifted through memories and household items often, looked for signs of it all beginning. You have scrutinized photos of Clare, searched for a marker, a hint in the openness of her eyes, the set of her mouth, that she was changing, preparing to fall away from you. You study them with a magnifying glass, but there is nothing, just your bright smiling daughter perched on the edge of a swimming pool. You have kept report cards, receipts from piano lessons, Brownie badges, macaroni art, but these offer no indications, these are not clues. You cannot reconcile these artefacts of Clare's childhood with the memory of finding her, at fourteen, in the garage with a boy, her panties clutched in a fist behind her back, and the smell in that hot, dusty space, the musk of your own daughter's body. Or with the sadness that slipped over her like a veil, dulled her into a quiet melancholy, that made her difficult to talk to, almost impossible to rouse out of bed in the morning. You cannot pinpoint the event that pushed her from childhood to adulthood. A heartbreak, a seduction? Was it an older boy? A group of girls? Was it the lure of the liquor you left unlocked in the dining room cabinet, the liquor you found, a few months later, to be nothing but coloured water? How long, you had asked your husband in front of embarrassed guests, how long do you think it took her to drink all that? You are ashamed to admit it, but you have even looked at your husband and wondered about sexual abuse. You are looking for an answer that will relieve your own culpability, something that will prove you, if not innocent, then at least misled.

You have refused to pack up Clare's room. Each day you stand outside the closed door and hope the inertia of everything in there – clothes, books, stuffed animals, dust – will stop the planet from turning. What keeps you from going in is the silence, the unbearable absence of sound in that room. So, while wandering through a mall one day, you decide to buy a stereo, something to keep you company while you gather Clare's things. You choose a small portable one, with a five-disc CD changer. You try to select five CDs that Clare would like, but you don't know what Clare likes, so you buy numbers one to five from the Weekly Top Ten rack. You charge it all to your credit card. When you get home, your husband is in the driveway in gloves and a toque, washing his car in the freezing cold. He offers to wash yours. "What's that for?" he asks, points to the large box in your arms. "Clare's room." He starts to say something low and serious but his voice is drowned by the spray of the hose dangling limp in his hand. You turn and walk away. Inside the house, you climb the stairs, balance the box against your chest. You turn the doorknob with two fingers, push the door open with your foot. You lean down, lowering the box to the ground, and what you see when you look up forces you to sit on the floor. The room is empty. He has made it there before you. Furniture, toys, clothes, all stripped away; even the curtains are gone. You try to remember pop star posters, school certificates, an endangered species calendar, the photos and stickers on her vanity mirror. When you open your eyes, there is only the dirty peach of the walls. You wrap your arms around the cardboard box. The corners pinch against your forearms and wrist, pushing you away, but this only makes you hold on tighter. You start to cry. Your husband appears in the doorway. "I thought it would be easier," he says. Before he can move to you, you shake your head, shout at him that he is not what you want. When you look up again, he is gone. You wipe your face with your hand. You kneel on the floor and begin to tear the box open, strips of cardboard and staples coming away in your hands. You set the stereo in the centre of the room, load in the CDs. You flip through the instruction manual, press some small metal buttons, set the machine for continuous play and turn the volume up high. You make sure the door will lock when you close it. You leave Clare's room, and slam the door behind you.

Days after the real estate papers are signed, the telephone rings. You have decided to stop saying hello. Instead, you lift the receiver and wait for the other person to start talking. Your husband's barely audible tones. A suggestion of going out for dinner smattered with *are you there's?* You are distracted by the muffled bass of the music coming from Clare's room, a surrogate heartbeat. You hear yourself agreeing to meet at a Japanese restaurant at six o'clock; you know he wants to talk about the new apartment, the move; you will have to tape the news. You put down the phone and immediately it rings again. You forget yourself and say "Hello," as the receiver touches your ear. You hear whispering, amplified, close to the phone, a woman and a man. "Hello," you say again, your voice dashing down an empty corridor. A muffled conversation on the other end and the sound of someone smothering the mouthpiece. "Clare!" you shout into the phone. A tumbling sound; someone grappling with the receiver. A sudden tinkling, like small bells. A man's voice, "Sorry, uh . . ." Then you hear it, clear in the background, the throaty ring of your own child's laugh. The man's voice again, snickering, "Hey, wrong number." There is a click and you are disconnected.

There are certain channels open to you when your child has been arrested more than once, been hospitalized more than once. A government-run courtesy that is not wasted on parents whose children are mere underage drinkers or weekend runaways; a level of service reserved only for those like you, who have spent time in a holding cell, once cupping a handful of your daughter's vomit as she wretched and shook in front of you, once cradling a maxi-pad between her legs after what she and police called a "bad date." You pull the business card out of your wallet and call a constable who calls your phone company. Within minutes you have the address of a telephone booth downtown.

The photo you carry is a recent one, a Polaroid you took in front of the police station two years ago. Clare's face, drawn and dark, a bluish shadow around her left eye. She is slouched against the cement wall of the building, her body like thin cord beneath the denim jacket, her left shoulder jutted up in defiance, the right side of her body turned into the wall as if she is about to recede into it. You waited on the sidewalk while the picture surfaced; Clare smoked a cigarette. A social worker in the waiting area had lent you the camera. "Take a photo of her now," she said. "You'll find her faster next time. Faster than with that, anyway." She pointed to the photo you were holding, Clare's eighth-grade school photo. Clare in a bright red cardigan with a white t-shirt underneath. Her smiling face, still round with baby fat, touched lightly with the powder blush, mascara, and lip gloss you had helped her with in the morning. Around her neck, a thin gold chain with a single pearl pendant, the gift you had given her for her elementary school graduation. This was the Clare you were searching for. And though physicians and nurses and therapists had told you that it was best to approach the process without expectations, you clung stubbornly, secretly, to the hope that this Clare would return. On the sidewalk, you showed the Polaroid to your daughter, asked her, "Is this really you?" Clare held the photo in her dirty hands, squinted through cigarette smoke, shrugged and handed it back to you. The white bottom of the Polaroid was smudged with her thumbprint, a dark trail of swirls and circles that seemed to lead nowhere.

The phone booth is at an intersection on a busy nightclub strip. Though it's February, and barely dusk, working girls in miniskirts stroll the curb, clutching their fake furs around them. They hover, then move quickly toward the cars that slow down. Some of them troll the sidewalk, sashaying backwards as they proposition the men who are walking. When a man seems interested, a girl opens her coat, gives him a preview. From a distance, you study these girls, their narrow, youthful bodies, their confident postures, their carefully styled hair. You are relieved that most of them look healthy, strong, that they smile and joke with one another. You watch how they keep their legs rod straight, as if executing a gymnastics bow as they lean down into the open windows of cars; you notice that some of them don't bother with underwear. You approach the girls one by one, careful to not interrupt their transactions. You tell them, "I'm looking for my daughter," and show them the Polaroid. Some of them shake their heads without looking at the photo, some of them hold the photo and stare at it sadly. A dark girl in a purple stretch-velvet dress squeezes your hand, her long pink nails denting your skin, "I hope you find her." An older woman in a full-length fur coat pulls a pen and tattered notepad from her pocket. "Give me your name and number, I'll phone you if I see her." You write down your name, Clare's name, and your phone number. You see that other pages of the pad are filled with numbers. To stay warm, you settle in at a diner on the corner, the Lotus Café, a place you have visited before. As it gets dark, you keep an eye on the phone booth, and the girls doing business. You watch many of them leave and return. You wonder where they take the men. Do they kneel behind dumpsters? Stay in the cars and drive to a secluded parking lot? You want to remind them to be safe, to carry mace and maybe a knife, to keep the car doors unlocked and their seatbelts off, to have another girl memorize the licence plate. Make sure you count the money first and never, never go with more than one man. These are things your daughter taught you.

You have often told Clare she was a difficult birth. You say it with pride, touching her hair, her hand, a shared trauma, a permanent bond. Thirty-two hours of labour and in the end, they gave you drugs, dragged her out with forceps. You had resisted the medication for hours, pleaded with the nurses, told the obstetrician you didn't mind going through pain for your child. The obstetrician laughed and said, "You'll have plenty of time for that later." What you remember most clearly about the birth are the wet, slippery sounds: her mucousy slide from your body, the delicate slurps as they suctioned her nose and mouth, her first gargling cry, your husband's sobs behind his mask, and, when she was brought to you, the tiny, almost imperceptible sound her mouth made as it opened and closed.

"If you're staying much longer, you'll have to order again." The waitress is collecting the plate from the Denver sandwich you finished hours ago. As she fills your coffee cup, you stare at her face; she is maybe ten years older than you. Her name tag says "Emily"; the cheerful energy of the name and the tired pallor of the woman seem horribly mismatched. On her lapel she wears a large novelty button, a portrait-studio photo of three kids and a teddy bear. "Are those your children?" you ask, pointing to the button. Emily looks down at her lapel as if to double-check. "Oh, no," she chuckles and shakes her head, "grandchildren." You nod and look at your watch, eight forty-five. You decide to go home.

The night is dark, but the streetlights are beacons. The strip is jammed with cars, a slow parade of men with their windows rolled down and their stereos turned up. The working girls compete fiercely: some go topless beneath their open coats, some hike up their skirts to flash their merchandise. Outside the nightclub across the street, a line-up has formed. You examine the pairings. Men who are too old, too bald, too fat, too ugly, with beautiful girls at their side. Girls with steady smiles and dead eyes. Over the clicking of your heels on the pavement, you hear their stray laughter, their young offerings. You imagine these girls with their heads thrown back, their mouths open wide, the lengths of their necks callow and exposed. You know if you approached the men, accused them, berated them, they would laugh and shake their heads, wave you off with their ringed fingers. And the girls, the girls would cower, cling to those men, stare at you with guarded eyes. Not one of them would come with you to your car, not one of them would accept your offer of a hot meal, not one of them would let you take them home.

Before running away from the last treatment centre, Clare told you she would never live with you again. You were sitting across from each other on white rattan chairs in a solarium, surrounded by glass and ficus trees. Clare had just finished a session with her therapist. She explained her need for space and independence. You felt a small stab in your chest as if someone had slid a safety pin through your heart. Clare asked if you were okay. You said yes. You didn't tell her that it seemed unfair; you had been fighting to get her back for so long and now that she was here, safe in this place, surrounded by doctors and counsellors, you were being forced to let her go again. You didn't demand the years you were owed, the fairy-tale months of living together as mother and daughter. Instead, you laughed, nodded, tried to seem light-hearted, understanding. You remembered feeling that small sharp pain before, but couldn't recall when. Days later, the police in your living room, your daughter once again missing, the moment occurred to you. Her first day of kindergarten. You had expected her to cry when you got her to school, to cling to your dress and beg you to stay. Instead, the moment she saw the playground, the dome-shaped monkey bars, the wooden fort, the swings, she dropped your hand. She ran across the grass toward the other children, strangers, as if she couldn't join them fast enough. You stood still, not knowing if you should continue forward, not ready to retreat. Halfway there, she halted and turned to face you. You smiled. She was scared, the yards of grass between you, an immense distance to her small eyes. She would run back to you, or wait for you to catch up. But instead, she waved and shouted, "You can go now!" Clare bounded away from you, her arms outstretched toward the swings, her ponytail fluttering back at you like a dismissing hand.

You sit in your car and listen to the radio news. A female broad-caster announces that a bomb has exploded in an embassy overseas; all twenty-nine bodies in the mass grave have finally been identified, all families have been contacted; the controversial ledger will be published in the next morning's paper. You rest your face against the steering wheel, feel the cold plastic against your forehead. This is real, you tell yourself, this is real. You sit back in your seat and close your eyes. The broadcaster is interviewing former neighbours of the accused. An elderly woman with an American drawl remembers that he posted a "no junk mail" sign on his mailbox. An older man, a retired welder, recalls him as friendly. "He seemed like a nice guy. He always said hello." A young mother of three, who declares over and over, Thank God my children weren't hurt, thank God my children weren't hurt, remembers that the dentist waxed his car an inordinate number of times. "Twice a week. I kept asking myself, why does he need it so shiny? I thought it had something to do with teeth."

It is the shuffle and clink against the car that startles you. Someone squeezing by. You look up and catch the backs of a man and girl walking. The girl, in a white leather coat that almost covers her short white skirt, takes long strides on high, chunky heels; the man, thin and older in a tight-fitting suit, follows quickly behind, looking around himself as he goes. You turn off the engine and get out of the car. You follow them down a short side road, then into the alley. They stop near the middle, against the back of a tall red-brick building. The alley itself is dark, but an emergency light farther down casts them in silhouette. There is an urgent smell of rotten fish and fresh urine; you press your palm over your mouth and nose. The girl says something, her voice too quiet for you to hear. The man shakes his head and the girl shrugs, turns away. The man says, "Hey," and grabs her arm. She yanks her arm away and holds out her hand. The man shakes his head again, pulls his wallet from his pocket. The girl counts the money, then slides the folded bills down into her shoe. She crouches in front of him, the pale of her hands reflecting some misdirected light. There is a quiet, rhythmic sound like soft panting, the musical jingle of thin metal bracelets. She is on her knees, her face buried in his open trousers while the man's head lolls back and forth. Her hair is twisted and gripped in his fingers, her legs, bent and stiff beneath her. You hold out your hand and trace the curve of her back in the distance. Sink into the awful hush, the muted groans and whispers, the tiny wet sounds, the dripping of water, the electrical buzz of the emergency light. You stroke the air in front of you, then look down at the ground, at the puddles of urine and wet garbage, the discarded condoms and needles. You will yourself to breathe, to take everything in. You force yourself to watch. When they finish, the girl stands, turns her head to the side, coughs. They both move away from you. The man walks to the back of the alley slowly, his hand dragging along the brick wall. The girl trots past him, veers left at the end of the alley, raises her arm to steady herself, her bracelets ringing like chimes as she turns the corner.

Your house is silent. In the upstairs hallway, you see that Clare's door has been broken open, the door frame split and cracked to raw wood. The carpet littered with thin, ragged splinters, pieces of the stereo, stray buttons and dials, shards of black plastic casing, twists of metal and wire. Mechanical entrails. Your first thought is that somehow this is Clare's doing. Then you notice the hammer. This is your husband turning inside out.

Your bedroom is dark, but your hands find your husband in his usual sleeping position, fetal, turned away from your side of the bed. Your hands press into his shoulders, his chest, massage the muscles in his arms. You ignore his tired murmurs and *where were you*'s as you climb onto the mattress, onto his body. You pin his shoulders with your palms, push yourself into him as hard as you can, rub your breasts over his chest; open your mouth wide as you kiss him. He is dazed, alarmed, arms at his side as you stare at him. You grab his right hand by the wrist and push it between your legs. He hesitates, keeps his hands still. You clench your thighs around his wrist, reach into his pyjama bottoms; you are coaxing him, begging him to become someone else. You drag your nails across his scrotum. He shivers and reaches up for your breast, squeezes it hard between his thumb and palm; you hear yourself moan. He grips your shoulder and turns you onto your back. He mounts you, pulls your panties down your thighs and enters you in raw, burning strokes. You slide your hands under his t-shirt and dig into his back; he whimpers. "I want to hurt you," you tell him as you dig your nails into his buttocks, "I want it to hurt." He whimpers again. He forces himself into you harder and harder, his hip bones spreading you, splitting you open. You feel a blunt pain through your stomach, the bed sliding, scraping against the hardwood floor. You cry out. Your husband stops, his whole body frozen above you, his eyes frightened wide, unblinking in long seconds of shame and ecstasy. He shudders. His body goes slack and for an instant you feel his full weight. You reach your hand to his face, to touch the sweat that has seeped from his skin, but he inhales sharply and moves off you. You turn your head and stare at him. His flushed skin, his startled eyes, his mouth open as he breathes. You want desperately for him to say something. You tell him about the news on the radio. He nods, wipes his face with the sheet, gazes up at the ceiling. His eyes start to close and you are afraid that he will fall asleep, leave you alone with a quiet house. You tell him everything then, slowly, deliberately. You begin with the phone call and the diner, the Denver sandwich and the waitress named Emily. You tell him about the alley, the smell, the needles. The girl, her arms, her knees, the man, her hair in his hands, her buried face. The wet sounds, the jingle of her bracelets. You tell him that she looked thin, but not too thin, not sick, not hurt. You stop. Your husband's face is tense and pale. For a moment it looks as if he is having trouble breathing, his chest strangely immobile, his jaw tight. You touch his arm and his face crumbles, he falls against you, cries into your breast, loud, heaving sobs, his chest shaking.

You stroke and kiss the top of his head, rub your palm across his back, soothe him with your voice.

While your husband is in the bathroom, you open the bedroom window, let the cold city air fill the room. You listen to the sounds of traffic and sirens, rain on the pavement, someone's radio. You lie down on the bed, naked, hungry and tired, let the city wash over you, your body all gooseflesh, the insides of your thighs bruised and aching, a hot and empty soreness between your legs.

East

The minivan sped through the night. Windshield wipers thwapped out a nervous beat. A death, a dead dog, was a serious thing.

Annie watched Jemma steer with her elbows, light a cigarette with her free hands.

"I told him," Jemma said. "I told Marcus not to buy them a fucking puppy, they were too young. What a prick. He said it was a snoopy." Jemma's hands waved above the wheel; tiny flecks of ash drifted in the air. "I said, you idiot, Snoopy's a beagle, that's a basset hound." She brought the cigarette back to her lips, took a deep, sucking breath. "And you know, it was just like I said it would be, they tortured the thing, squeezed his stomach, made him puke, made him pee. They thought it was a riot."

Annie squeezed her armrest.

"So today we're building a snowman, you know, a midget one before the rain melted everything away. I heard the brakes go, and I fucking knew that was it." Jemma tapped her cigarette against the edge of the console ashtray. "The woman who hit him wouldn't stop crying. God, I wanted to slap her. The kids are screaming 'Snoopy's brains! Snoopy's brains!' And fuck if I didn't have to clean the mess off the road, brains and all. I asked the driver, she was wearing gold costume jewellery, that should give you some indication, I asked her, would you please take my kids around back while I do this? She sat down on the curb and started hyperventilating. I had to call a fucking ambulance just for her. Anyway, all afternoon the kids were crying and carrying on. That's when I called the sitter."

Annie nodded, her eyes fixed on the lights of a semi curving towards them.

Jemma jerked the wheel to the right, pushed her hand into the horn. "Asshole!"

The semi's yawning retort trailed in the distance.

"Fucking Marcus, he tries to be divorced father of the year and what do I get? Puppy brains." Jemma adjusted her side mirror.

"I think I've heard enough about the brains."

Jemma pulled out into the left lane to pass a pick-up truck. A horn blared, high beams flashed. Jemma swerved back to the right. A low-slung sports car edged up, out of Jemma's blind spot.

"Sorry." Jemma cringed and waved politely as the sports car passed. She leaned forward and reached for the pack of gum on the dashboard. Steered with her wrists as she unwrapped a stick and folded it into her mouth.

Annie tugged on the shoulder strap of her seatbelt, was relieved to feel it hold.

In the gas station store, they wandered the junk food aisles, their hands opening and closing.

Annie chose four flavours of cough candy, opened them all and put one of each in her mouth, mumbled, "I think I'm coming down with something."

When they were finished, they approached the counter, arms full of chips, diet pop and licorice, chocolate bars, newspapers, women's magazines and the open cough candy.

"Number seven," Jemma said to the boy behind the counter.

The boy was a smooth, lanky thing with a lazy face and full lips that betrayed a future of one-way crushes, lovesick girls. Annie was used to that equation; in high school, she would have let this kind of boy make a fool of her.

He watched Jemma as she dug through her purse for her gas card, his eyebrows furrowed, his mouth tense. Jemma's looks often inspired a painful gaze in men.

Annie didn't think Jemma was especially attractive. Her face was plain, her body slim but nothing better than average. It was how Jemma manipulated her looks that seemed to draw men in. Her make-up was immaculate, her eyebrows brushed, her cheeks contoured, her lips lined and glossed. And her hair: long honeyed caramel layers that swam around her shoulders, framed her face in hand-twirled strands. Men went crazy over that hair. She wore clothes that hugged and criss-crossed her body and always showed some skin. She never wore flat shoes.

"Just a sec." Jemma was flustered, her hands full of old receipts, lipsticks and packages of breath mints.

Annie felt a bit sorry for her. All that primping and fuss. Annie was less desperate for attention. Her own outfit, a fitted corduroy skirt, rayon men's-style shirt, and Gortex jacket seemed more practical for driving around in the rain than Jemma's clingy, low-neck cross-over top and skin-tight jeans.

"Fuck, it's here somewhere."

The boy's expression said, take all the time in the world. He was looking down the front of her top.

Annie crunched a piece of cough candy between her back teeth; her mouth filled with cherry syrup.

The song that dripped from the in-store speakers was a saccharine ballad. A seventies hit about two rodents who fall in love.

Jemma punched her left hand down into her purse. "Fuck!" Lifted her right hand to cover her eyes. Her shoulders shook. The boy took a step back.

Annie moved to the counter, looped her arm around Jemma's waist, lifted her hand from inside her purse and danced her away from the boy.

"Remember this song?" Annie asked.

Jemma shook her head into Annie's shoulder and cried. "That fucking dog," she said, her voice thick with tears. "It was just a baby."

Annie pulled her close and sang in her ear; the syllables warbled with cough candy. "*Bah-dah-dah-dah-dah-dah-tango.*"

The clerk picked at his fingers.

"*Dee-dee-dee-something-jingo.*"

Jemma sniffled.

"He was checking out your cleavage," Annie whispered.

Jemma lifted her head, looked at the boy; her face was smeared and puffy. The boy smiled. Jemma moaned, rested her head back on Annie's shoulder.

"*Phone me 'cos you still got my stuff, looks like mushroom love . . .*"

Annie moved her around the front of the store, rocked her back and forth between the chip display and the magazine rack. They bumped against the bulk candy bins. Annie gave up on the lyrics and just hummed the tune.

At the end of the song, Annie sighed, pressed her cheek against Jemma's hair. The boy stared at them, his mouth stuck in an expectant smirk.

"What the fuck are you looking at?" Annie said. The cough candies made her voice unfamiliar, thick and hollow like a dumb jock's.

Jemma lifted her head from Annie's shoulder, turned to look at the boy. He lowered his eyes, moved back to the corner behind the cash register.

Jemma coughed, then covered her mouth with her hand and started to giggle.

Back on the road, Annie twisted a licorice stick in her mouth. "I'm pathetic."

"Who isn't?" Jemma was eating pretzels out of her lap.

"Peter's dumping me."

"No, he's not."

"I called him at midnight last night, he wasn't home."

"So?" Jemma reached over and dug through the plastic shopping bag beside Annie's seat, steered with her torso.

"I called him at six this morning and he still wasn't home."

"He's playing out of town." Jemma came up with a chocolate bar in her hand.

"I checked the game schedule."

"He got drunk and stayed at a friend's."

"He's cancelled our last two dates."

Jemma hooked her wrists through the steering wheel and peeled the wrapper off the chocolate. "Oh."

Annie watched the rain shimmy up the windshield, frantic drops of water fleeing the blade. "What kind of liberated woman gets dumped by a hockey player?"

"You'll find someone else." Jemma offered half the chocolate bar to Annie.

Annie shook her head. "He was ugly."

"And rude."

"No, I mean, he was ugly, I purposely chose an uglier guy so this wouldn't happen. Even ugly guys are dumping me now."

"He hasn't actually dumped you yet." Jemma threw the crumpled chocolate bar wrapper on to the floor.

"Whatever."

"You're too good for him."

"He told lies, you know, all the time."

"There you go. Who wants to be with a liar?"

"I miss him already." Annie stared out at grey streaks of melting slush along the roadway. "How long are we going to keep driving around the city?"

Jemma shrugged. "Till we're happy. Or we hit something."

The inside of the minivan was a womb, an upholstered bubble humidified and warmed by on-board climate control. Annie was lulled by the pulse of sad music, the ballad of a drained and broken man, another casualty of the seventies. *Looking for a chance that just ain't coming, you want to settle down but you can't stop running around. And all I'm trying to say is maybe, maybe, baby you could stay here tonight . . .*

She reclined her seat and turned onto her side, soothed her cheek against the cool leather. Her mind was full of the hockey player: the crooked ridge of his nose, his knuckly hands, his dentures, the pressure of his erection through the cotton of his chinos. His ugliness and arrogance excited her. Something arresting in the way he called her beautiful and made it sound like a handicap. She fantasized about him while he was away, masturbated in the bathtub with her legs around the tap. Imagined a roomful of handsome men unable to satisfy her, then Peter with his apish lovemaking, his unshaven face, his missing teeth; she'd grip the slippery enamel and hold her breath.

A shrill electronic ring. Jemma's cell phone.

Annie sat up.

Jemma checked the display and rolled her eyes, answered the phone. "What?"

The minivan drifted towards the solid yellow line.

Annie slipped her hand into the moulded plastic door handle.

Jemma over-corrected, catching the shoulder of the road for a gravelly instant. "She's not a fucking stranger, Marcus . . . just shut . . . just shut up, she's the babysitter."

Annie smiled. Jemma had her battle voice on. She felt almost bad for Marcus.

A year ago, when Jemma had left Marcus and the kids for the first time, he had called Annie every day, begged her to talk to Jemma. Jemma had moved in with a lifeguard from her children's community pool.

"Yeah, I don't know . . . I don't know . . . the gate was open. What do you mean what do I mean the gate was open? Oh, I see . . . maybe I left it open, is that what you're saying? Well, excuse me for being too busy raising your children to check the gate every five fucking minutes!"

Annie had talked to Jemma, and between Jemma's detailed descriptions of the sex she was getting, Annie tried to convince her that she was having some sort of married-with-children crisis and what she needed to do was go home to her family.

Jemma did go back, but not because of anything Annie had said. Marcus had hired a live-in nanny, a young Mexican girl with thick dark hair down to her waist. Jemma had phoned Annie in the middle of the night, screamed about being replaced. For weeks after, Jemma complained to Annie about finding metre-long black hairs all over the house, on furniture, on the floors, in the drains.

"Do what you want, do whatever you want. Just make sure you pay the sitter and she has a – hello? Hello?" Jemma threw the phone onto the dash.

"Everything okay?"

Jemma punched her fist into the steering wheel. The horn wailed. The family sedan in front of them swerved. "Right as rain."

Jemma was muttering along with the CD, hard rock crossed with gangster rap, *I am the man, you understand, bitch-lovin', pot-smokin' gangsta fan. I am the man, I am the man . . .*

The hockey player had been a set-up.

Ian in marketing at the brewery knew Peter from high school, was willing to use his connection to get an endorsement for their new "sport-focused" beer. The hockey player came in for a meeting. Annie listened as the marketing guys pitched, then displayed her print-ad mock-ups, the hockey player coming to a sudden halt in a divine spray of ice, his skate blades centimetres from the frosty bottle of beer.

At the end of the day, Ian had approached her desk, pencil drumming in his fingers. He told her the hockey player was willing to do the print endorsement, for much less than they had budgeted, if she would agree to go on a date with him.

Annie had laughed. "I can do much better than that, you know."

"Just a date," Ian said. "Dinner, a few drinks, no one's asking you to sleep with him. Well, not until we finalize the TV budget, anyway."

Because he was a local celebrity, she had expected some sort of fanfare, a limousine, a special table at a restaurant. Instead, he picked her up on foot, explained that someone had borrowed his car without asking. She found out later it was all a lie; his licence had been suspended a few months earlier. He wore faded jeans and a Genesis concert t-shirt and looked older than she remembered from the meeting. He stayed outside while she got her coat and purse so that he could finish the joint he was smoking. They went to a nearby pub and before his first pint was finished, he announced that she would have sex with him that night. He wasn't wrong.

Jemma was still lost in rap land.

Annie picked the newspaper up off the floor. She lowered the sun visor and turned on the vanity lights so she could read. The sports section was the first to go, she pulled it out and threw it into the back seat. She found the entertainment listings. "Want to go do something?"

Jemma shook her head, her lips still mouthing the lyrics.

On the front page of the newspaper was a photograph of a man. His head was turned as if someone had called him from behind, then snapped his picture. Annie read the cover story, then scrutinized the photo. The man was in his late forties, early fifties, balding but not trying to hide it, carrying it off in a distinguished, aloof sort of way.

Annie folded the paper in half, then in half again, so that only the picture showed. She held it up to Jemma. "Think he's cute?"

Jemma glanced at the paper. "He's alright. A bit old for you, don't you think?"

"Serial killer."

"No way."

"Yup. They just caught this guy with a bunch of bodies in his yard."

"Let me see that."

Annie leaned over and held the steering wheel while Jemma studied the picture.

Jemma dropped the paper back in Annie's lap. "Am I totally sick, or is there something kind of attractive about that man?"

Annie stared at the photograph. "You're totally sick. And there's something kind of attractive about him."

Annie fed Jemma chocolate-covered almonds. Hors d'oeuvres. She shook an empty potato-chip bag off her foot, rubbed salt and crumbs on the floor mat.

Rain sheeted across the windshield; Jemma had the wipers on high. The speed of the blades, the furious slapping sound, made Annie anxious.

The phone rang again. "Fuck." Jemma reached for it.

Annie turned down the music. She slipped chocolate almonds into her own mouth one by one. Maybe, she thought, it was time to get fat.

"What for? Why do you want to know that?"

Annie had always imagined that sometime in her life, late in her forties, after a husband, a house, some kids, she would let herself balloon. She would resign from the struggle to stay young and thin and beautiful, and simply let the pounds land. She would eat anything she wanted, whenever she wanted, she would throw away her bathroom scale.

"Look, I didn't need to take it to the vet, it was dead, its head was crushed."

She would join the ranks of middle-aged women who no longer cared that they didn't look twenty, who let their hips and stomachs spread into pastel coloured jogging suits, clothes that advertised a clear disdain for anything fashionable.

"In the garbage . . . yes, there is actual garbage in there with it."

Annie rattled the box of chocolates, tipped her head back and poured what was left into her mouth. She could be one of those endearing, sharp-witted fat women. The type with a huge body, and a pretty face, who provoked sympathy in friends and a contempt towards men, who as a sex, were clearly too superficial and thin-centric to recognize a good thing when they saw it.

"Yes . . . fine . . . listen . . . yes . . . listen, Marcus don't let them – fuck! I hate it when he does that!" Jemma turned to Annie. "He's having a fucking funeral."

"You're kidding."

Jemma didn't answer, just stared ahead at the road.

Annie held up the folded newspaper. "Can I bring my new boyfriend?"

Jemma didn't smile. "I'm tired of driving."

At the laundromat, the windows were fogged with heat.

Annie bought seven boxes of detergent from the vending machine, one for each time she'd slept with the hockey player. While Jemma stood and blocked the manager's view, Annie poured large white-powder hearts onto the tops of the back washers, seven in a row.

The two of them sat in white plastic garden chairs and watched the people come in.

An older woman chuckled when she saw the hearts; a dark-skinned man was puzzled and nervous, crossed the room to another washer, but kept looking over his shoulder, back to the one he'd left behind; a bookish man and his skinny wife were annoyed, pushed the powder over the side edges of the machine with the backs of their hands. A frugal older man collected the powder in his cupped palms, whistled as he funnelled the tiny granules into his plastic detergent container.

A girl with a silver-grey mohawk touched her index finger to the powder, then touched her finger to her tongue and winced. A college-aged couple, who looked like brother and sister, pushed the powder around to form their initials in the centre of the heart, then moved to do their laundry in another, heartless, washer.

Jemma lit a cigarette, offered it to Annie; Annie took a drag.

"You know," Annie said, exhaling, "of all the household duties associated with being a wife and mother, I think I would find laundry the least offensive."

"You ever notice in prison movies, they make such a big deal out of men doing laundry?" Jemma offered Annie the cigarette again.

Annie shook her head. "Men doing laundry is a big deal."

"Marcus did all our laundry. And the cooking. And the grocery shopping."

"Wow, was there anything that guy didn't do?"

Jemma smiled at Annie. Then raised her eyebrows and stuck out her tongue, wiggled it from side to side.

Annie laughed and felt herself blush.

They stayed until all seven hearts were ruined.

At Denny's, they sat across from each other, their feet propped up one another's bench.

Jemma recited the menu items as if they were sexual positions: "All American Slam, French Slam, Moons Over My Hammy . . ."

Annie noticed many of the men in the restaurant staring in their direction, smiling. She knew they were smiling at Jemma.

Their waiter was young. Steve, a dark-haired boy with sad eyes, who was light on his feet. He brought two glasses of water then walked over to the food pick-up area and asked the cook for the hockey score. He did a little victory twist before returning to take their order.

When he got to their table, Annie interrogated him as to the true nature of grits. "What are they made from? How are they made? Are they full of fat?" She watched as he steadied his smile, fiddled with his order pad, waited for her to let up.

He told her he wasn't completely sure, but he didn't think grits were fattening.

Annie was disappointed. She demanded that Steve expand on his answer, even though she would probably pass on the grits.

His smile wavered, he shifted his weight, scratched the centre of his chest with the top of his pen, shifted his weight again. "I – I can check with the kitchen," he said finally.

"No," Annie said, holding him there with her eyes, "I want *you* to tell me."

She kept this up until he called her ma'am. She glared at him then, and he collected their menus, hurried away.

Jemma sipped her coffee. Annie read the newspaper, a different one this time, a colour tabloid. Her new boyfriend in a bright orange prison jumpsuit.

The restaurant filled with the deep, clipped barks of men. Annie looked up. Six men in boots, down vests over dirty work clothes, strolled towards them on their way to a booth at the back. Two of them loomed close as they walked by. Their smiles angling for Jemma. Jemma stared ahead at Annie.

The last man stopped in front of them, cast a wide shadow across their booth. His crotch rested on the lip of their table. He leaned down, closer to Jemma. "Lovely ladies like you shouldn't be eating alone."

Annie pretended to look at the newspaper, but watched Jemma. "Neither of us is alone, moron."

Jemma stared into her coffee. The guy kept his eyes on her, moved his face close, his nose just grazing her hair, then tapped the table, and stood up.

"Cunt," he muttered to Annie, knocking her shoulder with his hip as he walked away.

"I hope he gets cancer," Annie mumbled. Jemma didn't seem to hear her.

The minivan was a capsule of luxury, a testament to how deeply and completely Marcus loved his dissolving family. Heated leather seats, adjustable in every direction, ten-disc CD changer, on-board DVD player with two viewing screens.

Parked at Prospect Point, Jemma and Annie slouched in the back seat, smoked cigarettes, watched *The Shawshank Redemption* on twin screens.

Jemma took a long drag of her cigarette and pointed at the screen in front of her. "See, laundry."

"I believed you." The movie was slower than Annie remembered. Tim Robbins looked too much like an overgrown toddler. "Your kids watch this movie?"

Jemma shrugged. "They don't know the difference. It keeps them quiet."

Something poked into the small of Annie's back. She shifted in her seat, but could still feel it digging in to her. She reached behind her and pulled out a pair of swimming goggles. Jemma had joined a swim team while she was living with the lifeguard. "You still doing this?" Annie asked as she dangled the goggles.

Jemma opened a can of Diet Pepsi. "Yup. Six a.m., three mornings a week. You should try it. Get you in shape."

Annie didn't need to be reminded she wasn't in shape. Jemma's fondness for exercise was probably her most aggravating trait. Annie felt along the seat for leftover chocolate. "Nah, goes against my master plan." She found a single chocolate-covered almond, blew on it to get the lint off, then popped it into her mouth. "Jemmy, my darling, some things are just too hard."

Jemma pointed at the screen. "Harder than digging your way out of prison with a spoon?"

Annie looked at the screen; Tim Robbins was again looking doleful. "Yes."

On the turn of concrete steps overlooking Burrard Inlet, a patch of the point dimly lit by the glow of the Lions Gate Bridge, Annie and Jemma shared a joint.

Annie was ready to go home, to have a bath and watch TV in bed. She felt cranky. Jemma was also in a mood, but she had whined when Annie suggested calling it a night. Maybe the pot would ease them out.

They huddled under the prickle of evergreen branches. The wind off the water blew right through Annie's rain jacket. "This is scenic."

"Sorry." Jemma held her leather coat closed with her hand. "If Marcus catches a whiff of that in the van, he'll be on the phone to his lawyers. He thinks I'm out of control."

"You are." Annie felt the instant satisfaction of veiling something pointed and true in the guise of a joke. "You've got to be the worst mother I know." Annie chuckled, sipped on the joint.

Jemma shrugged and took the joint from her. "Where'd you get this?"

"The hockey player."

"Oh." Jemma said. "Your ex."

Touché. Annie managed a smile. "Yeah, and with my new boyfriend still in jail –"

"Maybe you should sleep with Marcus," Jemma said suddenly.

Annie stared out at the bridge; she could feel Jemma's eyes on her. Perhaps the truth wasn't always the best idea. Annie shoved her hands into her jacket pockets, tapped the safety railing with her foot.

"I mean," Jemma took a short toke, "wouldn't it solve all our problems? He'd be out of my hair, you'd have a boyfriend, he'd have someone new in his life?"

Annie forced a quiet laugh. "Yeah, I don't think that's gonna work."

"Oh well." Jemma flicked the roach over the railing. "It was worth a try."

Annie played with the dome light, flicked it on and off, over and over. Jemma turned up the stereo as loud as it would go. Bootleg underground dance music – her newest discovery. Individual electronic instruments whirred in a massive pulse of distortion. Annie found the repetitive lyrics and driving beat comforting.

Sky girl, cry girl, you used to be my girl, sky girl, cry girl, you used to be my girl, sky girl, cry girl, you used to be my girl . . .

They knelt on the carpeted floor between the front and middle seats, grooved as best they could in the limited space. They entertained each other. Jemma worked her thumbs to either side like a possessed hitchhiker, her head thrown back, her jaw hanging loose. Annie shook her shoulders like an epileptic cage-dancer, her face frozen in an expression of incredible surprise.

Jemma collapsed on the floor, howling.

Annie reached for the cough candy. They crunched the pieces one by one, cherry, lemon, eucalyptus, until all of it was finished. They sprawled on the floor, their legs resting up on the middle bench of seats. Annie fanned herself; she was damp all over with sweat. The CD finished; the abrupt silence, like a vacuum; Annie heard a small, high-pitched ringing in her ears. "I think I'm going deaf," she said, sucking on her last piece of cough candy.

Jemma laughed. "I've got more CDs."

"No, that's okay."

"We could watch another movie."

Annie shook her head. She wanted to go home.

Jemma lifted her arm over her head, ran her thumbnail down the back of the bucket seat; it left a faint grey mark. "I'm going to miss this van," she said.

Annie patted the floor around her for more candy, but there were only sticky wrappers and the folded newspaper.

"Marcus is moving back to Ontario. Back to his family. He says he has no friends here."

"Why doesn't he just take the car? I mean, you'll need the van for the kids." Annie waited for Jemma to launch into another Marcus rant. But Jemma stayed silent and very still. Annie turned her head.

Jemma was staring up at the ceiling of the minivan. The outside corner of her eye moist, her smoky eyeliner streaked in a shadowy line down her temple. A muscle in her cheek trembled. She swallowed, her throat tensing then relaxing.

Annie had no idea what to say. She opened her mouth and cool, mentholated air streamed out, empty and useless. Her whole body felt bloated and stoned, everything heavy and tired. She couldn't lift an arm to offer her hand to Jemma; she was suddenly too sad to move.

When Jemma spoke again, her voice was raspy, like she was choking. "He's the better parent, Annie, I'm not ashamed to admit it."

The side of Jemma's face was shiny with tears. Annie puckered her lips and blew gently against Jemma's cheek. Jemma closed her eyes and smiled.

The highway was black and wet. Annie drove.

They sat languid and askew with their seatbelts off. The cabin alarm dinged continuously. Annie missed the reassuring pressure of the belt across her shoulder, the tightness around her waist; she reached back for the nylon strap.

"No!" Jemma shouted. She pointed a stern finger at Annie.

"The alarm is making me crazy."

"It's spiritual."

"It's annoying."

"Everything spiritual is annoying." Jemma emptied the contents of her purse onto the van floor, leaned down to push things around. "Just give me a sec."

Annie focused on the road, her hands steady at ten and two. She watched the white dashes as they blipped through the headlight beam, but the pace of the dashes didn't match the frequency of electronic dings. "Hurry up already."

"How many men does it take to wallpaper a room?"

"I've heard that one."

"Ha!" Jemma sat up. She held a large yellow Post-it pad.

"I'm glad you're taking notes. Can I put my seatbelt on now?"

"No!" Jemma peeled a note off the pad and stuck it to Annie's thigh. She held out a pen. "Okay, write the hockey player's name on the piece of paper."

Annie took the pen, printed as best she could while trying to keep her eyes on the road. *Peter.*

Jemma wrote on her own Post-it, then threw the pen onto the floor, pulled the lighter out of the console. "Okay, ready?"

Annie's eyes moved from the road to Jemma.

"According to *Cosmo,* this will be cleansing." Jemma held her Post-it by the corner and touched the opposite corner with the lighter.

The edge of the Post-it darkened and curled, popped into a small yellow flame. The flame spread sideways in a thin line, a border of fire that advanced towards Jemma's finger. The paper shrank to a smaller and smaller triangle until Jemma flicked it into the air and it flared into a tiny white burst, then singed into nothing, a crinkled grey ash, drifting back and forth between them to the floor.

"Damn, that was good." Annie laughed. She held the steering wheel with her left hand, peeled the Post-it from her thigh with her right, watched as Jemma lit the corner. The lighter touched the paper and the flame flared, brighter and angrier than Jemma's, the advancing line quicker. Annie waited for the threat of heat at her fingertips, then flicked. The paper stayed. She flicked again. She was stuck to the adhesive, she had held the wrong corner.

"Jesus!" Annie shouted.

Jemma smacked at the flame as Annie shook her hand. "Stay still!"

Jemma's palm caught the edge of the paper and the lit corner sprang from Annie's finger. Annie watched the flame as it arched in the air, a trembling tear of light, and landed on her right breast. The fabric of Annie's shirt sent up a thin stream of smoke. "Jem!"

"Shit!" Jemma opened a can of Diet Pepsi and poured it over Annie's breast.

Annie looked up and, startled by the sudden field of lights in front of her, channels of red and white points in the darkness, she turned the steering wheel sharply to the right and stepped hard on the brake.

The van pitched and growled on the gravel shoulder. The back skidded out to the left as everything slammed forward with a jolt. Annie caught the steering wheel in her ribs. Jemma slipped off her seat.

The wipers dragged across the windshield.

"Are you alright?" Annie whispered.

Jemma was crouching in the foot well; she patted her hands slowly over her body. She nodded.

Annie pressed her forehead to the steering wheel and tried to catch her breath. She felt the area around her ribs, but nothing seemed broken.

Jemma started to giggle, a stifled, nervous laugh.

On the way into the convenience store, they passed a group of kids with skateboards. Young hooded boys, with pierced, sulky girlfriends hanging off their shoulders, clinging to their hips.

"Hey, hootchie mama!" one of them called as Annie and Jemma passed. Annie gave them the finger.

The light inside the store was blue and hummy.

Annie grabbed a bottle of club soda on her way to the bathroom.

In the small tiled room, she took off her shirt and held it in the sink. The burn looked like a bullet hole. She wet her fingers with the soda and rubbed around the dark ring; the wrinkled black edges bled out into a wider brown circle.

Through the door, Annie could hear the soft clicks of Jemma's heels as she paced the store, the sounds of her speaking to someone, laughing. Annie sighed. She was really ready to go home now. She would call the hockey player from bed.

She poured more club soda, rubbed a palm-sized section of the shirt in her hands. The brown circle started to fade, but the hole, and why hadn't she thought of this before, was irreparable.

As she put the shirt back on, she noticed the skin darkening below her left breast. A sprawling bruise. Something the hockey player would come home with.

In the store, Jemma was leaning against the counter talking with the clerk, a twenty-something girl in a bright green polyester uniform. The girl had bright green streaks in her blond hair and was resting forward on her elbows, laughing at something Jemma had said.

"Hey!" Jemma shouted to Annie. "Wanna go to prison?"

"Not without a spoon."

Jemma laughed. The girl looked amused. "Seriously," Jemma said. "Your new boyfriend lives around here."

Annie shook the front of her blouse; the clammy wetness was almost unbearable. "Don't you think we should head home?"

Jemma drove them to the prison.

She talked and lit another cigarette. The windshield wipers were back to their frenzied pace. "Then she said, Everything bad is east. And I said, What do you mean? And she said, Think about it, what's at the western-most tip of the city? The university, right?"

Annie shook her shirt in front of the dashboard vent, enjoyed the warm air that passed through to her skin.

"So, it's downhill from there. As you move east the population gets poorer, there's religious fanaticism, racial intolerance. What else did she say? Oh, yeah, book bannings, drive-by shootings, murder-suicides. That's why they put the prison out there."

"As opposed to right next to the university." Annie turned off the fan.

Jemma shrugged. "It makes sense."

"Did you find out who killed JFK?"

Jemma pulled over to the curb. Beside them, a grassy hill rose up sharply, a steep incline that reached up to the prison wall. Dotted along the hill were small, bald, deciduous trees.

Annie dipped her head, but, through the rain on her window, couldn't see anything beyond the mammoth cement barrier.

Jemma handed Annie her rain jacket. "Let's go."

"Wait." Annie checked the console clock; it was past midnight. "I should call him now, before it gets too late." She reached for Jemma's cell phone.

She pressed the numbers slowly. The phone rang.

He answered a clipped "Hello?"

"Hi? Peter?"

There was a pause. "Yeah, um, Peter's not here." He spoke loudly, behind him a shushing noise.

"Oh. Is he out of town?"

"Nope. Just not here."

Annie was sure it was Peter's voice. "Do you know when he'll be back?"

"Nope."

"Can I ask who is this?"

A pause. "I'm his cousin."

She heard men chuckling and talking in the background. "Is something funny?"

"No. Look, I told you, Peter's not here." The phone filled with the sound of men laughing. "Do you wanna leave a message?" She heard a man in the background yell, "Just leave a fucking message!"

"Yeah, can you tell him, Annie called?"

"Annie." His voice started to falter; he was trying not to laugh. It was Peter. "How do you spell that?" he asked. The men erupted in guffaws. Another background voice yelled, "Go home, Annie!"

Annie pressed the end button.

Jemma raised her eyebrows. "Well?"

Annie tossed the phone onto the dash. "He wasn't home."

The security lights on the hill made Annie feel as if she was walking out of the night and into some false dawn. Or onto a movie set, the downpour of rain falling in such perfect angles, it must have been coming from a rain machine.

Under the lights, the grass glowed an insistent green Annie had never seen before, an artificial green. The buildings behind the wall were far away, and appeared to be fashioned out of cardboard boxes. Maybe it was a side effect of the pot they had smoked, but nothing seemed real any more.

The ground was loamy and wet. Annie pressed her foot into the grass and everything below her sole sank like a collapsing sponge. A pool of water rose up to meet her shoe.

"What are we doing here?" she shouted to Jemma over the rain.

"I don't know!" Jemma shouted back, the expression on her face somewhere between pleasure and confusion.

Annie's rain jacket was almost soaked through. They were not turning back.

As Jemma worked her way up the hill towards the wall, the heels of her shoes disappeared into the mud, then reappeared, thick brown stalks. She leaned forward to keep her balance.

Annie came up behind her, the wet ground closing around her shoes, her arms outstretched in case Jemma slipped back into her.

Eventually, they found the easiest way to get up the hill was by scuttling sideways, facing each other, like crabs.

When they reached to top, Annie doubled over, panting, her right hand on the sore part of her ribs, her left hand on the wall.

The wall was high and slick, the buildings too far back to see.

Annie's arms burned from the cold; her corduroy skirt, now rain-drenched, clung to her legs like a heavy skin. "Okay. We did it. Now let's go."

Jemma tried to catch her breath and talk at the same time. "Are you crazy?" Small clouds of fog rose from her mouth. "We can't stop now." She looked down and started to laugh. Annie followed her eyes. Jemma's shoes were submerged in mud, her legs growing out of the ground.

Jemma braced herself against the wall, wiggled her legs and, one after the other, lifted her bare feet out of the shoes. She did a little hopping dance as her toes sank into the mud. "Go ahead!" she shouted.

Annie's own shoes were her favourites, seventy dollars on sale, air-cushioned sole, square-toed with a modest wedge heel. "Okay," she said. "But I'm coming back for them." She pulled one foot out and stepped into the mud. The sensation was like having her foot swallowed by a swollen, icy mouth. She pulled out the other foot; the ground held tight to her shoes. Annie squealed as her second foot hit the mud.

Jemma clapped.

"Now what?"

Jemma looked at the wall. "Climb?"

Annie ran her hand over the smooth cement blocks. "Yeah, I don't think so."

Jemma made a half-hearted attempt to find a hand hold, but there weren't any. She looked around, then pointed.

Annie saw that farther down there was a spot where the buildings were closer to the wall.

As they walked the rain started to slow, but the ground remained difficult. Annie moved carefully, tried to avoid the sharp gravel and rocks near the wall, grabbed onto Jemma's arm whenever her feet threatened to slip. Jemma took a wrong step and ended up calf-deep in grass. She laughed hysterically as Annie pulled her out by the wrists.

They reached the point at which the buildings had seemed closest to the wall and looked up. A trick of perspective. The wall now completely blocked the view of the nearest structures. Only a building far, far back was visible, a wide rectangle with two floors near the top lit up.

Annie cupped her hands around her face to block the glare of the security lamps. "Look, up there."

Curved into the small frames of each window were what could have been people. Dots and squiggles in squares of yellow light. Men's bodies, undoubtedly, with their sheepish, unrepentant postures. Annie imagined them cocky, confident, at home in that warm dry place. She turned to Jemma.

Jemma was bent over, poking around in the mud near the wall. She took hold of something and stood up, wiped it off and showed it to Annie. A rock, muted yellow, the colour of old bones. She rolled it around in her palm. "Shall we say hello?"

Annie watched as Jemma stepped back and lobbed the rock into the air. It spun and arced through the bright sky, soared over the curved lip of the wall, then disappeared. Landed with a distant but satisfying *thuck*, something concrete.

Annie loosened her sinking feet from the mud, one then the other.

Jemma found another rock, a shiny black one. She hurled it and it glinted as it crested above the wall. The sound of it landing was tinnier. Metal.

"Have you had enough?" Annie was thinking about finding her shoes, wringing out her skirt, blasting the heater in the car.

Jemma shook her head and scrambled for a small boomerang-shaped branch that was lying at the base of a tree behind them. With both arms, she swung the branch. "Hey, assholes!" she shouted as it turned end over end in the air. "Why don't you come out here?"

Annie watched the shapes in the windows; they were still, unfazed.

Jemma unearthed a flat grey stone, smoothed her hand over its surface then threw it like a Frisbee. "You fucking freaks! I hope they rape the shit out of you!" The disc flew high above the wall for what seemed a great distance, then dropped out of sight and crashed into something glass. An alarm went off.

Jemma screamed and clapped, tried to jump up and down, but then slipped and almost lost her balance. Annie caught her hand, held her steady. The alarm continued ringing. "We should get out of here." The rain began to pour again.

"No way," Jemma said. "Not until you throw one." She bent down and picked up a rock, tossed it at Annie. Annie caught it with two hands. The rock was slippery with mud and cold, heavier than it looked. Annie gazed up at the windows. The shapes seemed to have moved, grown darker. She wondered if the men could see down past the wall, if they were chuckling up there, calling others to take a look.

"I hope you die in there, you pathetic losers!" Jemma screamed as she threw another rock. "You puppy-killing bitch! You make me sick!"

Annie unzipped her jacket to free up her arm. Took a few steps back. A beam of light nicked the corner of her eye and a large white circle flashed onto the wall in front of her. She turned and squinted, put her muddy hand to her forehead.

A policeman moved awkwardly, but quickly up the hill, a hulking figure in a dark rain poncho.

Annie whispered Jemma's name. Jemma looked over her shoulder and froze.

He stopped a few feet away from them and turned back to a police cruiser trailing along the road at the bottom of the hill; he waved his flashlight above his head. "Just a couple of women," he said into his radio.

The radio crackled and Annie heard a man chuckle. She stepped back and moved her hand slowly to her pocket. A souvenir.

The cruiser rolled to a stop. Annie saw the second policeman get out and walk to the trunk, open it up and lean down into it.

The first policeman pointed his flashlight at their hands. "Okay, ladies. Put down the rocks."

Jemma's rocks hit the ground.

"Let's see some ID."

Jemma stepped forward.

The policeman shone his flashlight in her eyes. "Just stay right there, ma'am." He stared at Jemma and shook his head as she struggled against the light. Her hair was flattened and clinging to her head and neck, her face stained with mascara and mud. "You want to tell me what you're doing out here?"

Annie spoke. "We were just –" The light landed on her face. For a second she couldn't see. She covered her eyes until the glare was off her. When she took her hand away, Annie was sure she saw the policeman smiling, nodding as he looked her over, as his hand reached under his poncho. She looked down at herself; the beam of his flashlight hovered on her body. Her jacket was wide open, her shirt and bra soaked through, her breasts and nipples clearly visible through the sheer, wet fabric. She pulled her jacket closed.

The policeman held a set of handcuffs. "Do you ladies live around here?" He was looking right at Annie now, his smile gone, his voice hard. "Have you been drinking?"

"No," Jemma said.

He turned. "Was I talking to you?"

Jemma shook her head.

The policeman moved towards her, his flashlight beam narrowing on her face. "So, you and your friend just came out here to throw rocks. You haven't had anything to drink. Whose van is that down there? You the driver?"

Jemma looked confused.

"Listen —" Annie said.

The policeman pointed at Annie. "You just keep that jacket closed, sweetheart. I'll be with you in a second."

He looked over his shoulder, down the hill to his partner. "You better get up here," the policeman said into his radio. "It's turning into wet t-shirt night."

The radio crackled with laughter.

Annie's hand moved to her pocket. She felt her fingers tighten, her arm swing out. The rock hit him from the side, just above the ear.

The policeman's body twisted as he took a lurching step forward. "Jesus!" And clamped his hand to the side of his head. He sank to his knees, the ground squelching beneath him in a quick, smooth ooze.

The second policeman scrambled up the hill, his flashlight beam a frantic tunnel of light. He slid back in the mud, clutching at the grass to keep his balance.

Annie looked over at Jemma. She was standing stunned, her arms wrapped around her chest.

The policeman on the ground moaned.

"Shut up!" Annie shouted. She tried to wipe the rain out of her face, but her hands were shaking. Jemma started to cry.

When the second policeman grabbed Jemma, Annie tried to pull him off her. He clipped Annie's forehead with his flashlight and Annie stumbled back. Then the first policeman was up and it was quick after that. Annie and Jemma handcuffed and pressed flat into the soaking-wet ground.

One of the policemen gripped Annie's hair, turned her face into the mud and held it there. She could hear the other, a few feet away, talking into his radio. She could heard Jemma whimpering softly beside her. And in the distance, the wail of sirens. Someone pulled at her hair and her head was lifted; she tried to draw a breath, but her nose and mouth were clogged with mud, her eyes blind. She thrashed her legs and shook her head, the centre of her chest burning and ready to explode. As her mind slid into darkness, she felt their eyes on her, heard their excited cries, the men in the prison. Crowded into their tiny windows, scratching at the glass, hungry for the taste of angry girl.

Young Love

A winter evening in Vancouver, a high-school parking lot, the inside of my Chevette lit up by the dome light. Outside, the darkening sky, the colours leeched out of everything: evergreens, grass, the mountains, all muted like dull iron, metal shadows. I rolled up my window and turned on the radio, punched through the stations, then turned it off again. Too many heartfelt, sentimental songs for a grey and lonely night – unrequited love, avenged love, young love, who the hell cared? I stared down at the two amphetamine capsules in my hand and sighed.

I was here to do a favour for my neighbour Janet. Cotton-candy Janet, jolly and pink, kind enough to raise money for a drug awareness program at her son's school. The irony was not lost on me.

In the dim yellow light, the capsules were a perfect blue. Easy as an August sky, tempting as a neighbour's pool. I swallowed them dry. Adjusted my fake nurse's hat. Stepped out of the car.

At the edge of the parking lot, a group of skate kids sat huddled on a low railing, hunched over cigarettes, their feet on their boards. Scrawny junior-high boys with long hair and baggy jackets, drawn like insects to the glow of the gym. I loitered near the doorway, gripped the metal bars of the emergency doors, indecisive. The open night pushed gently at my back, reminded me of cool sheets and the limitlessness of sleep, while waves of indoor heat, heavy with cologne and sweat, rolled against my face. The bass beat of dance music shook the wood floor, made the painted red and blue lines jump like pick-up sticks. The walls were alive with swirling coloured lights. My equipment bag felt full of bowling balls and rocks.

The centre of the gym was a dense and elastic mass of moving bodies, each back flagged by a thick black number on white paper. Small groups of teens gathered around the perimeter, their frames slouched and curved into apathetic question marks. Girls and boys sipped water from an array of containers: sports bottles, spigotted strap-on reservoirs, spring water bottles, thrift store canteens. It was almost too much, the relentless beat of the music, the careful attention to water fashion. I had just finished another double shift at the hospital, my ears trained to the quiet moans and requests of patients, my eyes on the keys to the pharmacy cabinet.

Up in the bleachers, the supervisory fathers stuck out like a herd of buffalo, sturdy ungulates in cotton pants and expensive sweaters. They were gathered together, mouths yawned wide in over-enunciation, heads nodding slowly.

I spotted Janet barrelling down the bleachers. Tonight she wore a rippling silk creation, a tent of a thing, with flowing, trailing pieces, all in a kaleidoscope of blues and greens; around her neck, a massive garland of seashells. It was either the pills or the lights playing off her fabric, but she looked like a giant tidal pool moving across the room. She opened her arms and splashed against me. The seashells scratched my collarbone, dug into my chest. She wiggled my paper hat, "This is great!"

Janet took my hand and dragged me across the gym floor. The heels of my duty shoes stuttered along the wood as I tried to keep step. She hauled me up the bleachers and I watched my feet as they dipped in and out of the alternating slats in a haphazard pattern. I was sure I would fall, take a header into the bleachers and be the first to require medical attention. Things like that happened to me. Things that made my face burn red, my saliva taste like lighter fluid.

The parents stood as we approached. Janet introduced me as "Mary, the single nurse who lives next door." The pills kicked in and for a second the world tilted away, the entire row of parents tipping back so that I overshot a handshake and poked a rotund father in the stomach. I apologized and said something about cholesterol; he flushed with embarrassment.

I said hello to a petite woman with short, black hair and Scottie dogs on her sweater and my peripheral vision flared, a huge spotlight turned on behind me, my throat pulsed. I talked myself through the usual fears, I will not have a heart attack, I will not stop breathing, any moment now this will feel good. And even as I said it, the high broke out across my body like a prickly white sweat. Everything around me looked suddenly brighter. I held it together, except for the sweating – I had no control over that. I shook hands with my arm pressed firmly to my side and silently cursed polyester.

I had struggled out of my unit scrubs and into the white tights and traditional white uniform in the front seat of my car. A conversation piece, an ice-breaker. The uniform was snug; I hadn't worn it since the Halloween before nursing school, back when a stranger told me I looked good as a nurse, a compliment that led me to consider the profession. The costume included an old-fashioned paper hat and a "Florence Nightingale" name tag.

"Do you wear that to work?" the woman beside Janet asked, her finger waving in the air.

I shook my head.

I could tell the mothers hated the outfit. They gave me that disapproving-mother look, the look that said, I was once spread-eagled in front of strangers with piss and blood and amniotic filth squirting out of my body, but this, this offends me. The fathers seemed somewhat more appreciative, though none of them appeared to be the skirt-chasing, sports-car-driving type. These were men who had reached the fork of middle age and taken the high road. They were fact-collecting types, men in comfortable sweaters and cushioned shoes whose lust for information, statistics, and useless trivia replaced a waning libido. These men were history buffs.

Despite my immediate dislike for the parents, or maybe because of it, I was nervous, and may have seemed eager to prove myself. I shook hands like a jackhammer, shifted my weight back and forth to the beat of the music, spoke too quickly. I opened my equipment bag several times to show them my supplies. They smiled apologetically.

One of fathers, a man who looked to be in his sixties, touched my elbow. "Aren't you a little too young to be a nurse?" he teased. "Aren't you a little too old to have a kid in high school?" I teased back. He stiffened. A woman behind him laughed.

Bob or Todd or Dodge, a short, wiry man with a trimmed moustache, confronted me directly. "So, what exactly is the pre-scribed treatment for dehydration?" A pop quiz. These people had some nerve. I turned to Janet, wondering if the man actu-ally expected an answer, maybe he was joking. Janet nodded; her mouth twitched strangely at one corner. I looked back at the parents; they were waiting. Perhaps they doubted I was real nurse. Suspected me a fake, a freak who put on the uniform and rode the bus all night, or a call girl for some medically themed escort service, a date-and-mate whore, someone who screamed "Code Blue! Code Blue!" during feigned orgasms. My palms started to itch. I adjusted my hat, pursed and unpursed my lips, tapped my fingernails against my name tag, and in a moment of inspired genius, threw in a shrug. "Water?" I answered, in my best airy, blonde voice.

The fat father laughed, a nervous and quick crescendo that sent his voice into the female register. The women smiled; their eyes, brimming with judgment, stayed anchored to their drinks. The older man nodded knowingly, as only older men do, then reached forward and patted my shoulder. His hand was heavy and hot; I was tempted to swat it away.

Bill, a younger-looking dad in a collared sweatshirt, leaned forward to Janet. "Maybe she can answer our question."

"Yes!" Janet squealed and grabbed my arm. "What type of doctor was Coombs?"

Thomas Coombs. I'd seen his face daily in newspapers and on the television in the nurse's lounge. The same image, Coombs cuffed and shackled, stooped in his lab coat, his face frozen in an expression of grief or severe exhaustion. I was used to seeing photos of murderers and rapists with confident stares, cocky jaws, cool arrogance. Coombs's eyes were pleading, his brow crinkled in disbelief, his mouth opened but turned down as if he was scared or about to cry. "I think he's a dentist," I told them.

"Yes, yes." Bill lurched forward. "We know that, but what kind? Endodontist, periodontist, orthodontist, denturist?"

Janet cut in, "You see, Kate here," – the woman with the Scottie-dog sweater gave me a small, excited wave. I tried to smile – "she had oral surgery twelve years ago, someone who filled in while her endodontist was vacation. She thinks it might have been Coombs."

The sweatered woman was perky, wide-eyed, vibrated with an "I only need three or four hours of sleep a night" kind of energy.

Bill jumped in. "I heard he begged the authorities to let him wear his lab coat in prison, but they refused." He looked to me for confirmation.

I shrugged. I had only ever seen him in his lab coat.

"I hear he asked for a special bed in prison, because of his back."

"It's his ass he should be worried about," another man said.

The women tittered.

"What about him being addicted to laughing gas and marijuana?"

"Who isn't?" I joked.

No one found this funny.

Janet scuttled me back down the bleachers to give me a tour of the gym: the DJ station, the energy-bar and cookie station, the water-refill station. The coupled parents manning these last two stations waved as we passed. Janet explained the structure of the dance-a-thon as we walked. The kids had been dancing since nine a.m. and would continue until the same time the next morning. They were allowed a five-minute break every hour and unlimited water. Pizza would arrive at eleven. I followed behind her, watched the back hem of her blue-green skirt drag on the floor like a constantly receding tide.

The triage room was set up across the gym from the bleachers, in the girls' change room. Two sinks and a wall of mirrors at the entrance, a row of grey lockers, and behind the lockers, showers and bathroom stalls. Janet had arranged for two cots, blankets, bandages, ice, and a water cooler. The instant I saw the cooler, I was crazy with thirst. Janet began a detailed explanation of who had donated each item and how she had convinced them to do so. I tried to hold on until she was finished talking, but in the end opted to nod and make interested noises in my throat as I filled several paper cones with water and downed them in quick succession. When I looked up, she was staring at me. "Are you alright?" She asked the question in a good-natured but nervous way, her hands fidgeting at her pillowy stomach. I almost felt sorry for her. For weeks she had been organizing this event, and here I was, slurping and jittery, a hopped-up fly in the ointment. My hand shook as I lifted the last cone of water to my lips and gulped it down. I smiled. "Rough shift." "Sure," she said; she twisted her necklace. I left my equipment bag – stethoscope, thermometer, ice packs, blood pressure kit, allergy kit, slings and splints, salinated sports drinks, condoms – in the change room, followed Janet back to the bleachers to watch the kids dance.

I sat next to Janet and her husband, Paul. I said hello to him and shook his hand, greeted him like a new arrival, but the loose grip of his palm, the strain on his face told me we had already done this earlier. "I like greetings," I said. "Some cultures greet whenever they meet. Meet and greet. You know, bowing or nodding –" I let my voice trail off. Paul turned to the man beside him. Janet chattered on about Miles, their son who was in the tenth grade and on the soccer team and starting to get phone calls from girls at all hours of the night, girls she didn't know. "They're unbelievably persistent," she said. I imagined girls with plaintive voices, telephone cords curled through their hair, stretched out on their princess beds, rings on their toes. Girls who could keep a boy on the line through supper, make him go all night.

Paul sat silent beside me. He looked like a lumberjack with his red plaid shirt, his thick dark hair and beard. He stared down at the gym floor and sipped from his paper cup of punch, held the cup daintily between his giant forefinger and thumb, took long pauses between sips. We were sitting close enough that I could feel the warmth rising off his arm and shoulder. He was big, his shoulder like a ham beneath his shirt. I could smell it on his skin, the maple syrup, the dull scent of smoked wood, a hint of Ralph Lauren.

"Is that cologne or deodorant?" I asked.

Paul turned and looked at me, then brought his cup to his mouth and took a drink. He went back to staring at the gym floor.

Janet twittered on beside me. Miles was thinking about colleges; he had his eyes on a few in the States, thank God they could afford it. I turned to see Paul's reaction. He wasn't paying attention. Janet had told me about Paul's work as a structural engineer, that he designed roadways for airport terminals, travelled all over the world. I wondered if he'd ever called an escort service from his room at the airport hotel. My eyes followed the individual strands of his hair, complicated bridges and overpasses. The top buttons of Paul's lumberjack shirt were open, and underneath he wore a white, ribbed t-shirt. The white zone is for loading and unloading only. I looked down and studied the rise of his pectoral muscle, the red plaid pattern of his shirt strained and askew. Paul turned and caught my eyes on him. I tried to meet his gaze casually. He shook his head, a smile pulled at the edges of his closed lips.

Janet was still talking. Miles had a summer job working at a soccer camp for the underprivileged, better than the job he'd had last summer, washing cars at a local gas station; during the school year he worked part-time for the Boys and Girls Club running after-school and weekend sports programs for kids.

Paul shifted in his seat, cracked his knuckles. He stretched and his elbow pressed into my side. "Sorry," he murmured.

I sat dead still, all the blood in my body rushing to the spot where Paul's elbow had touched me, an inch above my waist. An accident. Probably. I crossed my legs, then carelessly waggled my foot until it tapped his shin. "Sorry," I said.

He gave me a brief sidelong glance.

For a while, I didn't move. Janet was going on about how much Miles loved working with kids. She was playing with her necklace, the seashells clicking together. I could smell her perfume, something soft and floral.

I uncrossed my legs, pressed my palms into my lap, leaned back and let my knees relax. My left knee fell lightly against the middle of Paul's thigh. I waited. He didn't move, didn't look at me, just stared intently at the pattern of bodies on the gym floor below. I let Janet's voice fade into the pulsing bass of the music and tried to see what Paul was seeing.

The dance floor was a lush and colourful pageant. Dozens of girls with sweet, ripe faces and sweet, thin thighs. Confectionary girls who suckled lollipops and candy soothers, who clipped their hair in little-girl barrettes. Sophisticated girls with their bare midriffs and bare arms, their clothes perilously dependent on elastic, gravity, and licorice-whip straps. Healthy girls with their taut calves, their square shoulders, their tanned skin and effortless posture. Each girl took up so little space, an unwound paper clip, a piece of string. Their painted eyes more open and awake than I had seen eyes in a long time. Their hair, cut on angles, wound into coils, cropped tight or shagged out, every style a precision manoeuvre.

And the boys, their adolescent bodies all roped and sinewy under baggy clothes. Their fresh mouths, promiscuous grins, necks like finely tapered candles. Their chins jutted out or tucked under, sly. Their swaggering dance steps. Even the plainer ones, the awkward, furtive ones with questionable skin gave off a vibe, crackled with magnetism that hinted at a fathomless gullet of sexual energy.

Paul's leg was warm against my knee, a constant, deliberate pressure. I lowered my left hand to the bench, to the pocket of dark, empty space beside my hip. I started to sweat again. A dribblet of perspiration trickled down my side, soaked into the waistband of my tights. His hand came down over mine, a hot, heavy paw, a backwoods greeting. My heart pounded. I couldn't look at him. Instead, I looked down and saw my name tag jumping in rhythm; was it my heart or the music that was making that happen? Janet turned to me. I snatched up my hand and squeezed it in my lap. "Are you alright?" she asked. The row of parents beside Paul bent forward on the bleachers to look at me. "I'm fine," I told her and excused myself.

Inside the triage room I splashed my face with cold water and rinsed my mouth. I dug through my purse for some Ativan and slipped one under my tongue. I paced the room, checking the door every five seconds to see if he would follow me. My body started to cool down. I rubbed my bare arms, then climbed onto one of the cots and covered myself with the grey wool blanket. The view from the cot was strange, the harsh, white-tiled walls, the cement that formed a band below the ceiling, like a prison cell or holding room in a mental hospital. I pulled the blanket tight around me, but couldn't get warm. I rubbed my legs together, wondered if prison was like this, always cold.

The bars and wires of the cot pressed up through the thin mattress and into my back; it was like lying on a mess of garden rakes. I pulled the blanket over my face. Just above my eyes, a patch of diffused light filtered through the weave of fibres. A distant sun, a Winnie-the-Pooh nightlight.

I fell asleep, dreaming of nothing but sleep itself. White sheets, a king-size bed, feather pillows, long, cool nights.

When I woke, I felt better, like I had finally landed in my skin. I straightened my hat in the mirror, rubbed my index finger over my teeth. I found a Xanax in the change pocket of my purse, a long white tube of a pill. I broke it into half, then into quarters, slipped a powdery white chip under my tongue to keep the edge off.

I rejoined Janet in the bleachers. Paul had disappeared. The clock on the scoreboard said 9:17 p.m. Janet smiled and handed me a paper cup of punch. "Cat nap?" She was the kind of person who said cute things like that.

"Yeah," I said. "These double shifts are killing me."

"You need a boyfriend," she said. And I almost choked on my punch. I coughed into my hand and stared at her through watering eyes, but she just smiled and patted my back. I swallowed the rest of the punch carefully. The DJ was beginning a slow set. All the kids who had been taking a break, milling around in groups, now crowded onto the dance floor. The perimeter of the gym was desolate, no-man's-land except for a few partnerless cast-offs who stayed close to the refreshment table and two chubby girls who were stalking the DJ.

My mouth felt dry and I thought about getting more punch, but my muscles were starting to chemically relax and I wanted to enjoy the fade. Janet grabbed my shoulder and pointed to dance floor. "There's Miles!"

The only clear picture I had of Miles was from a photograph that Janet had shown me last year. "Look what I found in the attic!" she had called to me, waving a snapshot as she jogged across her lawn. I was on my way to a night shift, making the short but daunting journey from my house to my car. Her house was dark; I assumed there was no one home for her to show this to, that she had been watching for hours from her living room in hopes of catching me. I had no idea why she thought I'd be interested in her family pictures. In the photo, a buck-naked toddler-aged Miles was humping the leg of a mortified P.T.A.-type woman. The woman, who was sitting, had lifted her leg in the air, no doubt, from the expression on her face, to shake the horny critter off. But Miles was steadfast in his grip, his head thrown back, his face raised to the ceiling in beatific rapture. "Isn't he a hoot?" Janet asked, her hand clawing at my elbow. Apart from this portrait, Miles remained elusive, a silent, hooded teenager who moved in and out of my neighbours' house with stealth. A few times, as I'd passed naked from my bathroom to my bedroom, I caught something moving near the curtains in their house. I had always assumed it was Miles, though now the possibility of it being Paul was more interesting to me.

As I followed the trajectory of Janet's finger, I braced myself for a dark prince of perversion; I half-expected to see her naked son bouncing on the leg of a cheerleader. Instead, Miles turned out to be an average, if tallish, boy with light hair. He was draped innocently over a shorter, blonder girl. "Poor things can hardly stand," Janet said, her face spongy with endearment.

The other parents agreed, a soppy consensus. Rob or Todd or Dodge leaned forward in the row, "I hope you're watching for signs of exhaustion." I wanted to give him the finger, but nodded instead.

I stared at the dance floor and the edges of my vision started to blur out; I tried to go with it. The kids were all clinging to one another, arms like twist-ties around necks and waists. I watched an athletic-looking boy with a blond crew cut slide his hands over the tightly wrapped rear of a dark-skinned girl. I watched a nervous girl in glasses survey the room as a red-faced, red-haired boy kissed behind her ear; I watched a couple weave behind other couples to grope and neck as best they could until the movement of the crowd exposed them. I wanted to be down there, soaked in the messy perfume of sweat, the rush of wandering hands. Those kids, their gestures so cheeky and reckless, so laden with urgency and ambition, made me wonder how anyone who had had that in their life could learn to live without it.

I recognized the song that was playing, "Sexual Healing," and chuckled. I looked down the row of parents beside me. They were clueless and smiling; some of them tapped their feet and snapped their fingers absently. The woman in the Scottie-dog sweater swayed, her palms up in front of her chest in a sort of minstrel pose.

Behind her, two couples were talking about Coombs.

"There'll be a book and movie in no time."

"Who do you think will play him?"

"Martin Sheen."

"Too tall."

"Gene Hackman."

"No, someone smoother."

"Yes, smoother."

As the song finished, the DJ sped things up. Couples pulled apart, boys' hands and arms lingered on girls' bodies, reluctant to leave wrists, waists, pockets. The girls were drawn to the new beat, hips gyrating, shoulders shimmying. And the boys, unable to resist all that frenzied flesh, joined in. But amidst the collective motion, one romantic couple made a bold statement, danced slow to fast song, a girl with long brown hair, her arms hooked under the shoulders of a tall boy with dark curls. I wondered if Paul had looked like that in high school. I closed my eyes and imagined dancing with him, my arms around his neck, my head buried in his chest. His body strong and broad, so unlike the boys I had danced with, the unfortunate strays. There'd been Anthony, a Portuguese boy who got beat up every day after school and tried to grab my ass while we danced. And Shilo, who told good jokes, but wore glasses and had a skin condition, dry white flakes that sloughed continuously off his hands, arms, and face, a dermal snowfall. He'd been the first boy to kiss me, and behind his thin, dry lips, his mouth had been shockingly wet and salty, like a weeping wound. Paul would be better than any boy I had kissed in high school. I imagined his mouth delicately moist, sweet and woody like winter sap.

Someone touched my shoulder. I opened my eyes, my tongue still rolling in my mouth. Janet was standing; all the

parents were standing. She pointed down. "Someone's fainted."
I stood up and tried to see what was going on. A small divot
in the carpet of bodies. I adjusted my hat and moved carefully
down the bleachers to the gym floor. Janet followed. The kids
continued dancing, but craned their necks to see who had
fainted. It was the boy who'd been slow-dancing with the
brown-haired girl. He was crumpled forward on his knees; she
had been trying to hold him up through two songs.

Paul appeared out of nowhere, worked his arms under the
boy's shoulders, and half walked, half lifted him to the triage
room. The toes of the boy's athletic shoes grazed the ground,
tried to step this way and that, pulling his body in an awkward
zigzag march that Paul fought to correct. In the triage room,
he sat the boy on the cot and hoisted his sneakered feet onto
the mattress. I opened my equipment bag and turned to thank
Paul, to ask him if he'd come by later to check on things, but
he was already gone, the door closing with a slow, controlled
whoosh behind him.

The boy was woozy, but awake. I put a cold cloth on his
forehead and took another amphetamine to wake up.

When the boy was ready to sit up, I gave him a few paper cones
of water, checked his vitals. As I held his wrist to take his pulse,
I asked the usual questions, his name, did he know where he
was, did he know what day it was. His name was Josh and
he knew everything. I took his temperature, a little above
normal, nothing alarming. There was a knock at the door as I

slid my stethoscope under his t-shirt; I jumped, my hand on his skin. Janet washed in. "Is he alright?" The boy's body was warm and damp. I held up a finger to quiet her as I listened to his heart – fast, hard, and insistent. When I finished, I folded the stethoscope in my hand, told Janet it was simple fatigue, that Josh would need to rest for a while before going back out. Janet nodded, her mouth in an empathetic pout. She slipped back to the gym.

I filled another paper cone with water and sat down beside Josh on the cot. He downed the drink in one swallow, crushed the cone and lobbed it into the garbage can. I asked him if he had any chronic medical conditions or allergies. He shook his head. I focused on the tiled wall in front of us.

"What are you on?" I asked him.

He leaned away from me, raised his eyebrows, mumbled, "Yeah, right."

I smiled; I had used that one with my family. I could feel him looking me up and down, evaluating, so I turned to face him, expecting him to look away.

Instead, we had a staring contest. I sat perfectly still. His eyes moved slowly back and forth from the right to the left to the right, an intimidating tactic. Still, I didn't blink. I tried to read his expression, worry, disgust, annoyance, amusement, but couldn't pin him down. His eyes were pretty though, like a girl's, dark brown with amber flecks, a sweep of black lashes.

"It's a medical thing," I assured him. My voice sounded strangled; I tried to relax my throat. "No one else needs to know." The sweat started again under my arms, around my hairline; my neck felt tight and hot.

He looked at his palms, pressed the tips of his thumbs together, shook his head. "Some E in the parking lot, a few hours ago."

I nodded, breathed slowly as I waited for the flare. We sat there on the cot for what seemed like a long time, both of us staring straight ahead at the tiles.

"What about you?" he asked.

The grout lines blurred; for a second I wasn't sure if I had heard his voice in the room or just in my head. I glanced sideways to check his face; I expected to see a smirk, something I'd want to slap away, but his profile was relaxed.

"I saw you pop, just after you guys laid me down." He reached into his pocket and pulled out a pack of cigarettes. His hands were slim and clean, his nails rounded neatly across the top. He offered me a cigarette and I took one, even though I didn't smoke. He lit up, then held his lighter for me. The flame touched the edge of the paper. I puckered my lips, sipped on the filter until the cigarette was lit.

"Blues?" he asked.

I shook my head.

"Tigers?"

I nodded, sucked some of the smoke into my mouth, blew it out again.

"Can you hook me up?"

I shook my head.

"Come on," he checked my name tag, "Florence."

I put my hand to my face and laughed. My body trembled with a beautiful flood of adrenaline.

He stared at me.

"It's a joke," I said, taking a breath.

He grinned and shrugged. "Whatever you say." He smacked his lips.

I twirled the lit cigarette in my fingers. "How long have you been using?"

"Long enough." He took a drag of his cigarette. "That a good gig?" he asked. "Being a nurse?"

I shrugged.

"You must get some good stuff." His smile was expectant, the skin around his mouth smooth.

I wanted to change the subject. He seemed persuasive and though I didn't know the details, I suspected supplying pharmaceuticals to minors carried a stiffer sentence than stealing them for yourself.

The pills were going full force; I got that detached, heady feeling, time was rushing past or standing still. I needed to grab onto something before I floated away. "That your girlfriend out there?" I drew in another mouthful of smoke and exhaled quickly.

His eyebrows lifted, then furrowed. He was disarmed by my question; he sat back as if to examine me, his eyes moving over my face, trying to decode something. He shrugged slowly. "Just some girl."

I looked down at my knees and tried not to smile.

Out of the corner of my eye, I watched him suck on his lower lip.

"You know, you don't look like a real nurse."

I smiled broadly and against my will. "Really?" My tone was sarcastic.

"Really." His hand lifted from the cot. With his index finger, he traced a damp trail around my hairline.

I dropped my cigarette on the tile floor and ground it out with my duty shoe. I felt his thumb press against my brow bone, down the outside of my temple, across my cheek, his fingers under my chin. I turned my head. My eyes fixed on the lower part of his face, the skin of his jawline, his lips slightly parted. I waited. And waited. And when I was sure he wouldn't make another move, I leaned into him and pressed my mouth against his. His body stiffened for a second, then relaxed. He opened his mouth slowly; I closed my eyes. I took in his tongue, guiding it with mine. He tasted of cigarettes and sweet punch. We stayed that way for some time, kissing, me sucking on his tongue. My left knee started to shake uncontrollably. We stopped to watch my leg vibrate; then my arm joined in; we both laughed. I wondered how much I had taken that day, the Dexedrine, the tigers, the Ativan, the Percocet from the skinny Haitian woman who mopped the unit floors. My mind could barely make it back to my second shift, let alone add up the dosage. I thought of poor Janet finding me unconscious on the change-room floor, her hand clutching the seashell necklace at her chest, the horrified faces of the other parents. I thought of the ambulance ride, Paul on one side of me, Josh on the other as the paramedics slipped an oxygen mask over my face, tried their best to tame my heart. I imagined the rush of my gurney into the emergency room, the shocked faces of nurses and doctors who worked on my ward, the unit clerk's gasp as she emptied my purse onto her desk. They would all blame themselves, because that's what responsible people do. They would take turns at my bedside, they would hold my hand and tell me they loved me. I thought about the closeness of someone squeezing my hand, their fingers reaching to brush the hair from my forehead, the warmth of their lips on my skin. I thought about that closeness and nothing else seemed important.

I unbuttoned the top of my uniform, my left hand still shaky. I paused between buttons to watch Josh's appreciative eyes. He smiled a lot. I thanked God that I had worn a good bra.

The top of my uniform was open, my bra undone, though still looped over my arms, the underwire digging up into my shoulders. Josh's t-shirt was on the floor, his dance-a-thon number, 117, crumpled beside it. My tights and underwear were in a ball somewhere at the bottom of the cot; his jeans and stretch boxers were down at his knees. We were under the grey wool blanket, pressing and rubbing. His body was harder than I remembered bodies ever being. I crushed myself into him to feel the slats of his ribs against my torso, the sharp grind of his hip bones on my pelvis. The sensation of his knee knocking against mine sent a charge through me. His hands gripped at my waist, pulling, demanding. I sat up and reached for my equipment bag, condoms.

The door to the change room swung open. I heard someone say "Shit!" Then recognized the voice as my own.

Paul was holding two paper plates folding over with pizza. He froze. The room started to fill with the smell of processed meat and melted cheese.

I scrambled to close the top of my uniform. Josh yanked his jeans on and stood up. Paul balanced the two plates of pizza on the edge of the sink, then walked back out into the gym.

My body felt repulsively warm. I swung my legs off the cot and pushed the blanket away.

"Fuck!" Josh laughed. He was jubilant; he bounced back and forth on his feet, drummed his palms against his bare chest. "I could have taken that guy." He thrust a combination of swift punches into the air.

I picked his t-shirt off the floor and threw it at him. "Get dressed."

He slipped his arms into the shirt. "Hey," he said. "You gonna get fired?" His voice was almost hopeful.

I shook my head. "Volunteer."

He nodded, his hip against the sink, reached into his pocket and pulled out his cigarettes.

"No. Outta here."

"You wanna hear a joke? A priest, a social worker and a lawyer –"

"Now."

He lowered his chin and raised his eyebrows. Gazed at me with what I could tell was his best come-hither look. When I didn't respond, he shrugged and put his cigarettes away, walked towards me with deliberate strides and leaned down to kiss.

I jerked my head back. "Just. Go."

He bent down and snatched his dance-a-thon number off the ground, backed away. When he got to the sink, he grabbed a slice of pizza, took a vicious bite out of it, then raised the remainder in my direction, like a salute. On the way out the door, he smacked his palm into the door frame, hooted some sort of victory noise.

I untangled my tights and underwear from the bottom of the blanket, sat on the cot and tried to straighten them out. One foot of the tights was torn. I tried to throw them across the room, but they fluttered in the air like gauzy streamers then settled beside me on the cot. Tired to the point where real sleep, sleep without a chemical lullaby, that lasted more than two or three hours, had become an elaborate, unattainable fantasy.

I stripped off my uniform and bra, stepped into the girls' shower, turned the water on cold, and let the icy pellets pummel me. The sound of the shower was like a thousand nails hitting glass; the water stung my chest, my neck; it was refreshing and unbearable at the same time. I wondered what Paul was doing, pulling Janet aside, rounding up a posse of parents to drag me out of the gym. I thought about Josh again, the grip of his eager hands, the taste of his mouth. I forced my face closer and closer to the shower head, until it seemed the spray would cut open my eyelids, split my lips. I braced myself, slapped my palms against the tile, opened my mouth to feel the sting on my tongue, my gums; I choked and coughed as I tried to swallow. I thought about how tired I was. Tired beyond sleep.

I smacked the tile over and over, as hard as I could, pounded with flat hands, but the wall was solid cement and my pounding made no sound. Not a single reverberation. How strange it was, I thought, that so much in life passed without consequence. All those pills, those lost shifts, so many desperate things kept invisible and secret.

With my forehead resting against the wall, I drew a deep breath, tightened my right hand into a fist and drove it forward as hard as I could. My head swam with the clatter of spoons dropping, air rushed in between my teeth, my hand went numb for a moment, then came alive with a nauseating pain that shot from my knuckles to my elbow, then receded back and pulsed like a flame in my fist. I staggered, then quickly forced my left hand forward, a weaker throw, a pain that speared through my shoulder. I lost my balance and grabbed for the tap, but missed, slipped down to my knees and sat on the cold, tile floor, my body freezing except for my hands, which exploded with heat.

Back at the cot, I checked my hands to make sure nothing was broken, dried off with the grey blanket, stepped back into my uniform. The tights, the underwear and the sweating pizza slice

went into the garbage. At the mirror, I pulled my hair back
into a ponytail, my hands trembled and burned as I twisted
the elastic. My knuckles were red and starting to swell. I tried
to position the hat on my head, but my fingers couldn't open
the bobby pins. I crumpled the hat in the best I could do for a
fist, then dug carefully through my purse for more Ativan. All
I could find were the three quarter-pieces of Xanax. I decided
to save them.

The DJ was playing another set of slow songs. As I moved
past the swaying bodies on the dance floor, I noticed Josh in
the corner, running his hands over the bare arms of the brown-
haired girl. I looked up to the bleachers. Janet waved. Everything
hunky-dory. Paul was nowhere to be seen.

I climbed the bleachers slowly and sat down beside Janet.
The other parents were fading, but she was holding on, forcing
out that last bit of sparkle. She touched my wet hair, gave me
a puzzled look. "Did you shower in there?"

I nodded. My body started to shiver. "Cold shower. To stay
awake."

"You're crazy." Janet was the kind of person who could tell
you the truth without even knowing it. She touched my cheek
with her warm palm. "You're a Popsicle." She reached over to
take one of my hands, then stopped. "My God, what happened?" Her mouth was open with alarm.

"I fell." My voice wavered. "In the shower." I shook my
hands in front of me, not knowing what to do with them.

Janet lifted her hand and squeezed my arm. Her eyebrows gathered in a sympathetic furrow, her bottom lip softened down at the corners and she gazed into my eyes with so much unquestioning tenderness, I thought I would die. I rested against her and shook my head. She took my hand in hers and stroked it gently, carefully, her fingers tracing clouds and hearts below my darkening knuckles. She hummed soothingly to the music, the heat of her breath on my forehead. We both stared down at the kids on the dance floor and said nothing. Behind us, two fathers were talking about Coombs. "People like that don't deserve to live," one of them said. I felt tears welling up and decided to let them come.

Spinning drops of light passed over the high gym walls. The DJ let loose a spray of vanilla fog, and couples crowded to one side of the gym to dance in the haze.

"What happened to Paul?" I whispered.

"Oh," Janet made a sound I hadn't known she was capable of, something between an exasperated sigh and a snicker. "Revisiting an old friend." She pointed down to the parking lot exit. There was Paul, propped against the open gym door, smoking a cigarette. "He keeps saying he'll quit."

By the time the scoreboard clock read 2:30 a.m., most of the mothers, including Janet, were nodding off. Her head tipped onto my shoulder and I didn't move. The DJ started a reggae set. I watched the young bodies bounce drunkenly to the beat. Some girls started a reggae can-can line. They flipped their hair from side to side as they kicked up their legs. A group of boys ambushed them from behind, grabbed the girls around their waists and swung them in the air. It was like *Seven Brides for Seven Brothers*, the perfect musical formula, someone for everyone. My hands ached.

"I hate reggae," I whispered to Janet.

She mumbled; her head shifted.

"It's so damn happy. Let's get together and feel alright. Who believes that?" I looked down at Janet for at least a nod of support, but she was fast asleep.

While parents dozed, their children searched for someone to hold them through the slow songs. Janet slept with her head on my shoulder, twitching every now and then, once muttering something that sounded like, "Fuck."

Paul sat at the gym exit, smoked cigarette after cigarette. His head tilted back against the open door, one arm limp at his side, the other making the slow, lit arcs to his mouth as he gazed up into the night. I can only guess what he saw out there in the endless dark. A falling star, a glinting satellite. Something bright, something different, something beautiful and just out of reach.

I fell asleep, eventually, sometime between four-thirty and five a.m. The last thing I remember thinking about was the dentist, Coombs, imagining him, cold and uncomfortable in a jail full of strangers, wishing for his white lab coat, anxious over who would play him in the movie of his life and whether or not they would get it right.

Rollie and Adele

AFTER

Rollie can't sleep. He's wide awake and propped up on his elbow, his body sinking into the sagging futon, his heavy hip cradled in a cool, wet spot. He's staring at Adele, examining the kidney-shaped birthmark on her right arm, the smatter of chicken pox scars across her neck. He lifts the blanket to look again at her legs, her bony ankles, her crooked baby toes.

"Cold," she mumbles. She raises her hand and tugs at the covers, her new ring snagging a blanket thread. She twists her hand back and forth, then pulls. The wool tears, a small tuft of it carried off with her disappearing hand, a frayed dangling yarn left behind. Rollie smoothes the splayed threads into the blanket: Adele has been here.

He settles for her top half and sniffs the musk of her unwashed skin, of her hair as he nuzzles his face into the back of her neck. He slides his fingers under her arm to feel the damp that shadows her clothes with a dark half-moon.

Adele presses her arm hard to her body, traps him there. "Sleep," she insists, her hand reaching back for him, patting his thick waist through the blankets.

But Rollie is stubborn and wills himself awake. He fixes on the individual split ends of her hair, fine, bright strands that shiver as he breathes. He thinks backwards and forwards, like a man who has found an envelope of money on the street, understanding his life before this moment, understanding it after, but unable to believe the good fortune of this moment exactly. He tells himself there are many unlikely roads to happiness.

He finds a flush of acne beneath Adele's ear, strokes the small red bumps with the pad of his finger. Smiles.

BEFORE

Adele knew as she settled in the doorway, her chances were good. A tattoo place, a red neon tiger glowing in front of a black window shade; it had to be men working here. She had fucked up with the last place, thought "Your Taxes Done While You Wait – Free Coffee" meant men. Instead a short woman with a bird face and scuffed shoes had kicked her awake, told her to get lost, get a job. "You hiring?" Adele had asked. The woman stepped back into the storefront, locked the door from the inside, glared through the glass as Adele shook out her jacket, retied her shoes.

Adele knew that women didn't want to give her a break. They acted all bitchy and judgmental, as if a girl like Adele was spoiling it for them, embarrassing some grand plan. Adele tried to stick with men. But it was tricky business. There were plenty of men trolling the streets, offering to help girls out. Something for nothing. A hot meal, some new clothes, free junk. Most of them were pimps. And Adele steered clear of them. The guys who weren't pimps still expected something. One guy, good looking, in jeans and a rain jacket, had told Adele he was a professional photographer, that he needed a model, a girl who captured the look of the street. He had led her to a warehouse and beaten her with his raw fists until she couldn't stand up, taken photos of her face. A fat, unemployed daycare worker had wanted her to have sex with his dogs, a Doberman and a Great Dane, had asked her quietly over a dinner of macaroni and cheese. Just this morning an older man in a white car with slow, soundless windshield wipers had trailed beside her for two blocks, a shiny, insistent slug. She had watched him out of the corner of her eye, his one wormy hand on the steering wheel, his other hand invisible as he leaned down into the frame of the passenger's side window. He was wearing thin, wire-rimmed glasses and looked like somebody's balding uncle. Adele had noticed right away that the inside of his car was spotless, the upholstery vacuumed, the dashboard polished to a high sheen. He told her about his house, just outside the city, his grassy yard and spare bedroom. He told her he was a dentist and that if she came for a ride in his car, he would check her teeth. That made Adele laugh. The man reached over and opened the passenger-side door, held it ajar from the inside as the car continued to pace her. "Get in." He nodded as he said it. Warm air leaked out onto the sidewalk; Adele felt it against her wet knees. She thought about riding around just long enough to get dry, and what she might do for that, a hand job, maybe more. But there was something about the man, his clean car, his puffy fingers, the fact that he might want to touch her mouth. She stopped, waited for him to stop. He let go of the door so that it swung toward her like an open arm. Adele walked to the door, bent down so he could see her face, gave him the finger, doubled-back on the sidewalk and ran.

Adele squeezed her body tight into the door frame, knees to chest so the rain wouldn't wet her feet. Her jeans were still dry, but the back of her nylon jacket was soaked. She leaned over on her side so the damp part of her jacket wouldn't press through her thin top to her skin. She wished she hadn't gotten her hair wet. Her jaw began to quiver, a deep and frenzied shake. She tried to think about sleep, about food, something warm, but her mind filled with cold. Snow and hail, the Arctic, the inside of a meat locker. She thought about ice cubes and cold showers until her fingers, her toes, the side of her hip ached with a numbness that spread like sleep; then she was dreaming.

This time it was the Latino girl, squeak-toy voice and spindly legs; she had worked Adele out of her last five dollars.

From the doorway of a closed barber shop, Adele had watched her hustle. The girl planted herself in the middle of the sidewalk and offered everyone who passed Levi's 501's for five dollars. She showed off the brand new pair she was wearing, turned and bent over so people could read the label on her tiny behind. The women in their office clothes and sneakers didn't slow down; a few of them held up their hands as if to say, "Don't touch me." Some of the men stopped, listened to her spiel, smiled to each other when the girl showed them her ass. The teenagers laughed and waved her off as they moved down the street to the stores that sold bongs and pipes, advertised fast-growing marijuana seeds. Only the drunks and hookers stopped to ask questions, take a better look. No one was buying.

Adele called the girl over. She was uglier up close, her cheekbones pushing high up to her squinty eyes, her thin lips pink and cracked against her dark skin. Her brown hair was teased out, with thick copper streaks that made her face look wild and on fire. "Do you even have five dollars?" the girl asked as she cocked a hip at Adele. Adele showed her the worn bill. The girl relaxed then, sat down with Adele and shared a cigarette. Told Adele she was having a slow day, that she must have sold ten pairs the day before. Adele saw that the girl had stars stuck to her long fingernails, gold, silver, red and blue; the kind of stars Adele remembered getting on her spelling tests in elementary school. After the cigarette, the girl pulled a tattered measuring tape out of her pocket, wrapped the ragged edge around Adele's waist and hips, memorized the numbers. "Perfect fit," she promised Adele as she took her money.

Adele woke with a flinch, covered her face against the sting of light. Tears matted her lashes, filtered the world in a watery blur. She felt someone watching her and shifted back from the door, looked up. She blinked and saw a guy inside the shop, staring down at her through the glass panes of the door. He was big, tall and broad, with a round pink face and a dark beard that was touched with grey. He was dressed nice, in jeans, and a black leather vest over a black t-shirt. Adele wiped her eyes and nose as she stood, held out her hand and waited for a couple of dollar coins, a palmful of loose change. She watched him hesitate, his large hand resting on the lock. She prayed he would give her something. He moved quickly then, opened the door wide, gathered her under his arm and into the shop. He smelled like newspapers and toothpaste.

In the back of the shop, Rollie searched for something hot to feed the girl. Turkey gumbo. It was all he had, a case of it from a warehouse store outside the city. He opened three cans

and poured them into a pot on the portable stove. He watched
the girl take off her thin red jacket, lay it over the tattoo chair.
It hung heavy, soaked through. She stood by the chair in her
torn jeans and dirty peasant blouse, stared out the window at
the people passing on the street. The light from the window
glowed through the girl's blouse and as Rollie stirred the soup,
he let his eyes fall along the narrow outline of her body, a frail
shadow, the small flare of her hips as they dipped into her
jeans. She wrapped her arms around herself and her fingertips peeked back at him. He was sure he could see her body
vibrating with energy. He watched in awe until he realized
she was shivering.

He went into his tiny bedroom and pulled a blanket off
the makeshift bed, an old futon mattress on a sheet of plywood.
He carried the scratchy thing out to her, told himself it was
too rough for a girl, but what else did he have? He draped the
blanket over the girl's shoulders and she seemed thankful,
smiled as she pulled it tight. "Sit down and rest," he said.

She wandered instead, leafed through his design books,
touched the drawings on his walls. He followed her pale hands
as they traced the wings of an eagle, a crow. He stirred the soup
to keep his own hands busy. She tucked the blanket under her
arms, held the ends together in a small fist at her chest. The
length of the blanket swept out behind her like the train of a
dress. Rollie was already infected with her edgy beauty, the
dark line of her lashes, the restless tangle of her hair, the sharp
white of her skin. He shifted his weight from leg to leg,

wanting to scratch, to rub, to tamp down the prickling sensation that was moving up his thighs.

"Is this your name?" she called out. She was pointing to a photo autographed to him from a local wrestler.

"Yeah."

"Rawley?"

"Rollie," he said. "Like –"

"Like roly-poly," she smiled.

He sucked in his stomach.

He carried the soup out to her. The bowl passed from one trembling hand to another, from nervousness to hunger. She sat down on the floor and he worried about the floor being dirty. Then he felt self-conscious standing, hulking over her, and sat down quickly in the tattoo chair.

He watched her eat, the spoon disappearing into the hollow of her mouth, then emerging from her lips shiny and renewed, a crease in her brow as she caught a spoonful too hot. After the first few mouthfuls, her black hair slipped down around her face, dark ends dipping into the soup. Her slight body curved around the bowl in her hand, as if her whole being was drawing heat from it, as if she was afraid he might snatch the bowl away. She didn't speak until the soup was finished.

"You got a bath?"

Rollie shook his head. "Just a shower."

The girl leaned down beside the tattoo chair, rested her head on the floor and pulled the blanket up around her.

"There's a bed in the back." He pointed to the door with the plastic "Private" sign.

She closed her eyes as if weighing his offer, then shook her head. "One time I had dream about a bath," she said. "A hot bath."

Rollie went into the bathroom and started the shower, turned it on hot to warm up the room. A puff of steam rose above the red vinyl curtain. He cleared his toothbrush from the sink, turned the tap on and gave the basin a rub and rinse with his hand. He folded a clean towel and his own bathrobe, carried them out to her.

She had fallen asleep on the floor, between the tattoo chair and the heater on the wall. Rollie sighed; she was already gone. He shook out the bathrobe and laid it over her. Lifted her head, and slipped the folded towel between her face and the floor. He paused for a moment to feel the delicate weight of her head in his hand, the warm stream of her breath on his wrist.

This time Adele slept without pictures. Easy darkness and a soundtrack that washed in and out, an old radio song, her mother's laugh, someone's whispering. She heard customers as they stepped over her, tiny heels, heavy boots, throats clearing, their hushed exclamations of "Oh!", "Who's this then?" Quiet chatter.

She opened her eyes to the orange afternoon and a crisp, electric buzz. A young guy with a red goatee was sitting in the chair beside her. His jeans and t-shirt covered in chalky dust, his face rough and unclean. She watched him until he turned and caught her staring. He smiled and winked. She smiled back and sat up.

Rollie was on the other side of the chair, hunched over the man's arm. She gathered the blanket around her and stood, walked to Rollie's side and peered over his shoulder. The needle dotted the man's freckled skin, burgundy inked into the wings of a butterfly.

"You like that?" the man asked her.

Adele nodded.

"*Batesia hypochlora.* Resident of the Amazon." He held out his right arm; it was covered with butterfly tattoos.

Adele moved back around the chair, gazed at the markings on his skin; the colours were beautiful. The man raised his arm towards her and she took it in her hands, felt a warm heat through his skin, the tickle of soft hairs against her palm. Her fingertips traced the wings of each butterfly.

"That blue one's *Epitola badura.*" The man turned his arm back and forth in her hands, flexed his bicep.

Adele laughed.

Rollie turned off the needle, but kept his head down. "Look, you gotta sit still."

"Sorry," the man said. He winked again at Adele.

Rollie shook his head and started the needle.

Adele leaned her hip against the arm of the chair. "You get all those here?"

"Yup. New one every month." The man reached into his pocket, pulled out a small white card and handed it to her. "I'm in drywall."

HOOVER DRYWALL in bold black letters, a bright orange butterfly rising out of the word DRYWALL.

"That's me," the man tapped Adele's hand. "Donny Hoover."

Adele nodded and closed her palm around the card.

"You Rollie's girlfriend?"

The needle lifted away from Donny's skin.

"Nah, he just let me crash here."

The needle touched back down.

After Donny left, Rollie pulled down the blinds in the shop's front window, turned off his work lights. He went into the bathroom and brushed his teeth. Adele was sitting in the back of the shop on a stool, flipping through a tattoo magazine.

"He seemed nice," she said.

Rollie spit into the sink. "Yeah? You like that sorta guy?" He turned the tap on and let it run, then held his toothbrush under the scalding water, watched his fingertips redden.

"What sorta guy?"

Rollie shrugged, shook the sting out of his hand, turned off the tap. He wiped his palms on his jeans, wondered what to do with her, thought about taking her out for something to eat, maybe buying her a warmer coat. Then he had another idea. He pulled his denim jacket from a hook on the wall, threw it at Adele.

The jacket landed in her lap, smothered her magazine. "We going somewhere?"

"My mother's."

"What for?"

Rollie shrugged.

They took the Fraser Street bus out of downtown. Adele watched the girls working East Broadway, some of them smoking cigarettes, some of them shimmying their legs in the cold. Rollie stood up at Kingsway. Adele followed him off the bus and across the intersection, past a Christian bookstore with high glass windows, then down a street of small, sad houses with trampled lawns.

It was late in the afternoon and Rollie's mother answered the door in her bathrobe. Adele was startled by the woman's face, black pockets under her eyes, thinning blond hair set in a mess of curlers, skin wrinkled like a trash-can glove. Adele hadn't expected her to look so old. Rollie introduced her as Flo. "Flo's getting ready for bingo, isn't that right?" Rollie said. Flo nodded. The living room was stuffy with trapped heat, thick with the stink of old cigarette smoke. The furniture was faded and worn, cramped against the walls. Adele knew without asking that Flo lived alone.

Flo led them back to the kitchen, where she was starting a bowl of cornflakes. Adele watched her eat cereal and smoke at the same time, a spoon in one hand, a cigarette in the other. Adele waited for the old woman to sink her spoon into the ashtray or flick her cigarette into the milky bowl. Flo's fingers were dark with nicotine stains, her knuckles bulbous; her hands tremored each time she lifted the spoon to her mouth. Flo dipped her head and Adele glimpsed scattered patches of pink scalp. No wonder she was alone. Adele tried hard not to stare, not to imagine what was under the old woman's bathrobe.

Plastic key chains dangled in a row along a bare curtain rod above the kitchen window. Adele got up to take a closer look.

"Umm," Flo said, her mouth full of cornflakes. "Those are from all over the world. The girls from bingo bring them back."

Adele could see the girls from bingo hadn't been anywhere in a while. The key chains were old, clouded, covered in what looked like layers of kitchen grease and dust. It was hard to tell where any of them were from.

Rollie watched Adele at the window, wished she hadn't noticed the old key chains. When Adele wasn't around, he would tell his mother to take them down, throw them out. Ever since his father had died, his mother refused to throw anything away. Her cupboards and closets were full of useless junk, glass jars and margarine tubs, empty perfume bottles, the ribbon and string from cake boxes. The cupboard under the sink was stuffed with thousands of plastic grocery bags. Rollie had tried once to help her get rid of some of it, gathered a garbage bag full of worthless things as she followed him around the house.

Finally, in the living room, she had struggled to get the bag out of his hands, and when it looked like she would cry, he let go.

Adele turned from the window and again light poured in around her; Rollie smiled. Adele smiled back. Her front teeth were small and pointy and he imagined them against his neck, his arm. He kept his eyes on Adele as he spoke to his mother. "Is it okay if Adele has a bath?" Adele's eyes widened, she clasped her hands together. He looked at his mother. She nodded slowly. Took a long drag of her cigarette before mashing it out in the ashtray. "I'll get you a towel."

Adele followed Flo into the bedroom. The room was a mess, the curtains drawn, the air heavy with dust, the closet door open to a giant heap that spilled out onto the floor. Adele watched as Flo leaned into the pile, gripped the door frame for support. She rummaged around for a while, then stepped back, shaky and out of breath. She held out a brown towel. Adele took the towel and pressed it to her face. Cigarette smoke.

"You known Rollie long?" Flo asked, her back to Adele as she picked things off the floor and threw them at the already full closet.

"No."

"He seems to do all right with those tattoos," Flo said, her voice muffled as she dug around for something. "He always liked drawing, even as a kid."

"Is that right?" Adele asked.

Flo nodded, but didn't turn around.

Adele plugged the bathtub and started the water. She found a bottle of shampoo upside down on the mildewy back corner of the tub, unscrewed the top and sniffed. Apples. She shook the bottle in her hand as she left the bathroom.

In the bedroom, Flo was stooped awkwardly over the end of her bed, her forearm under the mattress.

Adele tilted her head to look at Flo sideways. "Can –"

Flo gasped and jumped with a start. Her arm waved up, her body jerked back. With her hand clutched to her chest, she held herself still for a moment, then closed her eyes and sat down on the corner of the bed. Pressed flat between Flo's hand and the collar of her bathrobe was a twenty-dollar bill. "Oh, bejesus, you nearly gave me a heart attack!"

"Sorry." Adele held up the shampoo bottle. "I wanted to wash my hair. Can I have another towel?"

Flo shuffled over to the closet, rooted around and came up with a towel, this one faded pink.

Adele smiled as she took it.

With his mother off to bingo, Rollie tilted back in his chair and concentrated on the sounds from the bathroom. A trickle of water, a slosh, the echoey stutter of skin moving against the tub. He imagined Adele's thin, soapy hands cupping and squeezing her breasts, her back arching, her knees open; he tried not to think of the bar of soap tunnelling its way between her legs, nesting inside her. He pressed his hand into his thigh. It had been too long since he'd been with a woman. He'd lost count of the months. He'd met different women, in the shop, in bars, at the Lotus Café. But either they were selling or they just wanted to talk, to smile at him like he was a brother, to tell him their troubles with other men.

The last woman was an Asian divorcee, a sentimental drunk he met at a bar. She cried about her adult daughter who had dropped out of medical school and had stopped talking to her. Rollie brought the woman back to his shop more to comfort her than seduce her. But after showing him some photos of her daughter, the woman started to cry again, then wrapped her arms around Rollie's neck and crushed her lipstick-smeared mouth against his. She tasted like old liquor and chili pepper. The lovemaking was sweet and slow, something Rollie hadn't expected. In the morning he woke to an empty bed, his blankets full of her older-woman smell, clove cigarettes and dried roses.

The bathroom door opened and Rollie sat up straight, put his hands flat on the kitchen table. Adele waved as she passed from bathroom to bedroom, her clothes piled up in her arms, a towel around her head and another around her body. Rollie was immediately jealous of the brown terry cloth, wished he

was the one wrapped around her naked skin. He bent forward
to peek into the bedroom, hoped to catch a glimpse of her
getting dressed, but the door was half closed, blocking his view.
He looked back to the bathroom. She had left the tub full;
through the doorway he could see the calm, liquidy surface.
Could he get in there, strip off his clothes and slip into the tub
without her knowing? He would soak in her water, take on her
scent and carry it with him.

Adele reappeared. She wore the same peasant blouse and
jeans, but her freshly bathed skin made them look cleaner. She
took a couple of steps towards Rollie, shifted her weight to one
foot and swayed.

"Listen," she said, her right hand stroking her left. "Your
mom gave me some money. She told me not to tell you."

Her wet hair was pulled back in a ponytail; Rollie enjoyed
the full view of her face. "Bingo money. How much'd she
give you?"

Adele held up two twenty-dollar bills.

That night, on the lumpy mattress behind the door marked
"Private," Adele offered herself to Rollie. She climbed onto him
as he sat, guided his hands under her blouse and stroked his
lips with her thumbs. His fresh-brushed mouth tasted hollow
and minty. She ran her fingers through his trimmed beard,
over his ears; she lifted her breasts to his face. But Rollie was
no good. His sad eyes, his soft lap.

She tried other ways. Slipped out of her jeans and panties, pulled him naked on top of her, wrapped her legs around his waist and rocked her hips back and forth. Still, nothing. She took Rollie's penis into her mouth, gently suckled it like a piece of fruit; it dribbled and shrugged but would not harden. She held the soft flesh in her hand, talked into it like a microphone, "Is anybody home?" Rollie pushed her away then, covered himself with a blanket, his face red with anger, or embarrassment.

Adele cooed to him, nestled under his limp arm, cuddled against his side to make him feel better. She whispered in his ear, told him her small secrets. The friends she had as a kid, the stuff she snuck from her mother's purse, gum and money and cigarettes, the girls who teased her, tortured her at school. She told him about her first time, the sullen grade nine boy who had watched over her while her mother worked afternoons. He had told her they were playing a game, to take off her clothes; she knew what he wanted. And since she had a crush on him, every girl at her school did, she wanted it, too. He was all elbows and knees, cursing and muttering while he poked at her. He ordered her to lie still, clamped his arm across her flat chest. She tried to kiss him twice and both times he pushed her head away. He had cried afterwards, calling her names, then smacked her face when she tried to comfort him, even though she liked him, even though he was supposed to like her.

Adele felt a tickle on her forehead. She reached up to rub it away and her fingers touched something wet. She looked at

Rollie who was propped on his elbow, his face hovering above hers. His eyes were closed, his lashes damp.

"We can try again later," she said softly.

Rollie blinked. Adele saw that the corners of his eyes were shimmery and bloodshot. He shook his head. "It's not that." He was trying to smile. "That's a sad story, is all." He put his fist to his mouth and cleared his throat. Then pulled the blankets over her body, tucked them down her sides. "You should get some rest."

Out in the shop, beside the heater, Rollie settled in with a blanket and pillow. He lay on the hard floor and in the near dark, stared at the shadows of snakes and stallions on his wall. He had wanted so badly to be with Adele, his insides were tensed and crazy. But he couldn't shake the thought that something was not right.

He had imagined Adele, how delicate but strong she would be, how heated and vibrant. The shape of her body, the eager expression of her face, the smell of her hair were all as he had hoped. But the vision of his own rough hands near her perfect skin, his coarse, bristly nakedness, the grossness of his shape beside hers, had disgusted him, made him afraid.

He turned onto his side, felt the weight of his body slouch down onto the floor. His hand moved to his stomach, a thick, soft, tumble of flesh. Why would she want to be with him?

He felt like he had taken a gift meant for somebody else. A terrible mistake. Tomorrow he would wake up and Adele would be gone, he was sure of it. And as sad as the thought was, it relieved him, calmed him into sleep.

Rollie woke to a prickling at his hip. He swatted at the air, then opened his eyes. Adele stood over him, smiling, a broom in her hand. "I'm trying to give this place a sweep, but something big's in my way." He wiped his face with his palm. The shop smelled like fresh coffee. He sat up and looked around. Adele had gathered up all the stray magazines into a pile by the window, cleared off the counter near the stove, washed the dishes. She poked him again with the broom and laughed. Adele was a dream from which Rollie could not wake.

Adele couldn't believe her luck. A place to stay, meals, and she didn't really have to do anything for it. She tidied the shop, picked up after Rollie, but mostly she sat around and read magazines, talked with customers. Rollie didn't seem to mind that they weren't having sex. He was still nice to her. He gazed at her when he thought she wasn't looking, fetched her treats from the store, word-find puzzles, horoscope books, in case she got bored while he worked.

She could tell that Rollie was a good person, kind. But she didn't understand his jitteriness. He let her rest her hand on his shoulder or kiss him quickly on the cheek, but if she tried to put her arms around him or kiss him on the mouth, he backed away. "It's not gonna hurt," she teased him. He just shook his head and blushed.

Adele knew that if Rollie was just being nice because he felt sorry for her, her good luck wouldn't last long. She had been with other men, older men who treated her like a lost dog or a child, cleaned her up and took care of her for a few days, then sent her back into the world as if a couple of hot meals and a shower would make the street easier. Eventually Rollie would want a woman in the proper way, a girlfriend. Someone who excited him, someone he couldn't keep his hands off. And whoever that woman was, she wouldn't want Adele hanging around.

Adele saw the girls who came into the shop, some of them working girls in thigh-high boots and tiny skirts, others college girl from the west side who paid with credit cards. She watched their arched eyebrows, their inviting mouths as they *ooh*'d and *ahhh*'d, flipped through Rollie's design books. They played up their little stripteases, unbuttoned their tops, loosened their bra straps, lifted their skirt or wiggled out of jeans and underwear as if it was nothing. Then pointed to a smooth, naked patch of skin, moved it close to Rollie's hands and said, "I want it right here."

Adele did her best to compete. With the money she'd taken from Rollie's mother, she bought some cheap clothes, chose them carefully: a short skirt, a clingy top, a pair of red heels that made her calves and thighs look stiff and new.

She paraded around for Rollie, spun so that her skirt twirled up around her waist, gave him her best pouty lip. Rollie smiled awkwardly, and nodded with appreciation. But nothing she did drew him closer.

The customers took to her. Rollie watched them chat with Adele, their easy words, the casual way they touched her arm, her hand. Men who had enjoyed tracking the path of the needle, watching the ink stain their skin, who had always asked questions while Rollie worked, now focused silently on Adele as she moved through the shop. The swish of her skirt, the bounce of her ponytail. She flirted with them, complimented them on the thickness of their hair or how they kept themselves fit, smiled at them slyly. She traded dirty jokes, the dirtier, the better. Her favourite was about a pregnant blonde and puppies. The men laughed and wiped their eyes, even if they'd heard the joke before.

Their talk was full of innuendo, back and forth like a raucous and bawdy Ping-Pong match. Sometimes they pulled Rollie in, but he only stammered or shrugged, missed the ball. He couldn't talk to Adele that way, couldn't talk like that around her. Rollie envied how comfortable the other men seemed, the effortless way they teased her, called her foxy and darling, offered her a ride in their lap.

Even the women customers were fond of her. Though Adele took longer to warm to them, eventually she was reading their horoscopes out loud, chatting with them about their families, their boyfriends. She found out whose boyfriend was going back to jail, whose father had bought himself a Jaguar instead of sending her a birthday present, whose baby had been fathered by her blind first cousin. She held their hands if they worried about the pain, showed them pictures from magazines to keep them distracted.

At night or in the mornings, when she and Rollie were alone, Adele carried on one-way conversations, updated Rollie on the gossip he'd missed. Rollie nodded and smiled or frowned thoughtfully as her words dictated. He didn't care at all about the private lives of his customers, but he took pleasure in Adele's voice, lively and bright, her animated retelling. He especially enjoyed the times when she got worked up over something, an injustice, a betrayal, an abusive uncle, a cheating husband. Her voice sped into a skid of words, her pitch squeaky and sharp, her hands flapping at her sides. He'd laugh at her then and she'd get indignant, put her hands on her hips and glare at him. This only made him laugh harder and she pretended to be mad at him until she, too, started to laugh. She'd pound his chest jokingly with her fists.

Once a week, they went to Flo's for Adele's bath. Being around Flo made Adele nervous. Her strange eating habits, the way her eyes followed Adele around the room. Adele could never think of what to say to her, so mostly she stayed quiet while

Rollie and Flo sat across from each other and had slow, half-hearted conversations about the people from bingo.

"Lorna thinks her neighbour killed her cat." Flo was finishing a breakfast of canned spaghetti on toast.

Rollie looked at Adele and shook his head. "Why would she think that?"

Flo coughed. "Her neighbour's one of those cat-haters."

Adele stood from the table, walked over to the wooden clock on the wall. It was shaped like a log cabin, with a window shutter at the top. The clock read five past eight, but it was the middle of the afternoon.

"Cats run away all the time," Rollie said. "It's probably lost somewhere."

Adele reached up and touched the minute hand, pushed it slowly around the face, hoped that at nine o'clock something would pop out of the window.

"It doesn't work any more," Flo said as she carried her plate to the sink. "My husband used to take care of the clock, but now that he's gone, it's all frozen up."

Adele pried the tiny shutter open with her finger. Inside the small, dark hole, a dusty boy and girl held hands, their painted mouths still smiling.

Flo was beside her now, shrunken and bathrobed, digging at her teeth with a toothpick. She pointed at the figurines and her hand shook. "They used to come out and dance every hour. It played a little song."

"If it's broken, you should throw it out," Rollie said.

Flo turned to Rollie. "That's your answer to everything, it's junk, throw it out."

Adele was surprised by the sharpness of Flo's voice.

Rollie stared down at his hands and said nothing.

Flo turned to Adele, "I put your towels in the bathroom."

Adele loved the bath. How her arms and legs were weightless in the water, how her breasts floated like two perfect globes. She loved that her body absorbed the water's heat, so that after drying and dressing she would still sweat under her clothes. She loved the smell of apples and soap that stayed with her for days after.

Lying in the bath, she heard the front door close as Flo left for bingo. Adele was trying to be smart about the money, only snuck it when Flo wasn't home, then only twenty at a time, careful to smooth down the bedding so the corner looked untouched. Adele kept the money in the inside zipper pocket of her nylon jacket. A thin layer of bills that she folded and unfolded, counted over and over in case things went bad.

It was hard having Adele around. She had started answering his phone, taking appointments for him. He was charmed and distracted by her careful printing in his appointment book, thrown into sad imaginings of when these names and numbers would be all he had to remember her by.

He stared at her face, her hair, already missing her.

"Are you alright?" she asked.

He nodded and turned away, embarrassed by the secret way he loved her.

While he inked, she ran errands for him. His eyes were drawn away from his work, to her entrances and exits. When she left to buy a magazine or pick up their lunch, he would lift the needle, sure that he was seeing her for the last time. When she returned, he was startled all over again by her young body, her dark eyes.

Some nights he took Adele to a bar where they drank and played darts. A smoky room full of men and the blare of hard rock music. Adele chattered on about the bands that rehearsed in the buildings along Hastings Street, the frenzied guitar licks and drum solos that spilled onto the sidewalk; he scanned the smoky room for the man she was supposed to be with, the man who deserved her. A trim, muscular type with a sharp, square jaw and a strut in his walk. A man who could be a lover to Adele, look good in photographs, buy beautiful things for her.

Men came up to Adele; some of them nudged Rollie's arm, asked, "You the boyfriend?" He would shake his head, shuffle to the side and give them room. They talked to Adele with their backs to him. He caught glimpses of her face over their shoulders, her eyes wide, her lips smiling. Rollie sipped his beer, wondered which of those men would whisk her away. At the end of the night, he was always surprised that she walked with him back to the shop, sure that this was night she'd give him a pitying look, point to an idling car at the curbside.

He got used to sleeping on the floor in the shop, the dry warmth of the heater. Adele sometimes came out, wrapped in a blanket, and asked him to sleep with her on the mattress, to keep her warm. He picked her up and carried her back to bed, tucked her in and stayed with her until she fell asleep. The more he kept himself from her, the more he wanted her. His desire for her heightened to an unbearable pitch in the early mornings and he masturbated to imaginings of her. Daydreams of Adele alone. Rollie was careful to keep himself out of them. Even in his thoughts, he couldn't bring himself to touch her. She was air, he was mud.

Adele had started feeling sorry for Flo. The filthy state of her house, the sad way she ate alone. Adele had tried to help her clean, ran water in the sink to wash some dishes, soaked a rag to wipe down the kitchen table, but Flo got agitated, pulled her by the arm until she sat back down in her chair. "Just leave it, just leave it," Flo muttered.

The two of them were alone in the kitchen; Rollie was outside fixing something in Flo's car. Flo was smoking a cigarette, eating a lunch of wieners and pickled beets. Adele read the advertising flyers that came with Flo's newspaper and twisted the ends of her drying hair to make them curl.

"Lorna won just shy of a thousand last night," Flo said.

"Oh yeah?" Adele flipped the page of a grocery store flyer.

"Charlotte says she's next, but I told her, it's my turn."

"You did?"

"I'm about due, don't you think?"

"Uh-huh." Adele looked up from her flyer and gave Flo a small smile.

Flo took a heavy drag of her cigarette and put down her fork. "I know you're taking money from me." Smoke streamed out her nose as she stared down at the ashtray.

Adele was stricken, gripped the sides of the flyer, tried to play dumb and scrunched her eyebrows like she was confused. But Flo didn't look at her. Adele followed the old woman's gaze to the key chains in the window. Adele kept her eyes there too, stuck to their helpless dusty hanging. What could she say? What lie could she tell?

"Rollie hasn't had a lot of girlfriends," Flo said.

Adele stayed silent, better to let the old woman get it all off her chest.

"People deserve to be happy," Flo continued. "Before Rollie's dad passed, I was happy."

Adele stared at the key chains, bit the inside of her lip.

"Does Rollie make you happy?"

Adele was taken aback by the question. She shrugged. A flutter of uneasiness crept into her chest and for a moment, she couldn't breathe. She thought about the gentle way Rollie treated her, his big, warm hands, his minty smell, how safe she felt at the shop. "Yeah," Adele said. "He does."

"And what about you, do you make Rollie happy?"

Adele turned to Flo. "I don't know," she whispered.

Flo's eyes were bright and glassy, her chin trembled and her mouth shifted into a crooked smile. She placed a heavy, wrinkled hand on top of Adele's. "Well, keep trying," she said.

That night, when Rollie came to kiss her goodnight, Adele lay still in the bed, did not purr or whisper or try to pull him close. She turned away as he bent down to kiss her forehead; his lips touched her hair. He carried his blanket and pillow out to the shop as if nothing were different.

Adele fidgeted and tossed, piled the blankets on top of herself, but couldn't get warm. She lay awake on the cold mattress, ran her hands over her breasts, her legs, wondered what had changed about her.

Rollie didn't seem to want or need anything from her. And didn't that mean he'd have no trouble letting her go? Her hands worried in her sleep, rubbed bare spots in the blankets. She dreamed of the street and shivered till she woke. Grabbed for extra clothes, Rollie's sweater and socks. But even with those on, she couldn't stay warm.

Rollie tried keeping his distance when they went out to the bar. He played video games or shot pool. Adele got mad at him for ignoring her, shouted at him in the street, but still went home with him. He tried talking her into going out with some of the women customers, a girls' night, dancing. But she shook her head, said she didn't care for dancing, besides, the girls were nice to talk to, but they weren't really her friends.

Donny Hoover came in with another butterfly. "She's still here," he said, nodding towards Adele who was sitting by the window, reading a magazine. She looked up for second, like she knew someone was talking about her. She stared at them, then went back to flipping pages.

"What have you got for me?" Rollie said.

Donny showed him a colour copy of a photograph. "*Graphium weiskei*," Donny said. "She's from Papua New Guinea." Donny's bicep bulged below the sleeve of his t-shirt; drywalling had kept him in good shape. Rollie wondered if he also went to a gym.

"What do you think?" Donny asked.

Rollie studied the image, the lacy outline of the wings, the stained-glass colours, turquoise, magenta, green. "It won't be cheap."

Donny shrugged. "Nothing is."

Rollie nodded. Donny's black pick-up truck was parked out front of the shop; it looked almost new. Rollie made an appointment for Donny later in the week. As Donny wrote down the day and time on the back of his own business card, Rollie said, "She gets bored sitting around here all day."

Donny looked back at Adele, then up at Rollie. "Well, you should take her out some time."

"Yeah, I should." Rollie stared at the butterfly wings. "Or maybe you could."

"Me?" Donny laughed. "Why would I do that?"

Rollie held onto the counter. "You have a girlfriend?"

Donny shrugged. "No one regular, no."

"So maybe you'll ask Adele out some time." Rollie felt a blunt pain behind his eyes, like a headache coming on.

"Sure, maybe," Donny said, his voice uncertain. "I mean, if you don't mind."

Rollie shook his head.

As he left the shop, Donny stopped at the door, said goodbye to Adele.

Rollie went into the bathroom, pressed a cold, wet cloth against his face.

In the sex shop down the street, Adele searched for something that would get Rollie's attention. The triple-X movies and magazines were too trashy. The sex toys would probably scare him, make him feel less of a man. Adele decided on a bottle of erotic massage oil. The man behind the counter demonstrated the product on her arm. He rubbed the oil in with his thumb, then blew on her wrist; her skin felt suddenly warm. He told her to touch her tongue to her wrist and she did: strawberries.

That night, Adele lit a candle and waited for Rollie to finish brushing his teeth. She led him to the mattress. "Take these off," she said, tugging at his vest and t-shirt. Rollie obeyed, lay face down on the bed.

Against the expanse of Rollie's body, her hands looked small, childlike. She rubbed the massage oil across his shoulders, worked her palms deep into him, pushed hard against the thick bands of muscle. Her hands circled under his huge shoulder blades; she used her knuckles to get at the tightest parts. She could hear his breath, slow and shivery, his small moans. She massaged down the sides of his back, then up his spine to his neck. She leaned down and blew a stream of breath across the tops of his shoulders. He was silent for a moment, then chuckled beneath her. She climbed off him and patted his hip. "Turn over," she said.

He rolled over and she straddled him, rubbing more oil into her hands. She started at his neck and shoulders, then worked her way down. She kept her eyes on his face as she massaged his soft chest with her thumbs and fingers; his eyes were closed, but she could see his face was tense. She dug her thumbs deeper to relax him. Her hands reached his stomach, grazed the buckle of his belt and his whole body stiffened. "It's okay," she said. She kneaded around his waist and stomach with her palms, let her fingers disappear completely into his flesh. She took a deep breath and blew circles around his belly. She kissed his stomach then grabbed playfully at his flesh, jiggled it. Rollie sat up. His large hand pushed against her shoulder and she slid off his lap and onto the mattress. He went into the bathroom and shut the door.

Adele lay back on the bed and waited for him to come out. After what felt like half an hour, she called his name, but he didn't answer. She got up and knocked on the bathroom door. "Just leave me alone," he said, his voice small and far away. Adele went back to bed and punched her hands into the pillow, buried her face in the blankets and cried.

She woke in the middle of the night to find everything dark, the bathroom door open. From the front of the shop, she heard Rollie's snoring, his easy solitary sleep.

His mother gave him the ring while Adele was in the bath.

"Your father gave that to me. Too small for me now."

Rollie nodded, turned the ring around in his fingers. A thin gold band, a cluster of tiny diamond chips in the shape of a heart. Something ordered from a catalogue. Rollie had seen enough rings on clients' fingers to know that this one was garbage, a piece of metal dipped in shavings. He angled the ring to catch the light, but there was no visible sparkle. The gold was tarnished, black around the setting. Rollie breathed on it, rubbed it with the edge of his t-shirt. Nothing changed.

His mother lit a cigarette. Inhaled. "I wasn't sure if you were, you know, making plans. Thought you might like to have it just in case."

Rollie nodded again, closed the ring in his palm, then pushed his hand into his front pocket and tried to forget about it. He didn't want to tell his mother that the ring was worth-less, a tacky piece of junk jewellery that only a cheap and selfish bastard like his father would have bought. That he would be embarrassed to give it to anyone. He couldn't help thinking about the years of servitude and adoration his father had gotten for that ring. His father, a lay-about, a man who rarely got out of his pyjamas, whose only skill was making up excuses for why he couldn't work. Rollie wanted to shake his mother, to hear her admit that she could have, should have, done better than that.

His mother got up to dress for bingo.

Rollie stared at the filthy kitchen window, the row of key chains dangling above it like a sickening fringe. He stood and stepped toward the sink. Reached up, wrapped his fingers around the curtain rod and pulled. The rod resisted at first, then broke from the wall in a sudden snap. The key chains flew around the kitchen. Some of them clattered into the sink and onto the counter. Others shot through the air and hit the far wall. The rod, broken in two, was limp and sticky with grease in Rollie's hand. He threw it to the floor.

"What the hell happened?" His mother stood in the doorway.

Rollie shook his head. "Nothing. I was trying to fix it."

The sound of the bathtub draining echoed from the other room. Rollie imagined Adele standing barefoot on the bathroom tile, opening her towel to him, her body pink with heat, clean and untouchable.

As Adele moved the towel over her body, she inspected herself. She looked older than she was, her skin puckering and drooping in places. Without her heels, the tops of her thighs wobbled, soft and loose. Her back was curved so that her breasts slouched forward; if she didn't stand up straight, she looked stooped. She wrapped the towel around her body. She worried most about her face. Checked it all the time in the shop's bathroom mirror. "Still beautiful," Rollie teased when he caught her doing it.

She wondered if Rollie had ever found her beautiful.

These days Adele thought constantly about the street. If she got a room somewhere, her money would only last a couple of weeks. Then it would be back to the shelters, lining up at the soup wagon while stray, dirty hands prodded her. The rain, the bad-smelling men, their greedy faces. She could try the parking garage again, the one with the lazy patrolman, the wire fence she could sometimes get herself under, the urine-soaked stairwells. She didn't like closed spaces, harder to get away from trouble. She knew in a month or so, when it got really cold, there'd be no spare change, people would rush by with their eyes down, their winter coats held tight. She would walk around all night to try and stay warm. She would try and get hooked up, sell some stuff. Start checking car doors. She would go back to dating.

Adele unwrapped her towel and shivered. The heat from the bath had already left her. She climbed back into the empty tub and pressed herself against its warm sides.

Rollie was on his way back from the bank. He stopped at the Lotus Café and ordered a grilled cheese sandwich and onion rings for Adele's lunch. He ate two slices of blueberry pie while he waited for the sandwich.

He strolled back to the shop, the perfume of fried food rising from the greasy bag in his hand. Halfway up the block, a group of skate kids crouched in front of a door, their faces pressed to the glass, hands cupped over their eyes. As he approached, he saw that it was the door to his shop; the delinquents were probably casing the place.

"Hey!" Rollie yelled. "Get away from there!"

The skate kids jumped up from the door and one of them locked eyes with Rollie, gave him a big thumbs-up. The kids laid down their boards and slid off down the street.

The first thing Rollie did when he got to the door was check for damage. The lock was clean, the panes of glass intact, no scratches or signs of jimmying. He was about to open the door when he looked up into the shop. His heavy hand slipped off the doorknob.

It was Adele. Her eyes closed, her lips slightly parted, her head tilted back revealing the full length of her throat. Her back arching, then curving forward, then arching again in a clumsy rhythm. She was topless. Her short, flowery skirt hitched up around her waist, her legs straddling the tattoo chair. In the chair, Donny Hoover, his hands all over her, in her hair, pulling at her shoulders, grabbing her breasts. His eyes were closed, his face a deep red, like a cartoon version of himself.

Rollie wanted to turn away, to run, but his legs were dead. The bag of lunch fell from his hand and he stumbled to the side of the doorway, where they wouldn't see him. His throat filled with tears, the two pieces of blueberry pie stung sour in his stomach. He took a deep, disbelieving breath and stepped to the glass, cupped his hands to his eyes, as the boys had, to see the two of them more clearly.

Donny's chest was covered in irregular patches of red chest hair that made Rollie think of weeds. His hands roamed ceaselessly over Adele's breasts and shoulders, grabbing and squeezing her flesh. His legs were bowed beneath Adele, motionless except for a twitch now and then, his feet limp and turned out, his shoes splattered with drywall mud. Donny's face was contorted in a grimace, his eyes squeezed shut, his mouth open and all his teeth showing, an expression so brutish and crude, it frightened Rollie.

Adele moved awkwardly on Donny's lap, shifting and sliding, adjusting and readjusting her position, clutching Donny's arm, then the seat of the chair, then Donny's shoulders, lifting her right leg forward, then back. Her face looked serious, her eyes intent on Donny's throat.

Inside the shop, the phone rang. Rollie backed away from the door, wiped his face with his hand. He expected the noise to startle them, to end their coupling. But Adele and Donny didn't stop. Rollie stepped forward again, riveted now by the sight of Adele's naked body. The phone continued to ring inside the shop, a persistent trill, a cloying alarm.

Rollie stared at Adele's thighs and buttocks, pale and dimpled under the flounce of her skirt. He had never noticed the tops of her legs were so doughy and slack. He watched the skin of her stomach jut in a small pouch around her waist as she leaned forward. He saw that her breasts, small as they were, swayed low on her chest, her nipples like long dark fingertips. Her skin had a sickly yellow hue; her hair, dull and greyish in the light of the shop. Her frame jerked roughly as she slipped to one side on Donny's lap, gripped the arm of the chair with her bony hand. Rollie followed her face as her head tipped back on her neck, her mouth stretching suddenly wide. He saw for the first time that Adele was missing some back teeth.

Rollie stepped away from the door, held his hand to his face. His skin was slick with tears. He tried to collect himself but a horrible tightness pushed at his chest and he erupted into a loud, shaking sob. The sound of his bawling surrounded him; some people across the street at a parking meter stared. He shook his head, then turned himself against the brick wall of the building, wrapped his arms around his face and cried. He choked on dirt and mortar dust as he blubbered, pushed his forehead into the crumbling brick.

When he finally calmed to a hiccupy whimper, he stood there, breathing the autumn air through his mouth, looking up and down the street, unsure of which direction to take. He glanced down at the pavement and saw the oily paper bag. He picked it up.

The smell of food made him suddenly hungry. He ate the sandwich where he stood, large, purposeful bites. The warmth of the melted cheese gave him some comfort.

He walked to the bus stop, sat on the bench, ate the onion rings one whole ring at a time. He crumpled the bag in his hands, threw it into the street, watched it dance and hop, drawn along by the wind, and then get flattened and dragged by the wheels of a car.

Across the street, in the park, the leaves were turning. Brilliant oranges and yellows, twisting from their rigid branches, falling to the messy earth. Junkies were splayed out on the grass, like fallen statues, their hands over their eyes, while dealers trolled the sidewalks for more customers. Birds darted from the treetops in daredevil arcs, splattered their white filth on the war memorial, then landed smoothly and pecked at the concrete ground. Rollie watched the world as if he had never seen it before, beauty and ugliness in everything; he could no longer tell the difference. He drew great gulps of breath, drank the foul, exhaust-filled air, and tasted in it the hint of a woman's perfume. He smelled the aroma of food from a nearby restaurant and the stench of old garbage, trash cans used as toilets. He stared down at his own body, the wide tub of supple flesh, his thick arms, the rise of his chest.

On the corner, a shabbily dressed old man was playing nonsense harmonica. Two shaved and tattooed girls held hands as they walked, kissed before crossing the street. Rollie checked the clock outside the money-lending store. In a half-hour or so he would return to the shop and fetch Adele, treat her to lunch someplace nice. He pushed his hand into his pocket, felt for his mother's ring. The metal was cool and smooth against his fingers. He slid his pinky in and out of its imperfect circle and rested back against the bus stop bench, looked up at the sky and searched the grey clouds until he found the hazy white shape of the sun.

Sisters

———•———

G race met him first. Outside the 7-Eleven. He was leaning against the glass, smoking a cigarette, wearing shades even though it was early November and heavily overcast. The sunglasses were what got her, the shiny gold frame, the large mirrored windows, the way they hid most of his pale, narrow face, revealed only the angles of his jaw. His leather jacket looked new, fitted and smooth. He was ignoring her, or letting her look, she couldn't tell which. She stayed on the curb and sipped her Slurpee, hoped he would be curious, want to talk to her. She played with the straw, dragged it in and out of the container, made a hollow, scraping sound.

"You skipping?" he asked.

She knew without turning around that he wasn't looking at her. "Second period. Math."

"Want a smoke?"

She shrugged. Bent her head to her straw so he couldn't see that she was pleased. There was a thwack as something landed beside her. His pack of cigarettes, Craven As. She found the lighter snugged inside, and lit one up. "Thanks." She reached back to him with the pack in her hand, kept her face still, didn't smile. He waved her off. "Keep it." "Thanks," she said again. The sound of her voice rang tinny and eager in her ears. He was facing her now, but whether he was looking at her, she couldn't be sure. She saw her twin reflections in his lenses: herself, but smaller, unrecognizable.

"They shouldn't put 7-Elevens so close to high schools," he said.

His name was Kevin. They drove to the Burger Brothers in his car, a rambling greenish-gold sedan. Grace nodded to the AM radio beat, classic rock, old Van Halen, Lynyrd Skynyrd.

"So, why you skipping?" he asked.

"Why not?"

"Where're your friends?"

She shrugged. "In class." She imagined Lisa putting her feet up on the empty seat in front her in Social Studies, third period.

"How come you're not with them?"

"What do you care?" She rolled down her window and drew a deep breath of cold air, let the wind cut at her face. She glanced over at him to see if he was irritated; he was smiling a thin, easy smile.

"You Native?" he asked. He said it like he already knew. "Part."

"Oh yeah." His smile broadened. "Which part?"

She looked away from him to hide the grin on her face.

As they entered the Burger Brothers drive-thru, she opened her purse, hoped she still had a few dollars. He put his hand on her wrist; his fingers were soft, hairless. "My treat," he said.

They ate their burgers in the car, in the parking lot. He rested his drink in the V of his legs; Grace held onto hers, the waxy cup sweating down her wrist, threatening to weaken in her grip. "So, when'd you graduate?" she asked him.

He chuckled and shook his head, dismissing her question.

Grace twirled a french fry in her fingers, tried again. "How old are you?"

He looked right at her and smiled. "Too old for you, Pocahontas."

She felt the skin behind her ears get hot; her mouth tasted like stale hamburger. He thought she was some kind of joke. She took long sips of her root beer and stared out the window.

He drove her to the lake. Kicked back against the hood of the car and smoked while she walked along the shore. The wind off the lake was cold, but she angled her face into it. She wanted him to watch her, for his gaze to bore holes through her clothes, singe her skin like the ember of a cigarette. She had stopped speaking to him at the burger place, but he didn't seem to care. Perhaps she was being childish. Could she go the rest of the day without saying anything? She picked up a few tiny stones, their edges worn smooth and round by the tide. She thought of whirling around and throwing them at the wheels of his car, shocking him, proving she was worth his attention. Instead, she shook the pebbles in her palm, threw them like dice, two by two, into the dark water.

Back in the car, he started the engine so they could get warm, listen to the radio. He lit two cigarettes and handed her one. She didn't say thank you.

"You pissed at me or something?" He took a drag of his cigarette and leaned back against his door.

His sunglasses bothered her now. She shrugged.

"What? You didn't like the lunch I bought you? The view isn't nice enough for you?" He was smiling, but there was an edge in his voice.

Grace shifted in her seat. "I didn't like what you called me," she said softly.

"Oh. I see." Kevin took another deep drag. "Fair enough. Fair. Enough." He was nodding.

She put the cigarette to her lips and inhaled, slowly, with relief.

"Here," he said. "How 'bout a peace offering?" He blew a series of smoke rings into the car.

She smiled, reached out and circled her finger inside one of them, watched it break apart, dissolve into the air.

"Hey," he said. "You ever been to the Rocking Horse?"

"No." There were only a handful of bars in town and Grace hadn't been able to get into any of them.

"Hmmm. You should definitely go sometime. It's pretty wild, you know? Some of the girls there just wear these skimpy bikini tops and jeans. You'd look great in something like that."

Grace felt herself blush. She wrapped her left arm around her stomach, took a drag of her smoke, shrugged.

"Well, you wear a bikini in the summer, don't you?"

"Sometimes." Her window was open, but the blast from the dashboard heater was smothering her face, making her uncomfortably warm.

Kevin stared at her like he was waiting for her to say something else. He flicked his cigarette butt out onto the dirt, then reached forward and put the car into gear. "You want me to drop you back at the school?"

Grace hung her arm out the window, watched the wind carry the thin grey trail of her cigarette until it was nothing. "Can't we go somewhere else?"

He put the car back into park and drummed his hands on the steering wheel. "You do wear a bikini in the summer, right? I mean, you don't wear one of those one-piece things like my grandma, do ya?"

Grace laughed, let the cigarette butt slip from her fingers out onto the ground. "No, I've got a bikini."

"Do you wear a bra?" he asked. "I mean, are you wearing a bra right now?" His voice was casual, like he was asking if she wanted a soda, or another cigarette.

She looked at him; his mouth was relaxed, his body slouched back into the seat, his sunglasses reflecting her own blank face. She nodded.

"Would you take your top off and show me?"

She laughed, a nervous spurt that sent a bubble of spit from her mouth in a high arc to the dashboard. The bubble rested there, glistened like a far-away planet.

"I mean, you wear a bikini in the summer, right?" He was doing something with his voice, on the surface it seemed light but underneath it was pressing, as if she was being unreasonable, keeping something obvious from him. "But look. If you don't want to."

"I don't want to," her voice a quick echo of his.

He bowed his head for a moment. Then turned to her and pulled off his sunglasses. His face was smaller than she had imagined, his eyes deep set and close together. His left eye, darker than the right, wandered a little. His eyelashes were long. Grace looked down. She could feel his eyes moving over her face. Something grazed her neck. She turned: his thin hand settled on her shoulder. She sat still.

"Grace." His voice was deeper now, softer and more earnest. "I can't tell you how many girls fall for that. I'm really glad you didn't."

Grace swallowed; she didn't dare look at him. The front of her face tingled. She felt on the edge of laughing or crying, but wasn't sure which. She stared at the dashboard.

"Hey," he said, gently. "Grace. Hey. You okay?" He put his arm around her shoulder.

His closeness felt good. She rested against him and rubbed her eyes. He steadied her.

"Are you crying?" His voice was calm.

She shook her head.

"Good," he said. "'Cos it would kill me to make you cry." He sat back and looked straight at her face. "I just wanted to make sure you knew how to be smart, you know? There are a lot of smooth talkers out there and you high school girls are sending out all the signals. You gotta be safe."

Grace nodded.

They spent the rest of the day driving along the highway just outside town. The windows down, the radio loud. She shook her hair so that the wind whipped it back around her face. Kevin hung his arm out the open window, smiled at her from time to time. "You're pretty cool for a high school chick, you know that?"

Grace smiled back. "Yeah. I know."

Nita has a work ethic, the other girls say. Even when it rains she goes out from five to eleven, stands under her red umbrella. She takes breaks if it gets too cold, sips coffee in the Lotus Café while the owner reads the newspaper, mists his plants. She rubs her calves together to get warm, pats her face with a paper napkin, careful not to smudge her eyes; she slips off her shoes, flexes her arches to hear the popping of small, lost bones. She puts the hours in, like a real job, not because she wants to, but because there is nothing else. When she can't stand it, even the thought of it, when she worries herself through two cups of coffee and a glass of water with the threat of bitter tastes, rank smells, she forces herself back outside, tells herself, you made this bed. Stands with her shoulders at her ears, her chin to her chest. Folded this way, she attracts them faster. The night is finished in a few awful smiles.

Grace looked for him all that week at the 7-Eleven: lunch hour, after school, while she was skipping classes. She smoked his cigarettes one by one, carefully, then kept the empty pack in her purse. She told Lisa about him, but Lisa only shrugged. "Does he have a job?" she asked. "Well, he must if he has a car." Grace sounded more defensive than she wanted to.

When he finally showed up, it was a couple of weeks later, outside her school at the end of the day. He was sitting on the rail that separated the grass from the sidewalk, smoking. Grace looped her arm under Lisa's and pulled her towards him. "Come on," Grace said. "We'll just say hi."

He seemed to stare right past them as they approached. Grace slowed her pace, wondered if he was waiting for someone else, another girl, if he would pretend not to know her.

She stopped in front of him. "Hi!"

He nodded. "I thought that was you."

Grace felt the breath leave her body.

"Who's your friend?"

"This is Lisa."

Kevin held out his hand; it seemed unnaturally long and pink. "Well, hello, Lisa."

Lisa didn't take his hand, kept her head down. "Hi."

"You girls wanna go somewhere?"

Grace looked to Lisa. Her mouth was set in a thin line; she turned her body in toward Grace, her shoulder blocking them from Kevin. "I'm gonna go home."

"What? Why? Don't you wanna go for a ride?"

Lisa shook her head. "Call me when you get in."

Grace sat beside Kevin on the railing while he finished his cigarette. They watched Lisa walk off down the street. "Your friend's pretty nice looking," he said.

Suddenly, Grace was glad to see her go.

He took her to the mall. Bought her fries and a root beer float at the food fair. She swirled the ice cream around in her cup and scanned the fast-food stands. "I wanna get a job here."

Kevin laughed. "Here? What the hell for? It would suck to work here."

"I need a part-time job, you know, to make some money."

"What do you need money for?"

"Stuff. Music. Clothes."

"What about your parents?"

Grace shook her head. Her mom worked in housekeeping at a private hospital; for years she'd been trying to get a union job at General. She gave Grace and her sister each seven dollars a week, for emergencies. They got new clothes at the beginning of the school year and that was it.

"Are they mean to you, your parents?"

"No, nothing like that. It's just my mom and she doesn't make a lot of money."

"Neither will you, working in a shit-hole like this. Can you type?"

"Yeah." She had learned the keyboard last year.

"Then you've got skills. You should be looking for something better. Something where you can move up."

Grace wiped her fingertips on a paper napkin; they came away still greasy. "Where am I going to find that?"

"Well, you gotta look for it. It doesn't happen overnight." His voice was sharp.

They sat in awkward silence. Grace had the uneasy feeling that somehow she had made Kevin angry. He sat with his legs stretched out into the aisle, his left arm hanging heavy over the back of his chair. He tore a napkin with the fingers of his right hand. After what felt like a long time, he sat up straight.

"Okay," he said. "Here's what I'm going to do." He reached into his back pocket and pulled out his wallet. "If you promise you won't take a job in this shit-hole, or any similar shit-hole, I'll give you an allowance. Nothing extravagant, just enough to keep you going from week to week." He placed a twenty and a five on the table.

Grace shifted in her seat. "I can't take money from you."

"Oh!" Kevin smacked his palm onto the table; Grace flinched. "You can't take money from me, but you'll take money from some fast-food grease pig who'll feel you up the first chance he gets?"

She stayed silent. What he said made her idea seem stupid, foolish. Why hadn't she thought it through? She kept her eyes on her fingers, her nail polish chipped under the shiny grease.

"Look," his voice was softer now, easier. "If it makes you feel better, when you get that office job, you can pay me back."

Grace stared at the money. Everything he said made sense. He was watching out for her, trying to keep her from making mistakes. She let her fingertips touch the edges of the bills. Her stomach started to feel thick and queasy. She drew her hand back to her napkin and tried to rub the grease off her fingers. "I can't take it," she said, her voice thinning in the air around her.

The manager of the rooming house in Vancouver says Nita pays him at the end of the month. A short, olive-skinned man who smokes a pipe and speaks in two volumes, mumble and shout, he collects Nita's mail, an inconvenience, those three or four envelopes a week, more than the one or two a month the other residents receive, a headache, illegal, he says. He sells things out of his office, VCRs, work boots, small Persian rugs. He offers Nita an electric shoe shiner for twenty dollars, then snorts when she turns it down. "Do I have any mail?" she asks. He is watching a soccer game on a tiny black-and-white television set; he shakes his head without looking up. "Are you sure?" He turns and stares at her, mutters something in a foreign language, then gets up and walks back to his office. He comes out with four brown envelopes. "This not post office, okay?" he barks. He stuffs his pipe with a stunted thumb while Nita counts out the rent money, a tidy plot of rectangles. He stares at the bills, then raps the square tip of his finger on the counter; the sound is like a fist on a door. "Thirty more!"

"What for?"

"Cable!"

"I don't have a TV."

"The building is getting cable, so now you pay for cable! If you don't have TV, that's your problem!" The manager goes back to his pipe.

Nita kicks the toe of her shoe into her ankle until she feels a bruise rising. She lays out three stiff bills.

The manager says she kicked his counter, left that white dent where the paint and plaster have fallen away. "Who pays?" he asks Grace. "You have money?"

Grace tries to show him a map; he shakes his head.

At the mall, Grace let Kevin buy her make-up, cigarettes, a blue rabbit's-foot key chain. He drove her to the park, where they sipped cans of warm beer that he had stashed in his glove compartment. He stayed with her until dinnertime, then drove her home.

"Where are you going?" Grace asked before she got out. The car idled rough on the gravel shoulder beside her house. The moment she asked the question, her body felt stiff and hot. She kept her hand loose on the door handle.

Kevin didn't look at her. "Out with friends."

"Oh," she said. "I don't have to be home for anything."

He laughed. "Yeah, but I gotta be somewhere. Without you." He poked his finger into the side of her arm, hard. "Now, get out."

She wanted to tell him to fuck off, but didn't. Instead she climbed out of the car and slammed the door. She slung her hips as she walked away from him, hoping his eyes were on her tight jeans. His car kicked up gravel and pulled away before she could turn around and check.

Over dinner, Grace asked her mother for a raise in her allowance.

"What for?" Her mother loaded food onto her fork, meat, carrots, corn.

Grace shrugged. "Just stuff." She poked at her meat with her knife. "New clothes."

Her mother shook her head as she chewed. "You already have plenty of clothes from Nita."

Nita looked up. Grace ignored her.

"People aren't wearing those clothes anymore, besides, they don't fit me, everything's too long, she's like a giraffe."

Nita seemed unfazed by the insult, kept on eating.

Their mother put down her knife and fork. "I don't care what anyone is wearing. Those are the clothes I paid for, so those are the clothes you have. If you want new clothes you can stop skipping classes and get your grades up to a decent level, then we can talk about you getting a part-time job."

Nita smiled as she helped herself to seconds. Grace wanted to stab Nita's hand with a fork. She pushed her plate away. "May I be excused?"

Her mother was lighting up. She pointed her unlit cigarette at Grace's plate. "I don't buy groceries so you can throw them in the garbage. At least finish the chop."

Grace sighed as she picked up her knife and fork, made a production of sawing her knife through the meat, so her mother would see what a bad cook she was, what a bad mother.

"I need that fabric for sewing class." Nita said.

Their mother nodded. "We'll go on the weekend."

Grace threw her fork onto the plate. "What? I can't have more allowance, but you're buying fabric for her? This is so unfair!"

"It's for school," Nita said.

"It's for clothes!" Grace shouted at Nita.

Nita's expression was vacant, like she couldn't understand why Grace would be mad.

Their mother rubbed her forehead. "It's a graduation dress, Grace. And when it's your turn to graduate, you'll get one too."

Grace glared at Nita. "How do you know she's even going to graduate? Her grades are crap. Ask her how many classes she's failing."

"Alright, that's enough."

"I'm actually saving mom money by making it myself," Nita said, softly.

"Oh, go to hell." Grace pushed her chair away from the table.

Upstairs, she locked herself in her room, listened to Def Leppard on her headphones and cried. She thought about Kevin, hated him and at the same time wished he were there to comfort her.

Before she left for work, her mother knocked on her door. "You gonna be okay?"

Grace didn't answer.

Hermia, the paranoid woman across the hall, leaves a gift for Nita every Friday night: two raw eggs tied in a handkerchiefed bundle to Nita's doorknob. Nita boils an egg for breakfast on Saturday and Sunday, heats the water in handleless pot on the hot plate. Once, Nita falls asleep with the warm egg in her stomach, leaves the hot plate on, the thin curtain swaying about it like a moth's wing.

She wakes to banging on her door.

"You setting the place on fire? You freebasing shit in there?" The manager's harsh bellow.

Nita jumps out of her chair and claps her palms on the hot orange edge of the curtain. "No, nothing, nothing! Eggs, just eggs!"

"Did it burn you?" Grace asked on the phone.

"Just my hand. He wants me to pay for the curtains."

"Maybe you should see a doctor."

"Forty bucks, Gracie, for those piece-of-shit curtains."

"Does it hurt?"

"What?"

"Your hand."

"Not really. Tell mom I miss her."

"Tell her yourself."

"You'd like the city, you know, it's huge, it goes on forever."

"When are you coming home?"

"Goodnight, Gracie."

The next morning Kevin was outside her house when she left for school. He was sitting on the hood of his car, holding two Styrofoam cups, wearing his sunglasses.

"Want a ride to school?" he shouted.

The morning air was prickly against her face. She pressed her teeth together, walked slowly to his car. He opened the door for her, handed her a cup of coffee. "I hope you like it black."

She didn't like coffee at all, but sipped the hot liquid anyway, tried not to wince when it scalded her tongue, slipped down her throat in a hot bitter film.

"So, what'd you do last night?" He bounced his hands on the steering wheel as he drove, his coffee cup nestled between his legs.

Grace stared ahead and said nothing.

"Oh, I get it," he said. He turned the radio on, not too loud, not too soft, then checked her reaction. "Are you cold?" he asked. He turned the heater on. Warm air blew against her neck. She closed her eyes.

At the intersection before her school, he glanced at her sideways. "We're almost there. You're not going to say anything to me? Not even thank you for the ride?

She forced a flatness into her voice. "Thank you for the ride."

He pulled up in front of the school. Turned the radio down and put his arm over the seat back. "Hey, listen. There's this party tonight."

She held the coffee cup to her lips, but didn't drink. "So what?"

"So, you should come."

She stared out her window at the school, the dirty cement building, the litter across the grass, the groups of kids with knapsacks and new jackets. Moments ago she had been desperate to get out of the car, to make a dramatic exit, now she wanted to stay. "Can I bring Lisa?"

"Lisa. Yeah, okay. But don't go inviting the whole school. This is a private thing, you know? I'll come by your house around eight-thirty."

Grace grabbed her bag and got out of the car. This time, instead of turning her back, she watched him drive off.

Nita spends her money at the Army & Navy, buys clothes: a flowery dress, a mohair jacket, a pair of black jeans. And she buys shoes, more than she needs, pairs with thin straps and tiny buckles. She wears each pair once, then packs them in tissue paper for some better time in the future, a closet full of tangled straps, crossed fingers. She buys food at the A & N, canned fish, dried noodles in boxes, bags of wine gums. She buys used paperbacks, science-fiction serials from a cart on the street. She buys weed on Wednesday afternoons down in Victory Park with the other regulars. Fat-bottomed baggies, a month at a time. This is where she meets James, the tall Native who plays hacky-sack by himself, his knees and ankles bouncing and lobbing the tiny beanbag in a complex series of catches and hits.

"He bounces it around and says nursery rhymes at the same time," she told Grace on the phone. "He sells CDs out of a hockey bag to these scrawny boys with skateboards. They're always hitting him up for crank and acid. Sometimes he sells it."

"Do you have any money left?"

"Hey diddle diddle, the cat and the fiddle, we used to say that one, remember?"

"You spent it all?"

"The dish ran away with the spoon."

"Nita."

"He said I was the dish. Don't worry, I'll get more."

Grace's mother stood in the bathroom doorway in her housekeeping uniform, smoking a cigarette. "Who's having this party?"

"I don't know, some people." Grace applied a careful trail of eyeliner under her bottom lashes.

"Well, where is it?"

"I don't know."

"Well, if you don't know where the party is, how are you going to get there?"

"Someone's picking me up."

"Who?"

"This guy that Lisa and I know from school, Kevin."

"Is he a good student?"

"Yeah."

"Is he Lisa's boyfriend?"

"No."

"Is he your boyfriend?"

"No, Mom, he's no one's boyfriend, he's just a friend." Grace pushed past her mom and ducked down the hallway, into her room. She emptied her purse onto the bed, then started to put everything back in, one item at a time, lipstick, spray musk, gum, lighter.

"I'm not even going to ask why you need that," her mom said, pointing to the lighter.

"Good. Don't."

"Look, Gracie. You can go to a party next weekend, when I'm off. I don't want to have to worry about you while I'm at work."

"So don't worry." Grace checked her face in her compact before throwing it into her purse.

"You are not going to some strange party by yourself."

"I'm not going by myself. I told you, I'm going with Lisa and Kevin."

"Okay. Fine." Grace's mom chewed on her thumbnail. "Take Nita."

"What?" Grace threw her purse back onto the bed.

"You heard me." Her mom turned and yelled down the hall. "Nita! You're going to a party with your sister!"

"Mom!" Grace pleaded.

"You want to go, you take her with you. And if either of you get into trouble, you're both done for, you hear me?"

Nita appeared. Hovered in the doorway, her same empty, blameless look.

Grace knew that Nita was pleased, happy to spoil Grace's plans, happy to finally have somewhere to go.

"Whose party?" Nita asked. "Where?"

Their mother waved her cigarette in the air like a wand. "Who knows who. Who knows where." And disappeared down the hall.

Grace and Nita waited outside the house, stamped their feet against the cold, did not speak. Nita had curled her hair, put on make-up, dressed in a striped top, a short black skirt and black tights. The make-up and hair made her look only slightly less plain, but the short skirt showed off her long legs. She had dressed that way on purpose. Grace's own legs were average, her figure voluptuous; her mother called her petite, which, she knew, was a polite way of saying short.

Kevin's car pulled up. Grace jumped into the front seat and closed her door, left Nita standing outside.

"Who's that?" Kevin asked, leaning down to see through her window.

"My sister," Grace said. "She's totally uncool. She doesn't have to come."

"Let her in," he said. "The more, the merrier."

If Nita's in a good mood, she goes down to the Mini-Mart and buys popcorn in the foil pan. Shakes it slowly over the hot plate in her room, watches the silver spiral unfurl and rise into a dome. She goes door to door, down the hall, offering. Hermia takes a handful, pours it into the pocket of her army surplus coat. Roy the alcoholic takes a fistful through the crack of his door, then pushes the door shut. Mr. Dell, the white-haired ex–piano teacher who only ever wears pyjamas and a bathrobe, who went to jail a long time ago for something to do with teenaged boys, likes to stand in the hall and chat as he plucks individual fluffs of popcorn from the pan.

"There isn't enough *neighbourliness* anymore. Stands to reason with that *simian* running the place."

"Yeah, how 'bout that extra thirty bucks he's charging?"

"What extra thirty *bucks?*" He says *bucks* like an angry chicken.

"For cable."

Mr. Dell shakes his head and waves his hand in a flourish. "Doesn't apply to *me,* sweetheart. No *boob tube.*"

"He actually said that?" Grace giggled on the phone. "Boob tube?"

Nita laughed so hard she couldn't talk.

Grace opened her door so that Lisa could squeeze into the front seat with her and Kevin, leave Nita in the back by herself. But Lisa said, "Why squish?", opened the back door, slid in beside Nita.

Grace turned around to check Lisa's outfit. A stretch-lace top and jeans. Lisa was "petite" like Grace and had pretty, doll-like features, wavy, blond hair, but she was small-chested and had no hips. When they were out together, Grace got most of the attention.

"How's school?" Nita asked Lisa.

"Fine," Lisa said. "How's school with you?"

"Okay. I'm taking Advanced Sewing. We're making our own grad dresses."

Grace shook her head. "Jesus, Nita, no one cares." She checked Kevin's face for a reaction, but he was focused on the road.

"That's cool," Lisa said.

There was a pause. Grace tried to think of something to ask Lisa, something that would make them both sound cool.

"So, what are you doing after graduation?" Lisa asked Nita.

Grace shot Lisa a dirty look. But Lisa ignored her.

"I don't know," Nita said. "I might go to college to study fashion."

"You have to have good grades to get into college," Grace said.

"Not fashion college." Nita said quietly.

Grace laughed. "There's no such thing as fashion college." She turned to Kevin. "Is there?"

"What?" Kevin looked confused; he hadn't even been listening.

"There's no such thing as fashion college?"

Kevin shrugged. "Beats me. I guess there could be."

Grace slumped against her door, waited for Nita to say something, but Nita was silent in the back.

Lisa leaned over into the front seat. "I have to be home by midnight."

The window was chilly and hard behind Grace's head. "Yes, I know," she murmured.

"Don't worry." Kevin turned to Lisa and smiled. "I'll get you home on time."

Lisa smiled back.

The party was in a small, run-down house. Grace could hear the AC/DC before they got out of the car. The front door to the house was wide open and though the late autumn air was cold and dry, the living room was a humid, smoky hive of bodies. The music hammered a heavy pulse into the floor. People were sitting, crammed onto couches and on the carpet, and around them, between furniture, against every bare patch of wall, others were standing. Most were drinking beer from silver cans, brown bottles, except for a few girls who sipped ciders and coolers. Empty beer cans and bottles covered the coffee table and mantel.

A small group of boys sat around the unlit fireplace, passing a joint. They all looked younger than Grace, maybe grade eight or nine; one had his hair in dreadlocks, another had the sides of his head shaved. A man with a moustache grabbed the boy with the dreads and swung him by the shoulders, side to side so that the boy's ass slid around on the tile like a floor polisher. The boy laughed and offered the man a toke.

Kevin had two cases of beer, one under his arm, one in his hand. He pushed his way through the crowd, saying his hellos over his shoulder; Grace, Lisa and Nita stayed close behind.

The kitchen was a bright white box, also jammed with people. Grace recognized two girls who were sitting on the counter by the sink. They had graduated from her high school a year ago. The blonde one, Valerie, was wearing tight black jeans with zippers down the sides. Grace had only ever seen those in magazines. Jan, the other girl, wore a black Iron Maiden t-shirt that set off her mane of teased red curls, her fair skin. Valerie and Jan were idolized at W. L. High; they'd both had full-time jobs while in school and had made enough money to rent an apartment together through grades eleven and twelve. As far as anyone knew, no high school student before Valerie and Jan had ever attempted such a feat.

Grace smiled at them; perhaps they would recognize her. Valerie caught her gaze, smirked, turned back to Jan.

"Where's the bathroom?" Nita asked Kevin.

Grace wanted to punch her.

Kevin tore open the first case of beer. "Yeah, I don't know." He handed them each a can. "There's gotta be one somewhere."

Nita pressed through the crowd in the hall to find the bathroom. Kevin shouted; the sound made Lisa jump, she put her hand to her forehead. He was waving to someone in the living room and before Grace could see who it was, he glided off.

Grace flipped the tab on her beer, sucked back the foam that bubbled up. The music seemed to bounce back and forth within the tight walls of the kitchen. Grace felt it vibrating in her chest. "Great party, huh?"

Lisa sipped her beer. "Yeah. I guess so."

A tall, heavy-set guy in a storm rider bumped past Grace to get to the fridge. He knocked her arm on his way back; beer splashed onto the leg of her jeans. "Sorry," he shouted.

"That's okay," she said, smiling, but he was already gone.

"Let's sit down." Lisa said.

"Where?"

Lisa pointed out some empty counter space beside Valerie and Jan.

Valerie and Jan were thumb-wrestling now, their long, painted thumbnails poised to do damage. The two of them laughed and squealed, as if thumb-wrestling were far more exciting than it appeared from the outside.

Lisa tugged on Grace's arm. They approached the girls.

"Hi! I'm Lisa. You guys graduated last year, right?"

"Hi! I'm Lisa!" Jan mocked in a high, squeaky voice. Valerie and Jan collapsed over each other, laughing.

Lisa looked down at her beer. Grace scanned the room for Kevin.

Valerie leaned forward. Grace caught a nasty waft of the hair spray that kept Valerie's wavy blond hair in a high feather. "What are you doing here? Shouldn't you be out babysitting somewhere?" Her voice was deep and rough like a man's.

"Can we sit here?" Lisa asked.

"Can we sit here?" Jan squeaked. The two of them started laughing again.

Grace elbowed Lisa. "Come on, let's go to the living room."

Grace and Lisa didn't find Kevin in the living room. They perched awkwardly on the hard arm of a brown corduroy couch and sipped their beer. Nita was sitting across the room on the couch under the window. On one side of her, a tanned girl in a white tank top was talking to a man crouched down at her feet. The girl's hair was straight and bleached white-blond; her lips, a shimmery pink, were closed in a polite, unimpressed smile. The man had his hands on her knees like he was praying to her. On the other side of Nita was a boy with thick, curly hair and terrible acne. He had a beer in each hand and was staring into space; his body seemed limp; every now and then he leaned over onto Nita and Nita pushed him upright.

Just keep drinking, Grace told herself, it'll get better.

And it did.

After almost a can of beer, the music wasn't as loud and the din of the room mellowed to a fragmented chorus of individual voices. Friendlier people nodded or said "Hi," as they passed from the corridor into the living room. Two guys named Tim and Harry, who looked old, in their thirties, stopped to talk. Tim asked what school they went to and what they were planning to do after graduation; Harry asked if they wanted to go out into the backyard and smoke some weed by the garage. Grace looked to Lisa; Lisa shook her head. "Well, if you change your mind." Harry smiled at Grace.

Lisa checked her watch.

"Will you stop doing that?"

"I can't help it, I'm bored." Lisa rested her head against the wall. "Besides, my beer's empty."

"Are those girls still there?"

Lisa stretched to see into the kitchen. "Yup."

Grace looked around the living room. "Where the hell is Kevin?"

"Maybe he's out back."

Couples in various stages of entanglement were huddled along the porch rail and on the steps down into the yard, but the largest group of people was gathered on the dark lawn beside the garage, away from the bright eye of the porch light. As Grace and Lisa moved across the grass, the heat from the house left them and they both started to shiver. Grace's eyes were slow to adjust to the dark. People seemed to be clustered in a pit of blackness. Small red points moved around in the air.

"Hey," a girl in the group said.

Grace saw the blurred outline of a thick, bare forearm. "Hey," she said back. The red points of light were floating in random patterns, slowing to a stop, hanging still, then moving again. "Have any of you guys seen Kevin?"

"I'm right here, baby," a deep, forced voice said. The group laughed. Grace could see better now. It was Harry who had responded; she recognized his moustache, the wide moon of his face.

"He was here a while ago," the heavy girl said. "But he went back inside."

Grace nodded.

Grace and Lisa walked back to the house, rubbing their arms to keep warm

"Hey, where you going?" Harry yelled. "The party's out here!"

Back in the kitchen, the counter girls were gone. Grace and Lisa grabbed a second beer and hoisted themselves up beside the sink.

"Do you think he left?" Lisa asked.

"No. He wouldn't do that."

Lisa gave her a look.

"He wouldn't."

James wears his long, dark hair in a ponytail. He comes by a couple nights a week. Taps on Nita's door around one a.m. They drink beer, smoke up and play cards, rummy and crib. For a treat, they do H. Lie on the floor, holding hands. "She

said she only does it with me," he says. "But I've seen needles and spoons that I know I didn't use." James calls her names, Sweet Toffee Girl, Nita Noodle, Thin Lizzy. Nita has names for him too, Tonto, Geronimo, Sitting Bullshit. Every once in a while, Nita puts her hand in James's lap and he lifts it out gently. "Can't do that, Nita." Sometimes, in the morning, he kisses her goodnight. Mostly, he strokes her hair and says her name over and over, "Oh, Nita, Nita, Nita, Nita."

≈

Two beers and an hour later, Lisa said, "He's not coming back."

Grace pinched the empty beer can in her hand then let it pop back out against her fingers.

"If we're gonna walk home, I need to leave now."

The living room had started to thin out a half-hour earlier, but now a second shift was coming in. A group of guys in hockey jerseys, balancing cases of beer on their shoulders. They yelled and whooped as they moved through the room; various people on the floor and couches slapped hands with them as they passed.

Grace nodded. "Let's go find Nita." They had crossed paths with her at various points, in the kitchen, in the living room, out on the grass. Nita had seemed perfectly happy sitting and talking to strangers, even if they were losers. Grace had pretended not to know her. She and Lisa drifted around like ghosts.

They walked through the kitchen and stood on the porch. "Nita!" Grace shouted into the dark yard. "I'm coming! I'm coming!" shouted back a fake falsetto. Laughter broke out among the hidden crowd. They waited on the porch, but Nita didn't appear. "Maybe she's in the bathroom," Lisa said.

Harry was in the bathroom. He had left the door unlocked and didn't answer when Grace knocked and called Nita's name. He stood in front of the toilet with his penis in his hand. "Hello ladies," he said in a calm voice. He turned to face them. Lisa pulled the door closed.

They checked the bedroom beside the bathroom and found a girl sitting on the floor in the dark. "Nita?" Lisa whispered.

"No," the girl said quietly. "This is Tracy."

"Sorry, Tracy."

The next bedroom door slammed shut, before Lisa could even get it open. "Some fucking privacy!" a guy yelled. "Sorry!" Lisa yelled back.

Grace listened outside the last bedroom before trying the door. She heard Nita's voice, that soft, round way of saying everything, which irritated the hell out of her. She reached for the doorknob. "Nita," Grace said, as she pushed the door open, "we have to go."

Nita's skin shocked Grace first, her bare arms and shoulders in the dim light. Nita was sitting cross-legged in the centre of the bed, her face blank with surprise. Kevin was lying on his side in front of her. He was propped up on his elbow, his palm on Nita's thigh, his back to Grace. Beside Nita, on the bed, a crumpled, purple and white striped mound – her top. Nita started to giggle, bowed her head down towards Kevin.

Kevin glanced back over his shoulder, then said. "You girls ready to head home?" His voice was steady, almost cheerful.

"What are you doing?" Grace meant the question for Kevin, but she couldn't take her eyes off Nita, her naked stomach, her white bra.

"What?" Nita smiled as she looked down at herself, then back up at Grace. "It's like a bikini."

Nita leans down into the windows of cars, tells the drivers to pull around the corner. Sprawling family sedans, dirty pickups. They take the corner slow, pacing her as she walks. She waits for the engines to turn off, for the drivers to wave the keys, lay them to rest on the passenger-side dash.

"They just want it quick." She explained it again to Grace on the phone.

"You go to a hotel?"

"Hardly ever."

"What if they want to take you home?"

"Never happened."

"Do they hurt you?"

"Not much."

"Mom wants to know where you're working."

"Tell her I got a job at a restaurant."

On the drive home, Nita sat in the front beside Kevin; Grace sat in the back, her body pushed tight against the frame of the car, feeling that at any moment she might open her door and jump out. Lisa complained about having a headache. Grace ignored her.

They dropped Lisa off first. She said goodnight, but Grace didn't answer. Nita turned around to the back seat and put her hand on the headrest in a little wave. "'Night, Lisa." She said it in a sweet, whispery voice that made Grace want to slap her.

When the car pulled up beside their house, Grace waited for Nita to get out. She'd been rehearsing what to say to Kevin, but none of it seemed right, nothing hurtful or humiliating enough. She wondered what he would say in his own defence, that he was drunk or stoned, that Nita had started it, that he was sorry. She wondered if she could forgive him.

The radio played Pink Floyd's "Wish You Were Here" as the three of them sat in silence. Nita was looking down at something in her lap. Kevin was staring out his window. Grace glared at Kevin in the rear-view mirror. Finally, Kevin looked up and met her gaze. She held him there with her eyes, hoped he could see what he was in for, that he wouldn't be getting off easy.

"Hey, Gracie," Kevin said, his nose and mouth framed in the thin rectangle of the rear-view; he was lighting a cigarette. "You want to head on inside? I need to talk to your sister."

Grace shoved the butt of her palm forward into Nita's headrest. The jolt pitched Nita's head forward, but she stayed silent, her eyes down.

Kevin opened his mouth to say something, but before he could, Grace was out of the car, slamming the door. She ran towards the house.

For half an hour Grace watched the car from her bedroom. She opened the window and the cold air rushed in; her body shook. She could see the small curve of her sister's shoulder and sometimes, her arm. Grace struggled to get a glimpse of Kevin, but he was hidden, shielded by the slope of the back window and her sister's body. She knew they were talking. She strained to hear the deep notes of Kevin's voice, the low shudder of his laugh, but no sound carried up to her.

It was Nita that Grace couldn't believe. Her own sister had lured Kevin away, then pretended she hadn't done anything wrong, said goodnight to Lisa in that fake, babyish voice, sat quiet in the car as Kevin booted Grace out. Nita, with her feigned innocence, her pathetic doe eyes. Grace hated everything about her.

At the rooming house, Grace cries into Nita's pillow, suckles the pillowcase corner, holds in her mouth the taste of cigarettes and old hair spray. She phones her boyfriend, Lee, from the pay phone in the lobby, chokes the silver cord in her fingers. Tells him the city sprawls out too far, that she waited too long, she should have come sooner.

She buys incense and candles and lights them around Nita's room, says prayers as best she can remember them. She opens the windows to let air into the room. Throws away the needles, crusted tin foil and spoons. She walks the streets with Nita's photo, a yellowing snapshot in a sandwich baggie. She turns corners only to realize she is walking in circles, passing the same panhandlers, the same huddled street kids, again and again. Even though it's June and warm, they are wrapped and shivering. She smoothes the curling edges of the photograph through the clear plastic skin. "She's older than this," she says. "Like me, but taller, prettier." "She might have been wearing a floral print dress," she says. "She has a very delicate face." She wanders the streets of the neighbourhood, moves from corner to corner with a spiral-bound notepad and a pen, draws maps for herself, trails Nita's fading scent, her faint marks. She's unable to write down enough, to find enough people to talk to. She walks until the blisters on her heels are unbearable, until her hand cramps.

Grace watched in the evenings, after dinner, as Kevin's car rattled up to the gravel shoulder and Nita ran out to meet him. Each time Nita got into the car, her body disappearing as she leaned over into the driver's side, Grace felt a thickness in her mouth and throat. They drove off in a spit of dust and pebbles.

Grace stayed behind and did the dishes with her mother. Grace dried and stacked without talking, tried to ignore her mother's complaints about hospital politics, her questions about school. Later, she went to her room, flipped through her homework, then phoned Lisa. She started in on Nita right away, how she couldn't stand living with her, how stupid she was, how she got to do whatever she wanted because she was in the twelfth grade, what a bitch she was for stealing Kevin.

"Well, he wasn't exactly your boyfriend." Lisa said. "And besides, he wasn't that hot."

Grace tugged at the fur of her rabbit's-foot key chain. "That's not the point." A thin, blue tuft came away in her hand. "I saw him first."

One night, just before Christmas, Nita announced she was getting a part-time job at McDonald's. "It was Kevin's idea," she said.

Grace tightened her fingers around her fork. The only thing worse than seeing Nita with Kevin was hearing her talk about him.

"Kevin this, Kevin that," their mother said. "This better not affect your schoolwork."

"It won't," Nita said. Her mouth crept into a smile as she chewed.

Grace kept her eyes on her plate. "I didn't know McDonald's hired retards."

"Grace," her mother's voice was exasperated; she waggled her knife. "If you can't carry on a proper conversation, then leave the table."

Grace stood, dropped her fork on top of her food, walked out of the kitchen.

Three weeks later, on a Saturday afternoon, the McDonald's manager phoned their mother, woke her from her daytime sleep to tell her Nita had been fired for stealing money from the till; the restaurant was considering filing charges. Grace stood in the kitchen doorway as her mother called in sick to work.

Her mother stayed in her nightgown. Her face unwashed, her hair frizzed out in a dark halo, she cleaned the kitchen, emptied out the cupboards, rewashed all the plates, bowls and glasses, then the pots and pans, scrubbed the cupboard shelves and doors. She covered the kitchen table with dish towels and piled the washed dishes there. After the cupboards, she did the drawers.

Around dinnertime, Grace fixed herself a ham sandwich, made one for her mother. Her mother said "No, thank you," went into Nita's room, sat in the dark, waited for Nita to come home.

Grace waited in her own bed, eyes closed. Cocooned under her blankets, she lay completely still, held her breath. Her bedroom door open, she stared out into the shadowy hallway until she fell asleep.

She woke to the sound of a woman shouting; it took some seconds for her to recognize the raw, hysterical voice as her mother's.

"How could you do this? How could you be so bloody stupid?"

Nita was crying, wailing. "I don't know! I don't know!"

"Look at me! Look at me when I'm talking to you!" The slap of her mother's hand. "Do you hear me?" Now her mother sobbed. "I did everything for you, everything."

The sound of her mother's voice made Grace's eyes fill with tears. She pulled the blankets up to her face, pressed them over her mouth. She heard her mother cough and blow her nose.

A door slammed, and moments later Grace heard her mother banging in the kitchen, opening drawers, closing cupboard doors. She heard her crying again, this time a soft, sustained whimper, like a hurt dog.

Before light, Grace woke, her hand gripped tight under her pillow, her lashes sticky. She sensed someone sitting behind her on the bed. She turned over and reached for her mother, to lay her face in her lap and feel her mother stroke her hair, hear her mother's hushed bedtime voice.

But it was Nita, sitting in her coat, her thin, pale neck rising out of the bulky wool collar. For a while, they didn't say anything, just stared at each other in the dark, the light from the hallway carving their faces into strange skeletons. "Kevin's taking me to Vancouver," Nita said. "Don't tell Mom." Nita leaned down to kiss Grace on the cheek. Grace turned away.

❧

Back at the rooming house, Grace boils water for noodles. Examines the contents of Nita's bathroom for clues: Nita shaves her legs and underarms with a yellow Bic and Irish Spring soap lather. She wears a perfume called "Tarzana" that comes in a small yellow and black aerosol tube. She washes her hair with Pert Two-in-One Shampoo and Conditioner, and styles it with Dep Strong-Hold Mousse and Sudden Beauty Hairspray. She paints her nails with Maybelline "Red Glamour" and uses Bonne Belle "Cherry Cola Crush" lipstick. She glues on fake eyelashes instead of using mascara, draws a line over her lashes with a fat black eye pencil, uses a sponge-tipped applicator to copper her lids. She doesn't use deodorant. None of this matters.

Without Nita, Grace was sure her mother had become kinder. She spoke in a gentler voice, didn't nag Grace about doing her homework or staying up too late. She touched Grace more, her thumb stroking Grace's cheek, her fingers lingering on her jacket cuff. Nita's things were still around: her dress patterns by the living room couch, her jeans and sweaters thrown over a chair in her bedroom, her hair ties on the bathroom sink; her absence was only temporary. Nita hadn't vanished; she was, after all, with Kevin. She was away on an unplanned vacation and would make her way home eventually, blushing and breathless, full of annoying travel stories.

Grace's mother saved a plate of food from every meal Nita missed; the plastic-wrapped dishes piled one on top of the other, filled every shelf of the fridge. Grace cleared them out, pried and pushed the congealed food with fork, watched it slip into the garbage. After two weeks of phone calls to the police, Grace's mother went to bed. She slept through entire days, her alarm ringing a few minutes before she had to leave for work. In the mornings, after work, she walked straight from her car to her bedroom. On her days off, she slept in shifts, waking every few hours to roam the house in her nightgown, to look in on Grace. She stopped cooking meals and Grace rarely saw her eat. When she did eat, it was like a child, a quarter wedge of apple, a half slice of toast. Even when Grace prepared a dinner and had it ready for her mother before work, her mother picked at the food and smoked a cigarette instead.

The police had sent Nita's information to all the major centres, Kelowna, Kamloops, Vancouver, Victoria. Grace told herself that Nita and Kevin probably changed their minds, could have gone to any of those places.

The phone call came at night, while Grace's mother was at work.

"Do you miss me?" he asked.

Grace was startled by the first sounds of his voice, so close, as if he were beside her, whispering in her ear.

"It's shitty down here, fucking winter in the city. Nothing but rain. We ran out of money. I'm trying to get Nita to get a job, but she's so fucking lazy."

Then mention of her sister's name shook Grace. She started to tell Kevin how upset their mother was, how Nita needed to come home. Kevin was silent on the other end of the line.

"I wish you were here," he said.

The tenderness in his voice caught Grace off-guard. She wanted to finish talking about Nita, to explain how her mother was behaving, but instead, she found herself saying, "Why?"

"Because," he said. His mouth was very close the phone, his words thick and echoey. "I wanted you."

Something lifted sharply inside Grace; her chest filled with a liquidy heat, she felt light-headed.

"Do you know your sister eats like a pig?"

She laughed, more out of nervousness than amusement. "Yeah," she said. "She likes her food." The moment she said this, she felt guilty. Kevin chuckled.

"Give me your number," Grace said.

"Can't," he said. "We don't have a phone. I'm calling from a pay phone. You better appreciate this, 'cos it's fucking freezing out here."

Grace felt herself smiling.

"Do you have any money?" He asked it casually, like he didn't care if she did.

"No." She wasn't lying.

"How 'bout your mom?" There was something different in his voice now, a hint of restlessness.

"No. She's keeping everything tight. Doesn't want me going next."

He sighed. "You should come to Vancouver. Before your sister eats me out of house and home."

They both laughed; this time, it was easier.

"I can't," she said.

"I know," he said. "That's what I like about you."

The next day, at school, Grace glided through her classes, smiled behind her books until Lisa dragged her into the girls' washroom and demanded to know what was going on. Grace shrugged. Pretended to check her make-up in the streaked mirror. "I'm just feeling happy."

Lisa threw her arms into the air. "Fine! Don't tell me."

"It's no big deal." Grace plucked a tiny flake of mascara from the end of her lashes, looked down at the gooey lake of pink hand soap that had pooled on top of the sink.

"Is it a guy?" Lisa was twisting the faucet on and off, causing the water to splash then stop, splash then stop. "Is it . . ." Lisa paused, lifting her hand from the tap, positioning herself to watch Grace as she said the name, "Lee?" Lee was in their science class. He sat at the end of their row, and had a sweet face, which they often admired in profile. Lisa swore she had caught Lee checking Grace out on more than one occasion.

Grace stepped away from the mirror. "Maybe." She leaned against the rim of the sink and part of her hoped Lisa would guess, figure it out without Grace having to say the words.

Lisa was nodding quickly, waiting to hear more.

"But what if it was someone else?" Grace scanned sthe wet floor, torn sheets of paper towel, an unused maxi-pad.

Lisa didn't answer right away. Grace looked up. Lisa was glaring at her, her lips pressed in a firm, hard line.

"Someone else who?" All the playfulness had drained from her voice.

"I don't know." Grace shrugged. She dragged the heel of her shoe across the floor; the rubber left a thick, black mark on the green linoleum. She tried her best to smile, to pretend it was a joke. "It's no one, silly. I was totally psyching you out."

Kevin called Grace every few nights. He complained about Nita, that she was lazy and couldn't find a job. "It'll get better," Grace tried to reassure him. "The city's different, Grace," he said. "It's hard. You don't know till you get here. Things are complicated." Grace told him about school, about Lisa. She asked him if he would tell Nita to call their mom, just to say she was okay. He said he would try, but it was hard getting Nita out of the apartment. He asked Grace again about money. After a month, he stopped calling.

James says that Nita isn't the first girl to leave him. "It's 'cuz I couldn't. I'm just not right. Sexually. She said it didn't matter. I could tell. She bought a new dress. I liked her. We played

cards. I really did. When I was young. Some uncle. It bothered her. Made her sad. I told jokes. Indian jokes. How many
Indians does it take to change a light bulb? She liked eggs. And
popcorn. I brushed her hair. She was too thin. She sang in the
bath. I miss that song."

❧

That winter, Grace watched her mother pile cardigan over
sweater over sweater. When the weather improved and her
mother shrugged off the layers of clothing, she was alarmingly
thin. Grace stared at her in her work uniform, shocked at how
the stiff blue polyester sprung from her mother's body; she was
a wire doll in a cardboard uniform.

Nita's life was a story Grace began to tell herself. A slow,
unremarkable narrative unfolding in a distant place. Nita
finally got an office job, nothing impressive, easy reception
work in a small, grungy office. The pay wasn't great, but she
liked the people. She was saving to buy a car, something used,
but reliable. She was thinking about taking a night-school
class, maybe trying to graduate.

At the end of tenth grade, Grace discovered that Lisa had
been right after all. Lee asked Grace to the end-of-term dance.
The four of them, Grace and Lee, Lisa and her date, Carl,
snuck out of the dance and back to Carl's car to guzzle Cokes
spiked with vodka. Lisa got sick on the way home, her head
lolling out the car window. Grace giggled until her eyes ran
with tears.

Over the summer, Grace got a job helping with a toddler daycare at the community centre. The days were too long; the highways out of town shimmering like snakes in the hills. In the evenings Grace found herself staring out the window, to the south, where the brush met the sky, to the west, wishing the sun would set. She kept her job part-time when school began in September. When she wasn't at school or at work, Grace hung out with Lisa, listened as her friend plotted their lives after graduation. Lisa kept an ice-cream bucket of old Barbie dolls, their clothes and accessories under her bed, a coercion device to keep her younger sisters in line. While Lisa skimmed rental listings in the local paper, searched for the perfect apartment, Grace played with the dolls, stripped their clothes, bent their legs back till their feet touched their ears.

"What about this one?" Lisa read a listing out loud.

Grace waited for Lisa to finish, then shrugged. Plans for the future made her uneasy, filled her with an uncertain guilt. She twisted the heads off the dolls, then switched them, pressed Barbie's head onto Skipper's body, and Skipper's head onto Barbie's.

The first call came on a warm September evening. The clouds nestled above the hills, a comforting humidity in the air. Grace was lying on her bed, sketching out a social studies essay, thinking about Lee and when she would see him again. She answered the phone, expecting it to be Lisa.

"Gracie?" a voice said.

"Yeah?" Grace flipped through her textbook.

"It's Nita."

Grace felt the bed fall out from under her, like she had tripped or stumbled in a dream. Her hand clutched at the blankets. "Nita? Oh my God, where are you?"

"I'm in Vancouver." Nita sniffled; it sounded like she had a cold. "Is Mom there? Can I talk to her?"

"She's already gone to work."

For a second, Nita didn't speak, and Grace wondered if that was it, if Nita would hang up.

"How are things, Gracie?" Nita's voice was slow, tentative. "What've you been doing?"

Grace stared up at her ceiling, the greying stucco arranging itself into confusing patterns. "Nothing much, school and stuff. I got a job at the community centre, I hang out with Lisa."

"She's nice."

"Yeah."

There was a pause. It seemed to be Grace's turn to ask something. "What about you? Where're you guys living now?"

"This place in the city." Nita cleared her throat. "You have a boyfriend?"

"Sort of. This guy, we've been out a bunch of times."

"Is he cute?"

"Yeah, pretty cute."

"That's good." Nita paused. "How's Mom?"

"Well, she was really upset for a while, but I think she seems okay now." Grace squinted and the ceiling drifted up, away from her. "How's Kevin?"

"He's fine. I guess."

Grace listened to the empty air of the phone.

When Nita spoke again, her voice was thin and quiet. "He took off. I tried to do things better, Gracie, so he'd stay, I really did. But you know me, I'm just not very good at anything."

Grace closed her eyes. She could hear Nita's ragged breath on the other end of the line, feel her sister waiting, hoping for something from her. But Grace didn't know what to offer.

"Anyway," Nita's voice started to shake. "I just wanted to tell Mom –" She was crying. "Tell her – I'm sorry I messed up everything. Just tell her I'm okay."

"When are you coming home?" Grace was surprised by the watery sound of her own voice.

"I'm not, Gracie, I can't."

Grace could feel Nita slipping away, as if she hadn't really left until this moment. "We'll send you the money. Hold on." She dug through her bedside table for a pen. "Give me your phone number, your address."

"I don't have a phone. It's not the money, Gracie. I just can't come home. I'll call you again. Say goodbye."

"Goodbye," Grace said, an involuntary response.

"She's no angel," the rooming house manager says. "She gets government cheques, in other people's names." He pulls out a stack of brown envelopes held together by a rubber band. "Look, look, all these people she pretends to be." He fans the envelopes. Grace catches Nita's room number on each of them. "I am keeping them for her, but I am charging her for the keeping when she gets back." "She owes money. For drugs." He nods emphatically. "These kinds of people, they just disappear."

Grace wipes away tears with the back of her hand as she lays out Nita's rent. "I'll mail you a cheque at the end of the month," she says. "Just leave the room as it is."

The manager shrugs.

After her first call, Nita phoned every couple of weeks. Sometimes in the day to have short, difficult conversations with their mother, but mostly at night to talk to Grace.

At first Nita said nothing about herself, asked Grace about Lisa and boys and things at school. Wanted to know what the kids she went to school with were doing. Grace filled her in as best she could remember.

After several phone calls, Nita began to tell Grace what she did with her days and nights. She spoke so matter-of-factly; Grace struggled to keep her own voice even, unsurprised. She tried to mention coming home casually, like it was something every girl in Nita's position might do. Nita ignored her, rambled on about the Lotus Café, where she drank her coffee, about the man across the hall in the rooming house who brought home young boy prostitutes and played piano for them so loud Nita couldn't sleep. "I'm not the worst one here," Nita said.

Grace got Nita's address just before Christmas so she could send her the red wool hat, scarf, and gloves she had bought to keep Nita warm in the city, the red umbrella to keep her dry. Grace kept the address folded in her wallet.

The last phone call from Nita came early in May. Grace and Nita laughed again about Nita's neighbour, Hermia, who thought the government was controlling people through barcodes and cellophane wrapping.

"What's the city like in the spring?" Grace asked.

Nita chuckled. "Wouldn't know. I've only seen this shit-hole part of it, and it's pretty much the same all year round."

Grace told her mother as they did the dinner dishes, her mother's arms deep in soapy water. "I'm going to visit Nita." Her mother's hands lifted out of the suds, gripped the edge of the sink. "It'll just be a week," Grace said. Her mother reached for a dish towel and dried her hands, her forearms. She turned and faced Grace. "Well, what can I do about it?"

"I just wanted you to know."

Her mother sighed. "Well, now I know." She rolled down her sleeves and walked out of the kitchen. Grace listened to her mother's footsteps as she went to her bedroom and shut the door.

In Nita's rooming house bed, Grace sleeps fitfully. Kicks at shadows near her ankles, fights a crushing weight on her chest, bangs her knee against the wall. She wakes in the morning, pushing hard against the black tide of sleep. She fights to surface, twisting and bucking, panting for breath, her hands bound in a strangle of sheets. She spends the morning packing her bag, tidying Nita's room.

In the early afternoon, she takes Nita's picture around one last time, back to the park, to the shops up and down Hastings Street. She walks the streets near the harbour and gets lost, finds herself under a viaduct with some passed-out drunks, scattered about on torn sleeping bags, squatting in makeshift tents. She asks directions to get back to the police station and double-checks the report she filed.

On her second pass of Hastings Street, she stops at a pawnshop window, casts her eyes over an arrangement of small china figurines: dancing boys and girls, a basket of puppies, rabbits having a tea party. Towards the back, she spots a mama tabby cat cleaning her two small babies. Animals caring for their young, cute and sentimental, the kind of gift Nita would give their mother. Grace counts what's left of her money, goes into the shop. She has the shop owner dig out a flattened box, tape it together, nest the figurine in bed of newspaper. As she pays, the shop owner notices her pad, her hand-drawn maps. He laughs. "You should go to Harbour Centre," he says, pointing up, up. "You'll see it all from there." He gives her directions.

Farther down the street, Grace finds it, an office building that advertises an outdoor elevator, a three-hundred-and-sixty-degree view of the city from an enclosed deck. She buys a ticket, steps into the elevator, gasps the moment the glass walls rise out of the building and into the air.

At the observation level, she presses her face to the glass, holds her breath and stares out at the city, serene and majestic under a perfect blue sky. Row after row of anonymous rooftops, the dense green patches of trees, the dark water of the inlet. She traces the streets below with her finger, the maze of roads travelling away, swimming and multiplying out to the horizon, stretching like ribbon to the ends of the earth.

Acknowledgements

Immeasurable thanks to:

My family, especially my mother, Nancy Chen. My partner, Robert Ahrens, for his infinite good humour, patience, and his excellent photo skills. My dearest companion, Laisha "rarely wrong, slightly psychic" Rosnau, whose words and friendship are a constant inspiration.

My editor, Ellen Seligman, for her amazing insight, intelligence, and enthusiasm. My agent, Anne McDermid, for her humour, style, and kind advice. Zsuzsi Gartner for big peppermint tea and unwavering effervescence.

Charlotte Gill, whose willingness to read went above and beyond. Lee Henderstein and Chris Tenove for their unabashed encouragement. Steve Galloway and all those lunches at Helen's Grill. Sally Breen and Carol Shaben for their careful counsel and snack foods. Olivia Scalzo, who is grace personified.

My first fiction teacher and mentor, Sally Stiles. The UBC Creative Writing Department, its instructors, and its many funding donors, as well as *PRISM international.* The B.C. Arts Council, the Banff Centre for the Arts, and the Canada Council for the Arts.

Munificent employers: Janice Bearg at the SFU Writing and Publishing Program, Andrew Gray at Booming Ground, Sharon McGowan and Peggy Thompson at Rave Film.

The thoughtful editors of *Toronto Life* magazine, *The Dalhousie Review, The Malahat Review, Prairie Fire, The Antigonish Review,* and *Grain* magazine. The lovely Yvonne Gall at CBC.